Love Letters

James Allen

HEADLINE
Liaison

Copyright © 1995 James Allen

The right of James Allen to be identified as the Author of
the Work has been asserted by him in accordance with the
Copyright, Designs and Patents Act 1988.

First published in 1995
by HEADLINE BOOK PUBLISHING

A HEADLINE LIAISON paperback

10 9 8 7 6 5 4 3 2 1

ISBN 0 7472 5150 9

Phototypeset by Intype Ltd, London

Printed and bound in Great Britain by
Cox & Wyman Ltd, Reading, Berks

HEADLINE BOOK PUBLISHING
A division of Hodder Houghton PLC
338 Euston Road
London NW1 3BH

Love Letters

Chapter 1

The love letters were in an old briefcase in a cupboard in the garage. The funny thing was, Kate had been looking for a screw. She laughed afterwards. Laughed until she cried.

They had a two-car garage which was rarely used except in the depths of winter. Even then, the garage would only take one vehicle because half of it had been converted into a workshop. Bob's Place. The sign said so on the door.

Her husband was sales director of an engineering company and for relaxation he made models: houses, level crossings, stations, farms. In the converted loft of their detached house he had created his own world of rolling countryside through which ran electric trains pulling coaches and goods wagons.

Kate only ascended to the loft as an invited guest. On one occasion she had said how marvellous it would be to invite children to play in this miniature wonderland. His reaction had been brief and abrasive.

These were not toys. These were crafted scale models of precision. This was his domain and no one else's.

1

'Good God, Kate. These are my creations. Hours of work. This is not a silly hobby. It's my way of relaxing after the pressures of the job.'

Somehow he was always able to end any discussion by referring to the pressures of the job. Not that they had really had a discussion that day in the loft. He had stated the position and she had accepted it, just as she accepted his was a demanding profession. All *she* had to do, he seemed to imply, was sit around the house reading or indulging herself in good works.

'Of course, I wasn't born into wealth and position,' he would say. 'I was out in the marketplace competing. Damn good thing, too. That's why I earn sixty-k per. That's why the BM is sitting in the drive.'

Kate didn't argue. She never argued. He spoke in business shorthand that sometimes she did not understand. She never suggested that she should get a job. Not a second time.

'A job?' he had said, the one time she had raised the possibility. 'What would you do? Don't be silly, Kate. You're my wife, the homemaker. Your place is here.' He had given her a brief cuddle of *bonhomie* more than affection. 'You're my little woman,' he had said, kissing her forehead. 'Your place is here.'

It was a comfortable marriage and a full life, until you looked closely. She hadn't looked closely for years. Perhaps she never would have, if she hadn't found the letters.

But he was away on an overnight trip when she went looking for a screw. The alignment of a cupboard door in the kitchen had sagged and it was no longer closing properly. It was a minor irritation in a kitchen where her husband liked everything to be in its place, in a house that ran like clockwork. He had meant to mend it himself but simply hadn't had time. Kate thought that if she mended it, he would be pleased at her initiative and skill.

A new screw was needed in one of the hinges. At least, that was her diagnosis. She went to the garage and opened his cupboard that had upon it the sign: Keep Out – Danger! Another sign, another joke.

Boxes and jars lined the shelves in neat order but there was a profusion of screws and she was confused. She dropped one of the boxes and a dozen half-inch diamond heads fell onto the floor. She crouched to pick them up, already regretting her intrusion, when she saw the briefcase on the bottom shelf. It was slim, zip-topped and made of imitation leather, and was pushed into a corner behind a stack of model-making magazines.

He had brought it home from a conference once, an example of the tawdry free gifts which delegates were being offered. It certainly did not fit in with £60,000 a year and a Five-series BMW. They had used it, for a time, to store old photographs, but she hadn't seen it for two or three years.

Kate replaced the box of screws and pulled out the briefcase. It made her smile that he kept old photographs here, in his workshop. She stood up and placed it on a bench. The zip rasped when she pulled it open, making her wince. A prelude to the contents.

From it she pulled half a dozen magazines and her stomach knotted with guilt and shock. They were glossy pin-up magazines, the sort she always avoided looking at when she went into a newsagent shop. Half-clad young women were featured on their covers.

Alone in the garage, Kate blushed. She put the magazines down and took a deep breath. Now she knew she should never have come in here, invading his territory. His space, as he called it. She tried not to think what it might mean that he had such a collection. Perhaps there was an explanation other than carnal?

Photographs. The briefcase had contained old photographs of them on holiday. When they took holidays. Before Bob had said they were unnecessary. She parted the two flaps of the imitation leather and saw there were photographs inside, along with several pieces of paper. Hopefully, she reached for them.

Even as she touched them, she knew they were not holiday snapshots. Her heart thumped and she hesitated before turning them over to look at them. These were polaroid pictures of a woman in her underwear. The pieces of paper were pages of letters.

With a sense of dread, she shuffled the pages and put them in order. There were two letters, both written in the same hand. They did not have the sender's address nor a date.

She read the first:

Sunday night

Dear sex pig,

I'm still aching from the fucking you gave me. When are you going to do it again? A weekend next time, not just a day. I want fucking until I can't

4

walk. Work something out with The Little Woman. Tell her you have to go away on business. Tell her anything but escape back to me. I want more of the same. A lot more. And any variation you can think of.

Yours in lust and with all my love.

Val.

She folded the single sheet of paper, put it back in the briefcase and opened the next letter, which was longer.

Wednesday

Dear sex pig,

I can hardly wait. Two whole days and nights. I've bought the new underwear. You'll have to guess which colour I'm wearing when we meet. If you guess wrong, you have to wait until we get there and make me come three times. If you guess right I'll suck your prick in the car on the way there. Will you be able to keep your concentration? How do you fancy a hundred-mile-an-hour orgasm? How do you fancy coming as we're going?

I enjoyed the quickie in the train. Fucking in a lavatory! No space to move, people outside, the train shaking. You shaking! Remember? I leaned over the loo and you pulled up my skirt and fucked me from behind. You dirty bastard. You enjoyed it, didn't you? Being dirty. You made so much noise I thought a conductor might bang on the door. If he had, you'd have probably let him fuck me as well.

It's because you have no inhibitions that you turn

me on. Is that why you called me Martini? Anytime, anywhere? We're well matched, you and I. The sex pig and the anytime girl. I've been thinking about it this week, you trapped there with The Little Woman and her pink bedjacket. You poor little beast. What do you do? Go to the loo and bang yourself off? Tell me your secrets tomorrow and I'll tell you mine.

I'll be ready for you tomorrow. I'm already wet now, just thinking about what we'll do in two whole days. Ooh, that's nice. Can you guess what I'm doing? That's right, I'm touching myself. I'm making myself nice and squishy. Oh, if you could hear the noise my fingers are making! Ooh! Two fingers inside me, now. Ooh! Three fingers . . .

Sorry, lover, but I can't wait until tomorrow. I'm going to have to come now. Too far gone . . .

That was good. Did it turn you on? Did it make your prick go stiff? I'll bet it did. Why not fuck Kate's bedjacket while you think of me?

I'll keep it wet and warm until tomorrow.

All my love and lust,

Val.

Kate folded the second letter and put it back in the briefcase. She looked at the polaroid photographs. Was this Val? Was this her husband's Martini? The woman in the photographs was dark haired and perhaps in her late thirties. Seven or eight years older than Kate.

Was she only thirty? Kate had to make a mental adjustment to think normally again. Was she really only thirty years old?

The Little Woman was thirty years old but felt ancient. The woman in the polaroid pictures was wanton. In some, her expression was sultry, in others intoxicated, but always lustful. Yours in lust. Her legs went on for ever, long legs in nylon stockings. The black straps of the garter belt and brassiere looked like webbing. A spider's webbing designed to enmesh men.

Abruptly, Kate put the photographs back in the brief-case with the letters. She picked up the magazines and slid them inside as well. The zip sounded more content as she closed it, as if it no longer had secrets to hide. She put it back in the cupboard where she had found it and left the garage. She vacated Bob's space in Bob's place.

Her actions became automatic. She filled the kettle with water, plugged it in and put a teabag in a mug. While the water boiled, she went into the living room and straightened the ornaments on the bookshelves. The imitation log fire glowed in imitation of a happy home. The room was cosy and warm. It made her smile.

As she went upstairs she realised she was humming tunelessly. What was the song in the back of her mind? 'Please Mr Porter'! Once she had identified it, she hummed it more convincingly.

But what was she doing here?

She had climbed the second flight of stairs and was in the spacious loft room, another area that was her husband's domain. She switched on the light and the sun shone over the land he had created. Fields, hillsides, forests and hamlets rested on rows of trestles and boards. Two stations and a goods yard. Trains in rows and tiny passengers standing on scale-model platforms waiting for the opportunity to go to the lavatory.

Kate had stopped humming the tune. The silence of the room filled her. The briefcase had been Pandora's Box. She had released reality, scratching and spitting, into her life. Her life. What life?

The kettle wailed downstairs and switched itself off. What day was it? Friday, of course. Friday and she had rituals to fulfil. Friday-evening shopping at Safeways.

Thoughts flitted in and out of her mind without apparent reason. She entered rooms as if checking them for intruders, but without fear, and was surprised when they were empty. Sometimes, she was surprised when she recognised the furnishings and realised she lived here. She tidied the living room again and checked the Radio Times for the programme she wanted to watch that evening.

Eventually, she put on her coat and went out to the car, after first checking that all the doors were locked. Bob's Law. Security. Make sure no one could invade their space while they were out.

Traffic was heavy on the main road but the fog had almost lifted. Was she really thirty years old? The Golf handled well in traffic. Perhaps next year they would change it, perhaps upgrade it to a GTI. Bob might be persuaded. A GTI would look good in the drive next to his BMW. Guilt at being uncharitable made her think of something else.

Roast beef or pork? Or perhaps Bob would want to eat out on Sunday? Every Sunday lunchtime without fail they went to The Red Lion. It had a dining room that overlooked the river and sometimes they ate there, sometimes she cooked a very late lunch. It depended on how he felt, how busy the last two days had been. How much pressure he had been under as to what he would want to do.

Kate wondered if he would want sex on Sunday morning. She shuddered and indicated a right turn. The click of the signal diverted her. A metronome of normality. She made the manoeuvre into the multi-storey car park that served the complex of shops. The shopping mall. The country was being swamped with Americanisms. She laughed out loud; a brittle, fragile laugh.

Her husband drove a BMW and she had a Volkswagen Golf. That didn't really leave her in a position to criticise outside influences on her life. Did it?

There were more cars leaving than entering. Was she late? She had a momentary surge of panic at being late. It was only eight o'clock. Plenty of time. What had she been doing until eight o'clock?

Kate parked the car, obtained a ticket from a machine and stuck it on the windscreen, then went to the lifts. One came, empty and metallic, a space tube to a different planet. The doors closed and she winced beneath the bright lights. They opened again and she stepped out into crowds, noise and coloured lights.

The maelstrom of humanity frightened her. She paused and turned away, coming face to face with her own reflection in a wall mirror. She didn't recognise herself. The clothes were familiar, Long skirt, white blouse, flat shoes, tan trenchcoat. But she didn't recognise the woman who wore them.

Her eyes stared back curiously. Was this her? Her hair was unpinned from the usual sensible bun she always wore and now hung around her shoulders. Her face was painted heavily in make-up. Black eyelashes, flushed cheeks and red lips.

Was this Kate or Val? Who was she?

Kate turned and walked away from the crowds. She left the precinct and gulped in the fresh air. It was the first week in September and there was already a night chill. But it was good to be walking, to let her long legs dictate direction. It was good not to have to think about anything. Roast beef or pork or scale-model copulation. Good to walk away.

After a while, her pace changed. She had left most people behind and had been swallowed by the darkness of the evening. Now she walked leisurely from one moonpatch of street lamp to the next, sometimes losing herself in the shadows in between that were cast by the trees that lined the pavement.

A car slowed to match her progress. The nearside window lowered electronically and a man leaned over from the driver's seat.

Lost? So was she, if she thought about it, but she didn't want to think about anything. She stepped to the car and looked in. The driver was small and tubby and wore thick glasses. Chins smiled at her as well as his mouth. His eyes danced over her face, his gaze was unsure.

'Are you looking for business?' he said.

Chapter 2

The question confused her and she smiled because it didn't make sense and she didn't want anything to make sense.

'What do you mean?'

He licked his lips. His eyes, big behind the lenses, now glanced up and down the road anxiously. The door of the car swung open.

'Oral,' he whispered.

'Oral?'

Kate got into the car. She was tired and he was offering her a ride. He wanted oral. What was oral?

He began to drive.

'How much?' he said.

How much? What was this game they were playing?

'How much for what?' she said.

'For sucking.'

He shuddered when he spoke as if the word excited him.

'For sucking what?' she said.

Kate was curious to see if he would shake again when he replied.

'How much to . . . to . . . to suck my prick?'

He shuddered.

Kate sat sideways in the seat so she could watch him. No seatbelt. She had not put on the seatbelt. What would Bob say? Fuck Bob. This was a game, like toy trains in the attic. Like polaroid pictures in the garage. How much to suck his prick? Even thinking the words made her aware that she was not in possession of her faculties.

Suck a prick?

Only once had she been subjected to the act. Her husband had forced her shortly after they were married. During lovemaking, he had straddled her face and she had wondered what he was doing. For a moment, she had thought he was having a heart attack But then he had held her head and pushed his erection into her face.

She had read about fellatio, had known of the practice, but had never been inducted into its performance. It was not that she would have been reluctant to try, if the approach had been different, but her husband had simply climbed up her body and forced it into her mouth.

Kate had not been experienced and his roughness and demands had confused her. Besides, she didn't know what to do. As well as fear of the unknown and of her husband's sudden brutality, there was the embarrassment of not knowing what to do. She had struggled and he had held her down. When his orgasm had approached he had lost his grip upon her and she had pulled her head sideways. He had ejaculated into her face.

Afterwards she had cried because she did not equate this with love and he had left the bedroom and slept on the couch. The next day, they did not speak of it. They had never spoken of it.

'How much?' she said.

Her words came through a mist. She was curious to know how much it would cost.

'Ten pounds,' he said. He glanced at her and away again. 'I never pay more than ten.'

'Ten pounds?'

This time she could not stop herself from smiling. A giggle crept into her voice. It was funny that a little fat man would spend ten pounds for the privilege.

'All right. Fifteen. But no more.'

'Fifteen.'

Kate said it seriously. She felt sorry for the little man. He was sweating. The heater was on boost and sweat beaded his forehead. Did her husband pay Martini?

'Where to?' he said.

Another question that didn't make sense.

'Where to?' she repeated.

'Don't you have somewhere to go? Somewhere to park?'

'Safeways.'

'Safeways?' He looked at her blankly and then grinned. 'Of course. Safeways.'

He turned at a junction and doubled back. Kate didn't know how long she had walked but it only took a few minutes to reach the car park. He drove the car up the ramp and circled the levels. She watched dispassionately, her mind not really present. They drove past her own car and he stopped on a higher level, driving nose-in to a parking space. No other vehicles were near them. Ahead, through the windscreen, she could see the lights of a high-rise apartment block fifty yards away.

Net curtains and tiny excuses for balconies. White plastic plant-pot holders trying to look Grecian, a sad row of washing and a bicycle on the tenth floor. Lights from television screens flickered and occasional shadows moved. Shadow people living shadow lives. Like her.

Who was she? The Little Woman or Martini? Or someone else she had yet to discover?

The silence was sudden when he switched off the engine. He turned off the lights, too, and the little display of green and amber and red bulbs died. She heard his seat belt clunk free and he turned to face her.

He reached into his jacket and she watched him take out his wallet. All his movements seemed slow. It was underwater ballet. Perhaps the windscreen was a television and all the occupants of the apartment block had tuned in to watch them. She looked back at the curtained windows and imagined cooking smells, children's cries and rows and people sleeping and making love, and maybe even making scale models of copulation.

'Fifteen.'

His hand offered her notes and she took them. Why was he giving her money?

'Thank you,' she said.

His hand touched her thigh over her skirt and she stared at it. Her look stopped him. His hand was small and fat. Fat fingers like sausages. He wanted to put his sausages upon her body and she panicked. He couldn't. She wasn't wearing the underwear. She remembered what she was wearing beneath the skirt and was embarrassed.

'No,' she said.

'Sorry.'

He moved his hand and she felt sorry for him again. He was easy to intimidate. He licked his lips. His eyes were on her blouse beneath the open coat. He reached out and she did not object. His sausage fingers traced the outline of her left breast through the cotton. They pressed gently so as not to offend her, testing the softness of the flesh.

Kate watched him. She was part of the TV audience. She watched his face, his eyes wide with want, his lips parted. She saw herself sitting passively, being touched. She was good at being passive and she wasn't embarrassed about her breasts. They were nice breasts. Firm, upstanding, substantial. After her shower when she had been playing squash, she had noticed how her nipples stood out.

It was funny, that. She always felt good after squash and after the shower. Vibrant, alive. Her nipples had been an expression of her vibrancy and she had admired them. It was another small game she played. Although she was naturally shy, at those times after her shower she was careless about dressing and stood around with her breasts on show for the other girls to see, and they saw. She had seen them look, noticed the admiration. It had made her feel good.

What were the sausages doing now?

Her blouse was open and the man had pushed a strap of her brassiere over her shoulder. His palm was sliding down over the sweep of her breast. She watched his hand push against the cup of the bra and palm the breast. He groaned.

What was he doing holding her breast?

'What are you?' he said.

The question distracted her.

'What?'

'What are you? You're not a straight fuck. I can tell that. You're different.'

'Yes. I'm different.'

'Some of the girls have a role. Some pretend they're schoolgirls.' He breathed heavily. 'Some are. Then there's discipline. You're not discipline?'

'No,' Kate said, quite sure of herself. 'I'm not discipline.'

'Are you a submissive?'

Kate smiled.

'I'm a housewife.'

He shuddered again. His hand made her breast quiver.

'Yes,' he said.

His gaze took in her hair and the way she was dressed.

'I'm a submissive housewife.'

The small man squeezed her breast hard and now it was she who gasped. He twisted her nipple between finger and thumb. She closed her eyes and felt tears.

'You're hurting me.'

He let go of her breast and she realised she had been holding her breath. She gulped air. This dream was beginning to feel wrong. She could sense a change in the atmosphere. She opened her eyes but he was still there and she was still in the car that was the focus of the apartment block of lighted windows.

'Suck this,' he said.

'What?'

The sausage fingers pulled her head down and she saw

in the shadows that he had released another sausage between his legs. But this one was fierce and hard. It rubbed against her face.

'No,' she murmured.

'Suck it!'

His words were a hiss.

Kate reached between them with her right hand and took hold of the hard, naked flesh. It throbbed in her grip. Her impressions were jumbled in the shadows but there was an overwhelming feeling of heat and urgency.

'In your mouth, bitch.' The small fat man had gained sudden, urgent authority. 'Suck it!'

'No, she pleaded, but the word made him even more urgent. He gripped her head in both hands. The heat against her cheek threatened to burn her. Wetness slid across her face and she opened her mouth and it went inside.

'Oh yes,' he said.

She held its base and he held her head, pushing himself in and out of her mouth. The size was a surprise and she tired to stop it penetrating deep into her throat, but his thrusts were getting stronger. The heat and the smell were overpowering and she wished the dream would stop.

'Suck, you bitch. Suck!'

The heat and the smell and the submissive housewife. She awoke from the dream to realise it was no dream. This was happening. She was sitting in a car in a public car park sucking the prick of a small fat man. He was making her. Holding her head down. He was fucking her face!

Her mind was full of mad images and words and thoughts. But she didn't know how to do it. That was all right. He was doing it. She just had to submit. They might be seen and her life of respectability would be put in jeopardy. She wanted to laugh but the wedge of flesh embedded in her mouth made it impossible.

This was disgusting. A depraved act in a public place. How had she allowed it to happen? Revulsion swept over her and her throat contracted. She struggled and he held her tighter. She would have been sick but the little man's erection seemed to become lodged in the contraction. He quivered and gasped and, once more, she wondered if this was the onset of a heart attack. Then he spasmed and she knew it was no heart attack. It was an orgasm.

The first spurts were deep into her throat and she swallowed out of self-preservation. The lesser spasms that followed were into her mouth and she held their discharge, wondering what to do with it. There was no choice. She swallowed that as well.

His grip fell away and she raised her head. He lay back on his seat, his lips parted, his breathing shallow. His eyes slid away from hers.

Her lips felt sticky and she licked them clean with her tongue. The taste was salty. It had left her with a thirst. She looked down at the man's lap and, even in the shadows, saw that the fierceness had been reduced to a soft snail.

He fastened his trousers.

'Do you want me to drop you somewhere?' he said.

He could have been talking to his wife. His wife. Was

he married? Did he have a Little Woman waiting at home?

'No,' she said.

'Well.'

The word was not going to lead anywhere.

He switched on the engine. She looked through the windscreen at the apartments opposite. Shame they missed the show. The dashboard lights came on. The engine purred, anxious to be gone.

'I'll look for you again,' he said.

She nodded and got out of the car. Before she closed the door, he leaned across the seats and said, 'What's your name?'

'Val,' she said.

Kate walked to one side while the man reversed the car from the space. He drove carefully back the way he had come. It was a BMW. Five series.

She walked in the same direction. There were few cars and fewer shoppers this high up at this time of night. She supposed it was dangerous for a woman alone. The thought made her giggle. Some man might accost her. He might push her into a car and rape her. Make her suck his prick.

By the time she reached the VW Golf she was humming 'Please Mr Porter'. When she reached for her keys, she found she was still clutching the fifteen pounds the man had given her. She pushed the notes into her pocket and stopped humming the song.

Kate got in the car and felt suddenly vulnerable. She locked the doors. The car faced inwards and all she could see was the concrete slab of the higher level, shadows and splashes of thin light on the oil-stained surface of the floor below.

Roast beef or pork?

Fuck roast beef or pork.

She drove out of the car park and through the brightly lit streets. She was going home. There was nowhere else to go but home. Maybe it had been destroyed by fire? Maybe the imitation gas-controlled log fire had developed a fault and destroyed the cosiness? No such luck. The handsome detached at twenty-three Maple Drive was still there.

Kate locked the car and went into the house. In the kitchen, she poured a glass of water and rinsed her mouth. She went upstairs to the bedroom, took off all her clothes and stood in front of the mirror. The red lips were smudged but that didn't matter.

Her body was fit and in proportion. She watched her diet and played squash. Her body was good. Wasn't it?

Defiance didn't suit her. She didn't know if her body was good or not. She was still in the middle of a nightmare. The love letters had destroyed her life and illusions. They had shattered her self-confidence. They had come close to destroying her self-respect.

And what had she done in response? She had gone walking in the wrong part of town and had been picked up by a little fat man with bad eyes. She had earned fifteen pounds for sucking his prick.

Kate bit her lip and looked at the bed. The memory came back as if from another life. The bed was covered with bits of pink wool. The scissors still lay amid the remnants.

Oh yes. She had cut the bedjacket into a thousand pieces, as well. A great act of retaliation.

The briefcase had been a Pandora's Box, all right. She had released all the ills of her world. A punishment from Zeus. But there had been something left in Pandora's box. There had been hope. Could Kate dare to hope?

Perhaps tomorrow. She fell on the bed amidst the pink wool. For now, all she wanted to do was cry.

Chapter 3

It was a dream. Just a dream. She had thought the other was a dream and had been able to taste it on her teeth hours later. But this was the past and most of the past was an hallucination, just as the future was a dream waiting to happen. Was there any difference?

Kate had been a tomboy at sixteen. Her hair was short and had been bleached light brown in the hot summer of that year. She had no boyfriend because the opposite sex frightened her. Horses were more reliable and Uncle Toby had three.

Ride them anytime, he said, and she did. Her mother encouraged her. It brought the three of them closer together. Her mother said Kate had been missing a parental influence in her life ever since her father had left home when she was six and had not returned.

You can't trust men, her mother said. At least, you can't trust most men. Toby was different, she said. But that was because Toby was her lover. Kate was not totally naive and understood the situation.

Her mother had been successful at running her own hotel business and Kate had had a cushioned upbringing.

They first met Toby when she was looking for stabling for the pony she hoped to get for her fourteenth birthday.

He was a land and property owner with a converted farmhouse in its own acreage. His land adjoined the hotel grounds. He was thirty-eight years old and had steel-grey hair in a military cut. His features were aqualine, his physique lean. He had never been married and was, her mother said, a catch.

Kate's mother was thirty-five, elfin-like and attractive, with dark hair that was bobbed short. The hotel business had taught her how to play people like anglers played fish. Kate had watched her switch on her sincerity and, just as quickly, switch it off again when it was no longer needed.

The two adults came to an arrangement. Kate could choose one of the three ponies he owned and use it as her own. It was a subterfuge that saved her mother the expense of buying one and allowed a friendship to develop. Kate first called him Uncle Toby for a joke and to imply the closeness of family. The joke stuck because it pleased her mother.

Even before that first time, she had sensed the danger of visiting the stables. Even when he was not there she felt she was under observation. She had her own keys to the house, which was extensive.

No expense had been spared on the conversion and it contained an indoor swimming pool at the back of the house with french windows that could be opened in the summer to allow access to the garden. After riding she would often shower and relax in the pool.

Occasionally, Sadie went with her. She was a year

older than Kate and was all long legs and long blonde hair. Sadie liked horses but preferred boys, and sometimes she would shock Kate with her stories.

If the house was empty, they would swim naked in the pool afterwards.

'What if Uncle Toby comes back?' Kate would say.

'Then he'll get a shock,' Sadie would reply with a wicked grin.

The thought of being caught was part of the danger, but not all of it. Kate was sixteen in the May of the long hot summer. It was a summer that seemed to last forever. Until the day they were caught.

Sadie had wandered the house naked and Kate had followed in her wake, wary of what her friend might do. In the study, the older girl lit a cigarette with a gold lighter. She opened drawers and moved items around the desk.

Kate was worried and uncomfortable until they were back at the pool. She had carried an ashtray so they would leave no telltale signs that they had been exploring.

The blonde laughed at her timidity and stubbed out the cigarette in the ashtray.

She said, 'Hide the evidence and put it back where you found it.'

Kate cleaned the ashtray and replaced it in the study. When she returned to the pool, Sadie was already swimming. She jumped in and joined her and they fooled around. Sadie entwined her limbs with Kate's and her hand went between her legs.

'Maybe we can invite Jamie next time.' Jamie was a

school heart-throb. Sadie groaned and rubbed herself against Kate. 'Just think if he was here now. What we could do to him.'

This was a game Sadie often played. Kate laughed and went along with it, but the thought of being with a boy made her nervous. Her friend's language made her nervous.

'I'll bet his prick is colossal,' Sadie said, thrusting her pelvis against Kate's hip. 'Jenny Smith says it is.'

'She should know!'

'She's had everybody in the Lower Sixth. At least, she says so. But Jamie. She says his is the best.'

Kate's experience of pricks was limited. A boy had made her hold his after a date and had panted a great deal while moving it about in her hands. He had eventually ejaculated, covering her fingers with stickiness. But while she had felt the dimensions of his prick, she had never seen an erect one and did not know how to differentiate between good, bad or indifferent. These conversations were an education.

'If he was here,' Kate said, 'what would you do?'

'I'd suck him. Put it in my mouth and suck him. Then he'd fuck me in the water. Like this.'

She rubbed herself against Kate again.

Kate shivered at the image that had been conjured.

'Have you ever sucked anyone, Sadie?'

'Of course.'

They twisted away from each other and Kate dived beneath the water. When she surfaced, the tingle of excitement died. It was replaced by fear and guilt. Always guilt.

Uncle Toby stood at the side of the pool watching them. Sadie was standing in the shallow end, her breasts above the water line. She stared with wide eyes and open mouth at this sudden appearance, so shocked she forgot to cover herself.

How long had he been there?

Sadie realised her breasts were naked and sank beneath the water. Without speaking, Uncle Toby turned and left the pool area. They exchanged looks.

Kate said, 'We'd better go.'

They climbed from the pool and went into the changing room, drying themselves in silence. Kate had a change of clothes and put on a short skirt, T-shirt, ankle socks and sandals. Sadie tugged herself back into her jodhpurs and a white shirt and tied her wet, long blonde hair behind her head in a ponytail. They had both left their riding boots outside.

Sadie said, 'We were only swimming,' as if rehearsing an excuse.

But they both remembered their conversation and their playful antics. What they had been doing in innocence might look different to an outsider.

They walked through the house towards the back door. He called them from his study.

'Would you mind coming in here?'

It was like being summoned by the headmaster.

They stood in front of him, guilty without trial, even though they had done nothing.

Sadie said, 'We were only swimming.'

He didn't speak but stepped forward and took Sadie's canvas haversack from her. He opened it, looked inside, and took from it the gold lighter. He put the lighter back on the desk and stared at them again.

Kate waited for her friend to say something, to make an explanation, to say it was a mistake, but she said nothing. This was Kate's fault for bringing Sadie here. That's what her mother would say. If her mother found out . . .

'Uncle Toby . . .' she began, but one look silenced her.

'Go and wait in the stables, Kate. I need to talk to Sadie alone.'

She did as she was told and stood in the yard. The sun that had been friendly and warm was now oppressive and hot and she had left her sunglasses in the changing room. She re-entered the house and quietly went towards the pool.

The door of the study was not fully closed. She expected to hear voices, to hear Uncle Toby reprimanding Sadie, but she could hear nothing. Had they gone? Had they left by the front door? Had he taken her to the police?

Kate shuddered at the possibility of the scandal and her own part in it. She was involved by association. Her mother would think the worst, particularly if he told her what they had been discussing, the language they had used. If he told her they had been naked and in each other's arms.

Her mother had been strict, her morality unwavering. They went to church every Sunday. Sex was dirty, she implied. The only true happiness could be found by saving your love for a good man. Kate knew her mother and Uncle Toby were considering marriage. Her fear was that what had happened that afternoon might have jeopardised those plans.

Seen from a dream, seen with hindsight, Kate knew her fears had been imaginary. But then? Deep in the memory, the fears were real and sixteen-year-old Kate was mortified at the possibility that she might have spoiled her mother's chance of happiness.

She went silently to the door and peeped into the study in case her unauthorised presence might cause offence. They had not gone. They were still there, standing facing each other, but they were not speaking.

Uncle Toby and Sadie were in profile. The girl stared up into his face with wide blue eyes. Uncle Toby reached out with both hands and began to unfasten the buttons of the white shirt she wore. For a moment, Kate did not understand. Sadie had not stolen the shirt. The shirt belonged to her. What was Uncle Toby doing?

The feeling in the pit of her stomach told her what was happening before her brain worked it out. The feeling was familiar. It was both delicious and depraved. It was the devil's temptation. It was sex.

She watched, unable to break her gaze, as he unfastened the buttons of the shirt with slow deliberation. Sadie stared and did not resist. He pushed it from her shoulders and the cotton slipped down her arms. She wore a white cotton bra. Kate remembered it had a rosebud embroidered between the cups.

The silence was intense. Kate licked her lips. Uncle Toby did the same. He placed his right palm upon Sadie's shoulder. The tendons of his hand tensed as he caressed the pale skin. His hand moved down her arm and he stroked her in soft, slow movements. His lips were parted and his face seemed heavier.

'You are a beautiful young woman,' he said.

Sadie said nothing. Her eyes seemed wider, as if hypnotised.

His hand moved upwards and slid the strap of the bra over her shoulder. The shirt hung around her waist, trapped by the jodhpurs and at her wrists. The fallen strap of the bra was limp, the cup still in place. His hand moved again, the fingers spread, down her chest and into the cup which now fell away. His palm became the cup and he held the breast.

Kate's face and loins were on fire. The devil had possessed her and she could not fight him. She could only stand in silence and watch.

Uncle Toby squeezed and caressed and Sadie closed her eyes. Her head tilted back, her golden hair catching the sunlight from the window. She looked like an angel waiting for forgiveness . . . or communion.

He let go of her breast and used a finger of the same right hand to hook the other strap and pull it down, taking the other cup with it. Her breasts were small, high and pointed. Kate licked her lips again. She had touched them in play in the swimming pool and had felt them brush against her, but that had been in play.

Now she stared at the breasts of her friend with a new understanding and a new desire. They were beautiful, a sacrament being offered in sacrilege. She almost groaned and closed her eyes to shut out the vision. She prayed for strength but had none so she opened her eyes to watch Uncle Toby take hold of Sadie's breasts in both hands.

He was content to contain them in his hands which pulsed as if he was gently moulding soft clay. He held them from the side and his thumbs circled the nipples. Sadie's lips parted.

Uncle Toby said, 'Have you really sucked a prick?'

The question caused her to open her eyes. She stared at him and sighed.

He added, 'Tell me the truth, Sadie.'

'No.'

'Why did you say you had?'

'Boys talk about it. They like it.'

'How do you know?'

'Because they talk about it. It excites them.'

'Has a boy asked you to?'

'One wanted me to.'

'But you refused?'

'Yes.'

'Why?'

'He didn't ask. He tried to make me.'

'What if I ask you, Sadie? Will you suck me?' Sadie ran her tongue along her bottom lip. 'You will, won't you, Sadie?'

His request was more like a command.

'Yes,' she said.

'Then do it.'

Uncle Toby put his hands on her shoulder, pushing her down, and she knelt in front of him in the study. She waited on her knees, her arms by her sides, while he unfastened his clothes. When his trousers gaped, he took hold of her head with his right hand and drew it towards his groin.

Kate held her breath. Her eyes were fixed on the point

of union but she could see nothing. The mythical erection they had talked about, that she had once held in her hand, still remained out of sight, hidden by his clothes and Sadie's head.

He sighed deeply. He held her head in both hands.

'Hold it,' he said. 'Use your hands.'

Sadie reached up and held it. She looked as if she were at prayer. Except for the shirt and brassiere that lay forlornly around her arms. Except for those deliciously pointed breasts that quivered as he slowly moved his hips in a gentle rhythm.

Kate contracted her vaginal muscles. She wanted to push herself against the door. She wanted to scream stop, to banish the devil. She didn't know it but she wanted to come. A noise escaped from her throat and Uncle Toby and Sadie stopped what they were doing.

He withdrew and looked first at the window but Sadie turned her face, which nestled against the open clothes at his groin, and stared directly into Kate's eyes. Her mouth was open, her lips shiny. She licked them with her tongue. Kate had expected to see distress in her eyes but she didn't. Instead, she saw a glazed wantonness. It was an expression she did not recognise.

Uncle Toby turned his head and his gaze began to sweep towards her. Fear of discovery overwhelmed her and, as he stared at the partly open door, she stepped away from it and out of sight. Had he seen her? She didn't know. She just had to get away from there before he came looking.

She found herself at the swimming pool and went into the changing room. There were her sunglasses. That was why she was here. She picked them up and caught sight of herself in the mirror. The expression on Sadie's face – the one she hadn't recognised – was now duplicated on her own.

Chapter 4

The changing time on the electronic bedside clock mocked her. It was a challenge to her inaction. She had cried, she had slept fitfully and she had dreamed. It had been a long time since she had thought of Uncle Toby, because thinking of him always confused her.

He had been a good man. Her mother had told her so. But Bob was not a good man. There was no comparison. Was there? Kate rationalised. She made excuses for her husband and blamed herself for prying. She even told herself there could be a simple explanation.

Different emotions came in turn, each one sweeping the last aside with its certainty and prejudice.

At three o'clock in the morning she got up and went downstairs in her pyjamas. She stood in the kitchen and waited for the water to boil, then made a coffee which she took into the living room. She sat in front of the cosy bloody imitation fire.

That's it. Swear. Let it out. Like last night when the unbelievable happened twice. She discovered the love letters and she sucked a man's prick in Safeway's car park.

35

She still didn't believe it. She had stared at her face in the bathroom mirror and had not believed it. When the memory returned so strongly she could taste his sperm, she had brushed her teeth. She had brushed her teeth six times but could not erase the memory of the taste.

Kate found it difficult to swear. She found it difficult to think vulgarity, never mind obscenity. Was she to blame for her husband straying?

The thought kept sparking in the back of her mind, a loose wire that made contact against exposed nerves. That time after they were first married, when he had tried to introduce her to fellatio; if she had submitted, if she had learned how, if she had not cried, perhaps he would not have gone looking for someone else.

Apart from the sex, they had been content. Hadn't they? They had shared so many things. Apart from his models and his workshop. Apart from her amateur dramatics and squash. Be honest, she told herself. They had shared a house and a social convention.

Sex had occurred on Sunday mornings and not even every Sunday morning. When it did occur he would move up behind her as she lay on her side in bed, still half asleep, finger her until she was wet and push himself inside her. He called it spooning, as if it were romantic, when actually it meant they lay like spoons in a canteen of cutlery.

But he had to give every damn thing a silly name. He would call it spooning and kiss her shoulder tenderly when he'd finished, then roll over and go back to sleep for half an hour until she had got up, cleaned herself and made breakfast.

All spooning had ever done was make her aware that there was a damp patch on the wall beneath the window.

But it was not the sexual unfaithfulness that hurt most. It was the fact that he had discussed her with this other woman. God, listen to her. She was already accepting her as The Other Woman in her mind, as if they were all characters in a play.

She was not The Other Woman. She did not deserve any title, apart from strumpet. She was Val or Martini, the anytime, anywhere girl. A strumpet who filled love letters with obscenities. A strumpet with whom Bob had discussed her, his wife.

The Little Woman. And that damned pink bedjacket. They made her sound middle-aged and boring. Unattractive and undesirable. They made her feel like suicide.

But she would not give them that satisfaction. The more she realised the depths of the betrayal, the more she wanted to fight back, if she only knew how. But fight back for what? To keep her husband and the models in the attic?

Kate felt the first surge of hope. She did not want to keep her husband. The more she thought about it, the more she realised what a disaster their marriage had been. They had hidden the disaster from themselves and each other by maintaining the pretence of a home and Sunday lunchtimes at the Red Lion.

'Looking tired this morning, Bob,' George Mellish would say when the men had pints of real ale before lunch and the wives had halves and pretended they liked it.

And her husband would say, 'Been spooning with my girl, George,' and the men would laugh knowingly and the wives would smile, and she would simper as he put his arm around her shoulder and gave her a squeeze.

Had she ever thought that was normal? But she had had nothing with which to compare it. Perhaps every other Sunday-lunchtime couple led the same sham lives. Surely not. There had to be more. But where?

Bob had always made the decisions since they met. She had been twenty-one, and he was eight years older than her and worldly wise. She had preferred literature to life and at first saw in him something of a Heathcliffe of rough hewn charm and action. Her dreams had not been fulfilled but then, neither had Cathy's.

If Kate no longer wanted her husband, what should she do about it? The first logical step would be to divorce him but how did she do that? See a solicitor? Leave home?

Home was now a loose term that meant the house and possessions they shared, but her spirits immediately rallied at the thought of moving out. Certainly not. If anybody moved out, it should be her husband. But how would he view it?

They had no children so how did judges divide a marriage?

All of a sudden, there were so many aspects that added complications that the logical first step no longer seemed so simple. But she had to persevere and she had to get it right because, for once, she wanted to win.

It was four o'clock in the morning when she went back into the garage workshop, got the briefcase and brought it into the house. She photocopied the letters on the machine in the breakfast room that he called his office. After studying the polaroid photographs, she copied them as well.

Now she would need a lawyer to advise her.

Kate was angry and hurt and she wanted revenge. Bob and his Martini girl had treated her badly. But she needed to plan carefully if revenge was to be sweet. She needed a lawyer to advise her and she also needed to rediscover herself, her own identity. She hesitated to use the expression but she needed to rediscover her sexuality as well. Had she never had any before Bob stifled her?

Her ambitions seemed too lofty. Despair swept in with doubts but just as quickly ebbed. There was a lot to be done, much to be attempted. In the final analysis, she was trying to salvage her life while there was still time. For a crazy moment, as her emotions tumbled, she thought that perhaps she should thank her husband for providing her with the reason for change.

At thirty she was still young enough to start again. Her marriage and life could have drifted on without the impetus to seek more. Her life could have sunk without trace into old age and regret.

The hope surged anew. Thank God she had found the briefcase. Thank God the strumpet had written the letters and her husband had been stupid enough to keep them. The polaroid photographs were on the coffee table in front of her. Long legs and stockings. Underwear designed for men and not for comfort. Underwear designed for sex.

Did she approve? Or did she condemn?

Her own underwear drawer did not contain frivolities, only cotton briefs and sports bras and tights. She wore pyjamas when she went to bed. Warm Pyjamas. And because she liked to read in bed she had worn a bed-jacket.

Could she compete? Was her body good enough to wear such garments? Did she want to? Did she really want to become a strumpet?

She remembered the fat man in the car and the taste of his semen. *Suck this, bitch!* She quivered and her stomach tingled. Now was the time for honesty. Kate licked her lips. In the car she had been frightened and ashamed. She had also been in control of the situation. She knew her strength, her fitness. If she had wanted, she could have broken free of the man at any time.

Discipline? She could have given him discipline and dominance. But she had allowed it to happen, right from the time she got into his car. She had been a submissive housewife, forced to perform a vile act that was against her nature, by choice.

Kate closed her eyes and allowed herself to listen to the whisper in her mind: she had enjoyed every minute of it.

Her tongue crossed her lips and she remembered again the taste, the darkness, the smell, the heat and the desperate urgency of that fat little man.

Suck this, bitch!

He had paid fifteen pounds to be able to say those words, to be able to fulfil his fantasy. The world must be full of men chasing fantasies. Women too.

Kate looked at the magazines which had remained

unopened. Now she turned the cover of the first and studied the photographs and read the letters and took her first steps into sexual fantasy.

Some of the letters could have been written by her husband's strumpet. They used shocking language and were explicit. Whether the incidents they described were true or not did not matter. The incidents could be true, but if they were not, the letter articulated a desire, a dream.

All you needed was imagination. Kate read on, from one magazine to the next. This was a new world of new concepts and possibilities. But so far it existed only in her mind. It was far removed from what she had thought to be normality.

But these were magazines that could be obtained on any high street. They were obviously popular and had a wide readership. Did George Mellish read them? Did the other men at The Red Lion read them? Perhaps even the women?

Kate was totally immersed. After reading them once, she read them again. The alarm clock going off upstairs in the bedroom made her stop. Seven o'clock.

Seven o'clock in the morning and she still felt angry and hurt and betrayed. She also felt tired and challenged and hopeful. Kate smiled and licked her lips again. Her nerves were flaky and the tingle was still there in the pit of her stomach, and she was embarrassed to acknowledge, even to herself, that she was aroused.

Upstairs, the alarm stopped. It would start again in ten seconds if she did not go and switch it off. During the night, its digital display had taunted her into making decisions. Now it was warning her that the night was over and the daytime was no place for false hope.

Her husband was coming home. That word again, home. She would have to behave as if nothing had happened. Her greatest decision would be roast beef or pork. She packed the briefcase so he would not know she had discovered its contents. By the time it was ready to be returned to the cupboard in the garage, the alarm started again, but still she did not go and switch it off.

It was a reminder that nothing would ever be normal again.

Chapter 5

After a weekend of humiliation, Kate had lost all the confidence she thought she had secretly acquired. After a weekend as The Little Woman she was drained of defiance. In its place was tearful despair.

Bob had come home with a tired smile, preaching platitudes about hard work and results and it all being worthwhile in the end. He had sprawled smugly on the settee and she had brought him a cup of coffee.

'Sweetheart,' he had said. 'Would you mind?'

Would she mind?

Kate had smiled and knelt by the side of the settee and had unfastened and removed his shoes.

Each small act, each submission, each compliance with the lie had eaten away her determination. She had had no choice but to keep playing the role, for she was not ready to confront him with what she had discovered. Would she ever be? she wondered.

On Sunday morning she awoke with him close against her back, his breath hot on her neck, his penis hot between her thighs. All she could do was submit and hope he did not take long.

Kate kept her eyes closed and tears ran silently down her cheeks. But even tears were too much of a defiance. She opened her eyes and stared a the damp patch on the wall beneath the window and tried to remember the name of the paint that proofed against weather and what colours she would pick for the new wallpaper.

As usual, he did not take long and, when he reached the satisfactory conclusion of his marital duties, he rolled over and went back to sleep. The sleep of the righteous, she supposed. The sleep of the good husband.

Her routine was set and she followed it. She slipped from the bed like a thief sneaking from the scene of the crime so as not to disturb him and went to the bathroom. She could not look at herself in the mirror because she knew her resolve was crumbling. She knew that without swift action she would be trapped in the old routine. Submissive housewife. The Little Woman.

She needed someone to confide in, someone to turn to for advice, but she had no one close. Only social friends. Only acquaintances. Only people with whom to exchange charades. Unless she could trust . . .?

They went to The Red Lion and George Mellish made his joke and Bob talked of spooning and she simpered as usual. She was drawn into conversation by Nancy Mellish and two other wives and found herself talking enthusiastically about her two half-days at the Oxfam shop.

'So rewarding,' one of the wives said.

'It's so good to help those poor unfortunates who have so little. Black people and poor people,' said the other, waving a hand to bridge articulation, 'and the rest.'

Kate excused herself and went to the loo. She couldn't

believe it. She had become so immersed back into character that she had been smiling, she had felt warmth towards the other women because they were sharing a conversation. She had felt empathy. She had been enthusiastic because two half-days at the Oxfam shop were the bloody highlight of her week.

If she had found anything sharp she might have been tempted to slash her wrists, but all that was to hand was loo paper and a Tampax dispenser. Perhaps she could choke herself to death? Suicide by sanitary towel.

Her despair was so deep she did not smile at the black humour. Instead, she splashed cold water on her face and smiled for the ladies outside.

When they got home, she took a sanitary towel that she had taken from the pub lavatory from her handbag and left it in the bathroom so Bob could see it and think she had started her period. It was equivalent to painting a red cross on the front door. Plague, Contaminated. Stay away. Not to be touched.

A small act of defiance.

After he went to the office on Monday she went back upstairs. She was exhausted. Living this lie was like living with a severe dose of flu. It was debilitating. She went into one of the guest rooms, drew the curtains and went to bed. At least here there were no memories or odours of her husband. She lay staring at the ceiling.

How had it happened? How had she made such a mess of things? How far back did she have to go? Uncle Toby? Her mother? Dreams don't just happen, they are prompted by the subconscious. Particularly dreams that were memories.

The weather was bad and she could hear rain being

thrown in against the window in stormy gusts. She preferred the summer. Hot weather and long days. Summer was eternal when you were growing up.

Kate had a sudden thought. How old had she really been when she was sixteen? A lot younger than Sadie. That summer had been really hot. That was why she now remembered it so vividly. Wasn't it?

Chapter 6

Afterwards, Sadie refused to speak of what had happened in the house and the friendship between her and Kate cooled. They no longer went riding together.

For a week, Kate stayed away from the stables. When Uncle Toby came to the hotel she was polite but made excuses to leave his presence. Eventually, when the three of them were together, her mother forced the issue by asking why she had stopped riding.

'The horses need exercising,' he said.

His smile was sure of itself.

'Go tomorrow, dear,' her mother said. 'Unless you'd rather come to London with me?'

She knew Kate hated London.

Uncle Toby said, 'I have a business meeting in Salisbury so I'll be away all day. You'll have the place to yourself.'

'Which will it be?' said her mother.

'I'll go riding.'

Kate was glad to be back in the saddle the next day. She was at the stables early but the Range Rover had already gone. She rode her own pony in the morning and a second in the afternoon.

It was marvellous to ride and feel the power of the beast between her legs. The feeling it gave her was akin to the other feelings she knew she should not have. The sexual feelings that overcame her unexpectedly and gave her moods and headaches. They were the devil's temptations but riding was wholesome. These feelings came from physical action and therefore were permissible. They were natural and good.

Thirty-year-old Kate distanced herself for a moment from the dream to wonder again: how old had she been when she was sixteen?

After the ride she unsaddled and released the horse into the grazing field. It was two-thirty and she was hot and thirsty. Uncle Toby had said he would be away all day but to be safe she should still go straight home. To be safe from what?

An image of Sadie kneeling in the study flashed into her mind and she shuddered. Perhaps she had been mistaken. And anyway, her safety was guaranteed by Uncle Toby's relationship with her mother. He was a good man.

Besides, the thought of the pool was inviting and the sense of danger maintained those feelings in her stomach, the ones she pretended were normal.

Kate let herself into the house. She left her boots in the kitchen and had a cold drink. A swim was exactly what she needed now. She pulled off the polo shirt she was wearing as she walked along the carpeted corridors to the pool but stopped with a gasp at the entrance.

Uncle Toby sat on the far edge, his feet dangling in

the water. His body was lean and tanned, the patch of hair at his chest as grey as the hair on his head. He wore blue shorts.

'Hi, Kate.'

'I thought you were in Salisbury.'

'Cancelled.'

'But I didn't see the car.'

'It's being serviced.'

'Oh.'

He laughed.

'What's wrong? Anyone would think you weren't happy to see me.' He slid into the water. 'Come on in. You look like you need it.'

'Erm. I don't know. I was going to go home.'

She realised she was holding the polo shirt across her front.

'Don't be silly. You're dying for it.' He grinned and splashed the water. 'Come on. Then I'll run you home in the MG. Wind in your hair?'

Kate rarely got to ride in the vintage MG that was his second car because it was a two-seater. Her joke was that her mother's hair was too short to live up to the sports car's image.

She was trapped. If she refused to get into the pool she would be admitting to him that she was suspicious of his motives. But what if Sadie had told him she had watched them that day in the study? What if he had seen her? Would she still be safe?

Did she want to be?

The changing room was a refuge. She pulled off the jodhpurs and opened the cupboard for a swimsuit but there were none. Now what did she do? She put on a towelling robe and stepped outside.

'No swimsuit,' she said.

'Didn't you bring one?'

'There were two here.'

'I gave them to your mother.' He grinned. 'Even swimsuits need washing from time to time.'

She smiled, relieved and disappointed.

'So,' she said, and shrugged. 'I guess no swim today.'

'Wear your underwear.'

Her face clouded.

'I don't know.'

'It's only like a bikini. Besides, I've almost had enough. Another five minutes and you can have the pool to yourself.'

Kate went back into the changing room and took off the towelling robe. Her bra and pants were white cotton. She looked at herself in the mirror. He was right, just like a bikini. She had seen bikinis that were a lot more daring.

In the reflection, she saw herself as she had always seen herself and did not appreciate the way the curves had subtly changed her skinny girlhood, or the extent to which her breasts had developed. Her breasts were a nuisance when she ran or galloped a horse. She did not see herself as an object of desire.

Hesitantly, she went out. She felt his eyes upon her body and flushed.

'That's the ticket,' he said, and swam away to the other side of the pool.

Kate slipped into the water and its coolness caressed and hid her.

'Feel good?' shouted Uncle Toby.

'Yes.'

She swam to the deep end and her limbs became languorous with the lack of weight.

'Did you have a good ride?'

'Yes.'

'You were out a long time.'

'I rode both Prince and Justin.' She looked down the pool to where he lay on his back, arms resting on the side. 'How did you know I was a long time?'

'I watched you first thing this morning.'

A nagging doubt entered her mind about all the other times she felt she had been watched when she thought the house was empty. All the other times she had swum naked in this pool, alone and with Sadie. All the other silly conversations they had had about sex and boys, all the other secrets they had shared.

Had she said anything about him when they had exchanged confidences? She must have. Sadie had been curious about how friendly he was with her mother. God! What had she said? Had he listened then, as well?

He swam the length of the pool towards her. She kicked off and swam the other way and they passed. In the shallow end, she stood up and brushed her hair back with both hands. He was swimming towards her and her heart thumped loud enough for him to hear. He went past and lay once more in the water on his back, resting against the side.

'Your mother should swim more often.'

'It ruins her make-up.'

He laughed.

'I think that's an excuse. I don't think she likes swimming very much.'

It was true. Swimming was extraneous to her mother's needs. In her view, any outdoor or leisure pursuit was unless it had a purpose that she could use.

Being busy was what interested her mother, running the hotel, doing things, going places whether she needed to or not. She was good at planning and stuck to her plans. When she and Uncle Toby spent an evening together, she planned it meticulously.

His smile was friendly. Her nervousness was ebbing away.

'She used to swim,' he said. 'When we first met. Do you remember?'

'Yes.'

That was because it was a way of becoming friends, of starting a relationship. Even then, her mother had preferred to sit at the side of the pool and watch.

'Do you remember the game we played?'

'Yes.'

'You nearly knocked my front teeth out.'

She laughed.

'You said I was like a torpedo.'

They had played innocently under her mother's gaze when she was fourteen and a lot skinnier. He had picked her up by the waist and thrown her backwards from the shallow end. Because she was light, and he was tall and strong, he had been able to lift her clear of the water and throw her a considerable distance.

After each throw and splash, she would swim back to him underwater and grab his legs and try to topple him.

Occasionally he let her. But one time, he bent forward as she surfaced too quickly and her head hit him in the face.

Her mother had used the incident as a reason to stop the game despite Uncle Toby's assurances that he was all right. Despite Kate's enjoyment. Or had it been *because* of her enjoyment? Had her mother been jealous that they were getting on so well?

He stood up and walked towards her, moving heavily through the water.

'Let's see if I can still pick you up.'

Kate could hardly refuse. She waited, the water speckling her face, until he stood before her. He was still a good six inches taller than her. She remembered the strength of his body from before. She saw that the hairs on his chest had become greyer.

His hands took hold of her waist and she held her breath. His eyes locked onto hers. They were smiling and confident. She smiled back.

'Ready?'

'Ready.'

He picked her up so that her thighs were clear of the water and threw her backwards. She arched her back, so that her feet cleared the surface, and went under like a porpoise. She had been frightened yet his hands felt so safe.

Kate swam back under water towards his sturdy legs, spread for balance, and swam between them. As she came up for air, he tumbled backwards and went under. When he came up, they both laughed.

'You're a bigger torpedo now,' he said.

He reached for her and she squealed and pretended to try to avoid his hands but he caught her and threw her. Again she swam back and went between his legs, pushing the weight of her body against him, but this time he did not fall. She put both hands around a thigh and tugged. He went under but grabbed for her and they wrestled.

Their limbs entwined, as her limbs had entwined with Sadie's, and their hands pushed and pulled at each other, but it was all in fun.

They came up for air.

'You're much more of a handful,' he said.

'So are you,' she said archly.

'What do you mean?'

'You've put on weight.'

'You cheeky young madam.'

He grabbed her and they wrestled close together, standing upright in the water. Her breasts brushed hard against the curling hair of his chest and sent tingles into her tummy, before he picked her up and threw her again.

She swam away up the pool and he followed, catching up with her in the deep end. They wrestled again, slipping beneath water, limbs brushing each other, bodies thrusting, arms holding, hands grabbing.

Uncle Toby's body was hard and manly. Sadie had talked about Jamie the school heart-throb, but he didn't compare to a real man.

He held her close, trapping her within his arms to stop her fighting anymore, and she relaxed against him. Slowly they sank beneath the surface, turning, drowning in each other's arms. The feeling in her stomach was as liquid as the pool and she had stopped wondering whether it was good or bad because it was total.

When he released her and they came up for air they were breathless, and not just from the immersion. His smile reassured her.

'Had enough?' he said.

She wanted to say no. She wanted to say let's pretend-fight for ever.

'I suppose so.'

'Still tired?'

'My legs ache.'

'You need a massage.'

'A massage?'

He laughed.

'One of my hidden talents.' He lifted his hands from the water and waved them. 'Healing hands. Come on.'

He swam to the side and hauled himself out and she followed. They went into the changing room where the towels and robes were kept and she gasped when she saw herself in the mirror. He stared at her reaction, then glanced at the mirror.

The water had made the cotton brassiere and pants transparent. Her breasts could not have been more naked. Her nipples were hard and pushed against the fabric as if trying to tear holes. Her dark pubic triangle was a matted forest that looked much more dense than when dry.

Kate put one arm across her breasts and a hand over the juncture of her thighs. Uncle Toby laughed.

'It's a bit late to cover up now, Kate.' He put an arm around her shoulder and, without the water and the game, his skin burned against hers. 'No need for false modesty.'

He kissed her on the side of the head, as a close friend and protector might do, before reaching for a towel. He dried his face and patted his body but she remained frozen.

'Come on,' he said jovially, and began to rub her back with the towel. 'We're going to have to get these dry before you can go home.'

His hands in the towel massaged her buttocks and her thighs. They smoothed her legs. He threw the towel to one side and handed her a dry one. He was still standing behind her and, as she held the towel to her bosom, he fumbled with the clasp of the brassiere.

'They're tricky when wet,' he said, as if he unclipped wet underwear all the time.

The clasp came apart and he pushed the straps from her shoulders. He had pushed the straps from Sadie's shoulders, too. Before, before . . .

He stepped away and threw her a white towelling robe. He put on another one and, turning away from her, bent over to pull off his wet shorts. He threw them on a chair.

'You come with me, young lady. I have the secret of soothing tired limbs.'

He rubbed his short hair with a towel and went to the door of the changing room. She removed the bra and, still holding it in one hand, slipped into the robe. She crouched and pulled off the wet cotton panties. Her eyes fixed on his blue shorts.

Beneath the robes they were both naked. She didn't want to think of reasons for what was happening. She picked up the shorts and wrapped her underwear in them, then followed him out of the room to the pool side.

'What about these?'

She held up the garments in her hand.

'Dryer in the utility room.'

Kate knew where it was. She had used it before. The utility room was near the kitchen and he followed her along the corridor. She opened the machine but he took the items from her.

'They're still sopping,' he said.

He twisted his shorts so that excess water splashed from them onto the stone floor, then threw them inside. She held her breath as he folded her bra so that the cups were together and gently squeezed them. That also went into the machine. Now he held her panties, a handful of transparent cotton, the panties she had worn all day.

Was it her imagination or did Uncle Toby take longer than necessary unfolding them, fondling them and squeezing them before he put them in the machine?

Kate's were still swimming. It was as if his hands had been fondling her.

He switched on the machine.

'They won't take long,' he said. 'Now let me introduce you to my oils.'

She followed,for she could do nothing else. She was a part of his plans, trapped in a maze that could lead anywhere. It led upstairs to a spare bedroom whose curtains were drawn. The covers had been removed from the bed which was covered with a white rubber sheet.

Kate had never seen a rubber sheet before. It made the breath catch in her throat with its wickedness. The sense of danger threatened her again and she hesitated on the threshold of the room.

'Welcome to my massage parlour,' he said.

He sounded so normal, looked so normal, and she was being a foolish girl again. Nothing terrible could happen to her. He was going to take her home soon in the MG, back to her mother. Away from the memory of the pool and they way their limbs had touched.

Besides, he was a good man.

Uncle Toby faced her, his smile friendly, his manner professional. He held up a small towel.

'Lie on the bed, face down.' Kate walked to the bed slowly and put her knee on it and he laughed. 'You have to take off the robe first. Here.' He gave her the towel. 'Cover your bottom with this.'

He left the room and gave her the option to comply or make an excuse. But really she had no excuse. Her underwear wasn't dry and she didn't want to offend him by suspecting his motives. The tingle was still in her stomach. The tingle wanted her to lie on the bed.

Kate took off the robe and threw it on a chair. She shivered with the guilt of being naked and lay face down on the rubber sheet. It was surprisingly yielding and soft. She reached behind her to drape the towel over her bottom.

'Ready?' he called.

'I think so.'

He came back into the room, his smile still in place, holding a glass bottle.

'Aromatic oil,' he explained.

She lay flat, her arms by her side to hide her breasts, and watched him remove the stopper from the bottle and pour some of the contents into the palm of his hand. He put the bottle down and spread the oil on his palms. He offered a hand to her face and she sniffed.

'Do you like it?'

'It's nice. What is it?'

'Patchouli. I'm not sure your mother would approve. It smells like cannabis.'

He reached over her and his hands stroked her shoulders. They slid over her skin because of the oil. His fingers dug into her muscles.

'You're tense,' he said. His voice had changed. It had become softer, more intimate. 'Relax.'

His hands worked her shoulders and the back of her neck. His thumbs circled outwards before following her spine. She was in his control and no longer had a say in what was happening. But all that was happening was a massage. And he was good at it. Kate began to relax.

'That's better. Now, put your arms up. Rest your head on your hands.'

Kate did as she was told, trying not to lift her upper body to reveal the swell of her breasts. It was a more comfortable position. His hands worked her shoulders and arms, they moved lower down her back. Periodically, he put more oil on his hands and she found that not only his manipulations were soothing but so was the aroma.

It seemed natural for her to be lying naked on a rubber sheet, her body sheened in oil and sweat in the

59

closeness of the shaded room. The rubber was sensual beneath her. The high excitement of earlier had been suffused by a glow that permeated her whole body.

The bed was an altar and she was a sacrifice. Her eyes were closed and his hands, those strong hands, moved silkily over her. They no longer spoke and she drifted on a gentle level of pleasure. She was being touched with reverence by a handsome man.

He moved to her legs, starting from her ankles, soothing oil into her calves, easing the muscles with fingers and thumbs. His hands moved higher, onto her thighs, and she remembered how they had brushed together in the swimming pool, how hard and manly he had been.

If she kept her eyes closed no one would see. No one would know. Nothing would happen.

He held her left thigh in both hands. The fingers moved up and down rhythmically. Oil was palmed into her skin. His fingertips slipped beneath the towel on the inside of her leg. They were a fraction from her secret place and it was too late to close her legs. All she could do was keep her eyes closed and pretend.

Closer, closer. Was it a wish? Her hips moved imperceptibly. Had he noticed? Her mind refused to consider consequences. She switched it off and lay prone and at his mercy. Submissive.

The fingertips oiled the flesh at the very top of her inner thighs and then slid away, beneath the towel and over her buttocks. The towel was pushed higher but she did not mind. She had no mind. No resolve, no option but to be silent and submissive.

He moved away from the bed and she sighed in disappointment.

'Turn over,' he said.

His voice was no longer jovial. It was low and breathless. Turn over? modesty made her reach for the towel at her waist. There was only one towel.

'Don't be silly,' he said. 'Turn over.'

'Don't be silly. Being silly was being immature. Besides, the feeling in her stomach demanded that she turn over. She did so. Her breasts were naked but the room was dim. She held the towel over her vagina and draped it across her hips.

The rubber sheet was liquid. Like the water of the swimming pool. Oil and sweat had lubricated it. The sensation added to the unreality of what was happening.

She glanced at Uncle Toby but he looked different. Sadie had looked different; when she had looked at herself in the mirror in the changing room, she had looked different. Did she look different now? His face was flushed and his mouth was open. His gaze was fixed upon her body and he was no longer Uncle Toby. He was simply a man.

Her eyes caught his. He smiled. It was a secret smile. It implied their secret. Their complicity. Her nipples tingled, her breasts quivered. She closed her eyes.

His hands began their work again upon her shoulders and her neck. They moved downwards onto the upper slopes of her breasts. They dipped around her ribcage and slid up onto her stomach below them. The thumbs circled gently, the fingers spread.

Kate's breathing was shallow. Her mind was blank, all thoughts were concentrated on the quivering of her breasts.

The hands moved, slowly and confidently. The moved

upwards, pushing the flesh from below, until they covered the soft mounds. Uncle Toby held them for a delicious eternity without pressure. Her nipples burned against his palms. His hands flexed, as if testing the elasticity of what he held, and he massaged her breasts in his hands.

She had been holding her breath and now released it in a long sigh.

He added more oil and his hands were slick as they manipulated the soft globes. Slippery noises were the only other sounds apart from their breathing. He worked on them for a long time before finally relinquishing them and moving to her thighs.

His massage began above the knee and slid swiftly higher. The fingers released the tensions of tired muscles and replaced them with tensions in her stomach. He was working her right leg, his hand sliding over the smooth tender flesh of her inner thigh. The towel was a flimsy defence and she did not object when he removed it.

Now she was totally naked and she felt total freedom. As long as her eyes remained closed. As long as they continued the pretence of a massage.

He dug an oily trail along the groove where her body met her thigh. His fingers slipped past the fringes of undergrowth of her pubic hair and she held her breath but, instead of touching the ache between her legs, the fingers slid around her inner thigh. As if by accident, the back of his thumb brushed against her sex and made her whimper.

Kate was not in control of herself. She was lost in a fantasy behind her closed eyes. Her senses were in the greatest turmoil she had ever known.

'Turn over.'

She didn't recognise his voice. It was soft and hoarse. She turned over, sliding on the rubber sheet and lay her head upon her hands.

He poured oil onto her bottom, dribbling it onto both cheeks. She felt a stream of it slip into the channel in between. His hands massaged it in, his fingers dipping more carelessly now into the junction of her thighs. Fingertips brushed her most sensitive area and a blackness filled her mind.

Kate heard something drop on the floor but was too far from reality to work out what it was. The bed sagged with his weight and she gasped as he straddled her. He was naked. His thighs pressed against her thighs. Like in the swimming pool when they had pretended to fight.

Uncle Toby leaned forward and his hands began to massage her shoulders. His weight shifted onto her bottom. A hard maleness pressed into the groove between the cheeks. As he massaged her shoulders, he rocked against her. The iron rod moved in the aromatic oil slick. It was hot, fierce. It slid and slithered against her softness and now Uncle Toby was groaning.

Soft groans that were emitted each time he leaned forward and his maleness slid and pressed hard against her bottom. His hands moved from her shoulders and slipped beneath her body to palm her breasts. He lowered himself upon her, as if they were pretend fighting, but she was not fighting back. She had given up any battle and remained passive and unresisting.

At the back of her mind was the ever-present knowledge that this was not right, but that added to the twist

63

in her stomach. Her feelings had never soared so high, her body had never felt so alive and if this was a game devised so that Uncle Toby could lie close against her she did not care.

His tensions must be greater than hers. She could feel his tension, fierce against her softness, and she was grateful she could help him find relief.

Their bodies slid against each other as if they were eels, the hairs on his chest scratching her back, the hairs at his groin set her insides ablaze. She wanted to squirm back but dare not in case it broke the sequence of his plot. She remained submissive, passive, a sacrifice.

Uncle Toby gripped her breasts and his face nestled down against hers. His breath enveloped her, a long breath, an escape, and he shuddered upon her bottom, his fierceness pulsing in the groove between flesh and he spilled more aromatic oil upon her.

He lay there for only a moment afterwards before moving quickly from her. She remained face down and eyes closed. Nothing had happened. It had been a dream. He wiped the small of her back with a towel and coughed.

'Best thing,' he said, 'is a shower.' His voice was normal again. 'Wash away the oil. You use the bathroom, I'll get your things.'

Kate listened to him leave the room. She lay for a while with her eyes closed and wondered if it had happened at all. She reached behind her and touched the small of her back but it had been wiped dry. Her hand slid over her bottom and between the cheeks. They were still slippery. Her fingers traced the curve and went between her legs. The lips of her vagina were open and she touched it experimentally, shuddering at the sensation.

That was wrong. She could not touch herself, not like this, in the middle of the day without reason. Without the pretence of sleep. She slid off the rubber sheet. It glistened. Her robe was on the chair. She should do what he said and have a shower. The oil might stain her clothes. It might make her mother ask what she had been doing and she would not believe her if she said nothing.

But that was the truth. Kate had done nothing.

Chapter 7

Kate had never done anything positive. If she had been asked last week for a word to sum up her life, she might have chosen flexible. Her husband could have said malleable. But now she believed the little fat man with the sausage fingers had probably got it right. Submissive.

Lying in bed was no answer. She got up, showered and dressed. There was one person she could talk to, but it was so against her nature to confide that she needed to invent an excuse to even make the journey. At least the rain had stopped.

She drove into town, parked near the town hall and went to the library. She had books to return and maybe she would see Paul. He was a librarian who was also involved in amateur dramatics. He acted and occasionally directed.

Kate didn't have the confidence to appear on stage, even when Paul had tried to coax her into accepting small roles, but she was content to be involved behind the scenes. She helped in the props and wardrobe departments.

Paul was a friend, she supposed, although a diffident

one. It hardly amounted to a relationship but they had a platonic understanding. At least they didn't have to use pointless chatter when they were together. If they had little to say, silence was more comfortable. At times, she'd caught him staring at her when they went for coffee or a drink in the pub after rehearsals. He would smile and shake his head when he knew she had seen him.

Kate wondered if he were laughing at her, but even if he was she didn't mind. He was gentle and without malice. An ordinary man of forty, just as she was an ordinary woman.

Her hidden motive remained latent until she arrived at the library. Then she caught herself remembering as if by chance. Paul was divorced. He had been through the whole process. He would know what to do. But could she ask him?

He was pinning old photographs on a board in the foyer to publicise a local history week. She waited until he caught sight of her. His smile was always slow, as if he had all the time in the world. Perhaps that was what came of spending your life in a library.

'Hello, Kate. Finished them already?'

'What?' He was looking at the books she held in her arms. She had only taken them out of the library just before the weekend. She hadn't read them. 'Oh, yes.' She grinned 'We had a quiet weekend.'

'Sometimes they're the best.'

'Are you busy?'

'Not very.'

'I wondered . . .'

Kate was on the brink again, hesitant about involving

Paul in her problems. It occurred to her that she might have to confess what she'd discovered. Confess? Why had it become her confession?

Because she was The Little Woman and being The Little Woman meant being a failure.

'Why don't you get rid of those,' he said, nodding at the books. 'Then I'll buy you a coffee.'

'What? Oh yes. These. I'll only be a minute.'

They went to a tea shop above a confectioners and shared a silence. Her doubts were back, robbing her of speech and courage. Why fight it? She was what she was and nothing could be changed.

'What's wrong, Kate?'

'Wrong?'

His smile had become sad. She liked his smile and his face. It was safe. A funny way to describe a face, perhaps, but it was safe. Maybe she felt safe because he didn't particularly care about his appearance. His suit wasn't fashionable or pressed and his hair was always a mess. She felt safe because they were no threat to each other. Because they were perfect for a platonic friendship.

'I can see it in your eyes. What's wrong?'

He stared into her eyes and she felt he could read her mind.

'My husband is having an affair.'

His face registered genuine sorrow. He reached across the table and touched her hand. The contact made her start and him self-conscious. He withdrew his hand.

'I am sorry, Kate. Really sorry.'

'I'm not.' She shook her head and felt tears closing in.

69

'It's not a marriage. Never has been. I want a divorce.'

His eyes widened at the revelation.

'It's over?'

'Yes.'

'There's no chance of reconciliation?'

'I don't want a reconciliation.' The anger returned unexpectedly. 'I want a life.'

He sat back and drank coffee. His eyes watched her over the cup.

'Why are you telling me, Kate?'

'Because you're a friend and because you're divorced. I want you to tell me how I can get a divorce.'

'It's a fairly simple process. As long as you're sure.'

'I'm sure.'

He talked and she listened. Eventually, he asked her if she was certain her husband was having an affair. She gave him a photocopy of some of the polaroids. After a moment's hesitation, she also handed him copies of the letters.

'I found them when he was away. By accident. I wasn't prying . . .'

Even now, she was worried in case he thought she had overstepped propriety. She tried to make her face a mask. Someone, eventually, would have to read the letters. Eventually, they would become evidence and the property of the courts. In a way, she was testing her resolve by showing them to Paul.

'Oh, Kate,' he said. 'I'm so sorry.'

She didn't want sorrow.

'They've talked about me. Laughed about me. They make me sound plain and boring. Am I, Paul? Am I plain and boring?'

'No, Kate. You're beautiful.'

His answer confused her. His face was no longer safe. They looked away from each other, both embarrassed.

'I'd better go,' she said. 'See a solicitor.'

Martin Bell was about the same age as Kate but far more assured. He sat behind a large desk and she sat in a chair in front of it. He took preliminary details and explained procedures. He, like Paul, talked about reconciliation. Although his words were addressed to her, he spoke to a spot about three feet above her head.

'Divorce is expensive, Mrs Adams. Two can live as cheaply as one if they stay together. If they part, they can have the devil's own job making ends meet.'

'I want to get rid of him,' she said.

'You're sure he is having an affair?'

Now he looked at the carpet.

'I'm sure.'

Kate opened her bag to take out the photocopies. Someone knocked on the door and he said enter. A young woman in a tight skirt came in and placed a file on his desk. He gave her a full smile and said, 'Thank you, Jennifer,' and watched her rear as she went back to the door and left the room.

'You're sure?' he said to the carpet.

'I found letters and photographs. I photocopied them.'

She got up and handed them to him. He perked up when he saw the photographs. He read the letters but returned to the photographs.

'Very good,' he said, without being specific. 'Where are the originals?'

'At home.' The word made her wince. 'I can get them any time.'

'Of course, the civilised way to divorce would be to discuss the matter with your husband and agree to separate.' He continued to look at the photographs. 'For two people of like mind it does not take long to obtain a decree.'

'I don't want to be civilised, Mr Bell.'

'You don't?'

'I want revenge.'

He looked up and stared at her for the first time.

'Revenge?'

'I want this other woman named. I want to hurt him. Embarrass him.'

'Financially?'

'Of course, financially.'

'Then we will need more evidence.'

The solicitor made a phone call and arranged an appointment for her that same afternoon with a private investigator called Stanley Bevan who worked from the Bank Building near the town hall.

Her heart fluttered as she read the sign on his door. She had never met a private investigator before, although she had read plenty of detective stories.

Stanley Bevan ushered her into his office and they sat either side of a cluttered desk. He was a retired policeman, fat and fifty, and he sweated in the central heating. He looked nothing like Mickey Spillane's Mike Hammer.

The man patted his stomach and said, 'They call me Flat Stanley.'

Kate explained her visit. She had a second set of photostats which she gave him. Like the solicitor, he preferred to look at the photographs rather than Kate. Once again, her husband's strumpet was making her feel inadequate.

The detective took personal details about her and Bob. He explained they would have to discover the identity of the woman, follow her husband until they were together and then attempt to procure audio or visual evidence of a sexual nature.

'It could be expensive,' he said.

'I don't care.'

'I suppose Mr Bell suggested talking to your husband?'

'He did.'

'And you said no?'

'I don't want my husband to know anything until everything is settled.'

He shrugged.

'There is still the expense, Mrs Adams. A negotiated deal with your husband would be cheaper.'

How could she negotiate a deal with her husband when she was trained like one of Pavlov's dogs to remove his shoes and take him coffee and simper to order?

'As I said. I don't care what it costs.'

'But will you be able to pay?'

This was something Kate had anticipated. She removed two hundred pounds in cash from her handbag and handed it to Flat Stanley.

'Is this enough for a deposit?' she said.

'We call it a retainer, Mrs Adams.' He smiled. 'It's enough to get us started.'

73

'Is there anything I can do to help?' she said.

'Yes,' said Flat Stanley. 'There is.' He looked at the details on his notepad. 'You don't work, do you?'

It sounded like an accusation.

'No.'

'No children?'

No, thank God. Not to him.

She shook her head.

'And no real commitments?'

He was doing a good job of putting her life into perspective.

'I have no commitments.'

'Then I suggest you go away for a week. Could you manage that?'

'I think so. Why?'

'To give your husband the opportunity to be unfaithful. He wouldn't be suspicious about you going away?'

'No.'

He wouldn't care about her going away. He would probably welcome it.

'So you can do that?'

'Yes. I can do that.'

'Preferably abroad so he knows you're out of the way.'

'All right. Is there anything else?'

'Yes. You can let us into your house before you go. We have a few electronic gadgets we would like to fit. Would that be in order?'

'That would be fine.'

He looked at the photographs of the woman in black underwear and smiled to himself. Kate could imagine what he was thinking. That he didn't blame her husband

74

for straying when he had such a straight-laced wife at home.

A week later, Flat Stanley had confirmed the identity of the woman as Valerie Hudson, aged twenty-eight and single, an insurance investment consultant who lived in a flat that she owned in the centre of town. He and his assistant had also spent a morning at twenty-three Maple Drive.

Kate, upon the advice of her solicitor, had photocopied various legal documents and a share portfolio and had delivered them to his office.

Her husband had been less than enthralled when she told him she had received a letter from an old school friend who lived in Malta. She said her name was Sadie. But when she added that Sadie had invited her to visit he suddenly became interested.

He urged her to go. The change would do her good.

Chapter 8

Uncle Toby had taken Kate into his massage room once a week until September. Until a day like today, she thought, as she boarded an Air Malta flight at Heathrow.

A lot had happened in the last week. Enough to stop the memories and the dreams. There were times when she could not believe she had actually put in motion the start of divorce proceedings. That she had a solicitor and a private detective acting on her behalf.

It had been necessary to see Paul at the library several times for silent but comforting support across the shelves of books or cups of coffee. She had gained strength from him, particularly when he had said he was no longer sorry for her, but proud of her.

But, until now, all that she had started had seemed to be temporary. They were actions she could stop. Even when she had arrived at Heathrow she knew she could still cancel the trip and the inevitable confrontation with Bob. She could avoid unpleasantness and return to her role in her husband's scheme of things.

Boarding the aircraft was not just confirmation of her intent. It removed her from a position of doubt and the temptation of calling the whole thing off. Entering the pressurised cabin was taking an irrevocable step into the future.

The pilot was in charge of her destiny now. The worries of home were behind her. She settled into her window seat and studiously read her book through the pre-flight preliminaries. When they took off she watched as they left a miserable day on the ground and climbed through clouds towards the perpetual sunshine above.

It had been a day like this when the trips to the massage room had ended. A day like this when Uncle Toby had married her mother at the end of that long hot summer.

Had she always hidden from reality? Was that why she had submerged herself as The Little Woman? Why she read so many books of fiction? Had reality been the massage room and everything since self-deception?

Sixteen and hot in the summer. The beast between her legs beneath the saddle. And afterwards, the beast inside herself that led her to swim in underwear that became transparent and to go into the massage room with Uncle Toby.

It became an unspoken ritual and she was good at rituals. They would swim in innocence and tumble and play in the water and their bodies would touch and become aroused. And after he had patted her dry, gently and without sexual inference, he would say, 'Time for your massage,' and she would go upstairs and lie on the bed.

Always the same, until he changed the rules. She closed her eyes as they left the clouds and the sun shone brilliantly in its peerless blue domain. She closed her eyes and remembered.

Kate lay face down on the white rubber sheet, her body slick with oil. Uncle Toby lay upon her back massaging her bottom with his iron manhood and his groin.

This was as close as she got to swooning. A turmoil of feelings she did not fully understand and which she could never fully satisfy. When he orgasmed upon her buttocks, her insides would tense with delicious sinful delight. Was she also experiencing an orgasm? She did not know and dare not ask. They still did not speak about what they did and the only words were those of his commands which she obeyed.

He moved himself almost leisurely upon her and the fire that lay in the groove between her cheeks made secret slurping noises in the moisture he had poured and created.

Because they only spoke of it in coded language, the performance had become what she had first imagined it to be: a sacrifice. Her body was the offering which he used, and oh how she loved to be used.

In between the performances, she tried to close her mind to it, for it did not sit comfortably in her thoughts when she was in her mother's presence or when the three of them were together. She also had to contain herself when he showed particular attention to her mother, and she was shocked to recognise jealousy in herself. This was the man her mother was going to marry. Kate had no right to be jealous.

Yet, even though she subdued her desires and wallowed in the guilt, she could not stop herself from wondering if her mother had ever enjoyed an Uncle Toby massage. For some reason, she assumed she had not. She assumed the massage was special to her and Uncle Toby.

He moved and his hardness slid and slithered. His hands massaged her breasts. His thumbs rubbed her nipples. A ritual of massage that never included a kiss or the touching of her vagina.

Kate wished he would invent another ritual.

Uncle Toby climbed from her body without climaxing.

'Roll over,' he said, and she obeyed.

She lay supine, her arms by her side, her legs slightly apart, her breasts pulsing with warmth, her eyes closed.

'Are you relaxed?' he said.

He was breaking the ritual. Her insides quavered at the possibilities.

'Yes.'

'But not relaxed enough. I can feel your tensions, Kate. Different tensions.'

She said nothing but lay in silence, her body attuned, her vagina tingling. He was standing by the bed. She sensed him reach over. His hands held her breasts.

'Do you know the tension I mean, Kate?'

'No.'

She felt foolish because she didn't know how to answer.

He took hold of her right hand and placed it over her pubis. Her hand lay like a shell upon the patch of hair, the fingers dipping slightly over the mound below which pouted the lips of her sex.

'You have a tension there, don't you, Kate?'

'Yes,' she whispered.

'A tension that needs to be released. Do you want it to be released?'

'Yes.'

'Do you know how, Kate?'

'No.'

'Have you ever touched yourself there?'

'Sometimes.'

'Did it bring relief?'

'Sometimes I went to sleep. Sometimes it made it worse.'

'It made the tension worse?'

'Yes.'

Her breathing was becoming more strained. She had never told anyone these secrets before and yet, lying here, naked with her eyes closed, she felt unable to do anything but tell the truth. She was compelled to tell the truth.

'Have you ever climaxed, Kate?'

A sigh escaped her lips.

'I don't know,' she said.

'Then you haven't.' His fingers pressed upon her fingers so that they dipped into the moist valley between her legs. 'It's time you learned how.'

He pushed harder so that her fingers slipped between the swollen lips of her vagina and entered a new silky oiliness.

'Touch yourself,' he whispered. 'Use your fingers. Stroke your sex. Make it tingle.'

Kate did as she was told and continued even when he removed his hand which had guided her there. She had

81

touched herself before but had always stopped when she got too excited because she did not know what would happen, because she was afraid of falling into a fit or making a noise and being found by her mother.

Her fingers probed and stroked and the delicious languid feeling in which she had been wallowing rose to a keener level. Her stomach was light, her thighs quivered. She groaned.

'Does it feel good?'

'Yes. Oh yes.'

'Find the rosebud.'

'The rosebud?'

His hand guided her fingers again. She allowed it to, making her hand an extension of his. He moved her finger into the apex of her opening and onto the hard little bud of flesh that was always ready to tingle. She gasped again.

'That's it,' he said. 'Does it feel good?'

'Yes.'

'Use your other hand as well, Kate. Explore yourself. Touch yourself. Stroke those tensions. Use that rosebud. Do it, Kate. Do it.'

Kate did it, slowly at first but without embarrassment. This was another part of the massage and the ritual. She was an acolyte under instructions. She had to obey.

The more she touched herself and the more excitement and desire she released, the more abandoned she became.

'Roll the rosebud,' he whispered.

She did and she moaned.

'Use your fingers,' he whispered.

82

She did, opening the lips of her vagina with her other hand, dipping beneath the folds of flesh.

Uncle Toby was kneeling by the bed.

'Push your fingers inside yourself.'

She did, and two fingers entered into the hotness up to the knuckle.

'Move them, Kate,' he urged. 'Move them in and out. Push them deeper. As deep as they will go.'

Kate did as she was told. She rolled the rosebud between the fingers of her right hand and pushed two fingers of her left in and out of herself rhythmically. Her thoughts were hazy, her body full of coalescing tension. Her knees were rising from the bed and her vagina was contracting around the fingers.

'Do it, Kate. Do it to yourself.'

Uncle Toby's voice seemed distant. The only sound she could hear was the squelching of her fingers as they fought the suction of her vagina. A squelching that was intimate and private and sinful.

'Do it, Kate!'

Her feelings seemed to be rushing together, combining in a tidal wave. She could even hear the distant roar it made in her ears. The roar was drowning the sound of her fingers, almost drowning the sound of Uncle Toby's voice.

'Let it come, Kate! Let it come!'

The sensations were centred in her vagina. It was as if her fingers were rubbing at raw nerve ends which, in turn, were twisting in her stomach, making it light, making her feel ethereal. She was on the verge of fear because she had never felt like this before. The fear fought with excitement and an emotion she didn't recognise. Only later would she realise it was lust.

'Come, Kate! Come for me! Come!'

The orders were distant but had to be obeyed and besides, the tidal wave had taken on a power of its own and she could not stop it if she tried.

Her thighs began to clamp around her hands, her back arched from the bed and her mouth opened. The tidal wave engulfed her vagina and the nerves twisted and sparked along her body, all the way to her skull, and her mind exploded.

Kate shook uncontrollably and a cry wavered from her throat, a long plaintiff cry that lasted as long as the tremors lasted, as long as her limbs thrashed upon the rubber sheet.

After the storm, she lay exhausted, but it was a beautiful exhaustion. Her spirit floated in a different sort of languidity, as if she had shed all troubles and pains and she wallowed in peace and delight.

'Was it good?'

'Mmm?'

'Was it good, Kate?'

Uncle Toby was asking her a question. But it was such a silly question. Was it good? It was miraculous.

'Yes,' she said, her eyes still closed. 'It was good.'

'Did you enjoy it?'

'Oh yes.'

'Then do it again.'

The command surprised her. Could she do it again? Was so much pleasure available any time at her fingertips?

'Again?'

'Yes, Kate. Make yourself come again.'

She moved her fingers experimentally and thrilled when she discovered the nerve endings were still attuned and waiting. She groaned.

And she did it again.

And again.

Every time afterwards when they went to the massage room, he would annoint her with oils and handle her body in the most intimate of ways but without touching her vagina. His fingers would prepare her sensibilities and he would lie upon her back with his iron rod slotted between the cushions of her bottom and move it like a piston in the slippery valley.

Then he would sit by her side and watch as she lay upon her back and massaged herself into oblivion, her cries sometimes wistful because it was ending, sometimes yelped because of the intensity.

She would make herself come at least three times and became adept with her fingers. Always she did it with her eyes closed. She knew Uncle Toby watched but to look back would have been to break the spell.

After she had pleasured herself to his commands, he would tell her to roll over and she would obey and he would once more take his position upon her back and rock against her buttocks until he came.

Once she had learned the technique of how to give herself pleasure, she practised it almost every night in her bed. At first she lay face down so that her cries would be buried in the pillow but eventually she was able to control the sounds that were an expression of her release.

When she entered the massage room she left all guilt

or doubts about right and wrong behind. The room was insulated from outside influences. It was a secret room for secret practices that no one else would ever discover.

But at home, the guilt was intense when she fingered herself to orgasm. She felt as if her mother suspected what she was doing and knew she would not approve. They had never discussed sex properly and if the subject had ever been raised obliquely her mother had let her disapproval show.

Intimacy of a sexual nature should only be practised within a proper relationship. Kate got the impression that her mother believed it was something women had to endure for the sake of their marriage. That it was something a husband expected and a wife provided as a reward for him being a good man.

She was certain her mother had never experienced an Uncle Toby massage.

The ritual lasted until the wedding. Both Kate and Uncle Toby knew that then it had to stop.

An autumnal day with dead leaves blowing in the streets beneath grey skies. A day drained of colour and life, a sepia day when Kate felt she was attending a wake rather than a wedding.

Part of her life had died but she was no longer jealous of her mother. Uncle Toby had become two people to her. The man with a friendly grin and generous spirit who was her mother's consort, and her secret masseur whom she kept behind closed eyes and whom she knew had to remain a fantasy.

Now the fantasy was over and she was sad but not jealous at losing him for she had never possessed him.

He had possessed her, but only for the duration of the visits to the room with the rubber sheet.

Chapter 9

Nero approached her the first morning when she had coffee at the harbourside. She had smiled politely and tried to ignore him by reading the *Times of Malta*. The newspaper was less compulsive than *The Times* of London. It was also a flimsy tabloid and did not provide adequate cover. Nero sat opposite and persisted.

'You are right to be wary,' he said. 'A beautiful woman must always be wary.'

Beautiful woman? Kate almost smiled at the blatant flattery. She knew she was not beautiful. Rather ordinary, in fact, which was exactly why she was alone in Malta and on the run. It sounded dramatic but she supposed it was true. When you fled a broken marriage she supposed you could describe it as being on the run.

She concentrated on the newspaper.

'My name is Nero.' He grinned. 'Like the emperor. I have a boat in the harbour. The big one, white with blue trim.'

He pointed and she looked from behind the sunglasses but without moving her head. The boat was modern and sleek. She studiously continued to read.

A woman alone would always attract a certain kind of man. Even a woman like her. She bit her lip in frustration. Being self-deprecating was a hard habit to break after life with Bob.

Her body, she often thought, looked better in a swimsuit than in clothes because it was trim and without excess weight. It also had a suntan. Although she had only been in Malta two days, the basis of the tan had been acquired on a two-week trip to an outward bound camp in Cornwall.

Another holiday alone, apart from two other volunteers and thirty fifteen year olds from under-privileged backgrounds.

Mrs Kate Adams: housewife with time on her hands and always available for charity and volunteer work. She remembered and smiled. A woman for whom two half-days in an Oxfam shop were the highlight of the week.

The self-pity annoyed her. She folded the newspaper and put it down. Nero smiled and introduced himself. He held his hand out formally and she shook it out of politeness and told him her name. He wanted to keep holding her hand, which embarrassed her, and she retrieved it.

He was about forty years old, a small man, no more than five feet six inches, but strongly built. His skin was darkly tanned, his hair black and curling with grey at the temples. He wore old baggy blue shorts and a blue polo shirt and a gold chain around his neck. On his wrist was a gold watch.

If, perish the thought, she had been looking for an

affair, it would not be with someone like him.

'You are English,' he said. 'Yes?'

'Yes.'

It was not so hard to work out. The *Times of Malta* was published in English and an English language copy of a Jeffrey Archer novel was on view in the bag at her feet. Besides, the island seemed to be populated exclusively by British tourists.

'This is your first time in Malta?'

'Yes.'

'Where is your husband?'

'In England.'

He raised his eyebrows.

'He allowed you to come alone?'

'Yes.'

'He is a foolish man.'

The flattery was annoying because it was patronising. He was chatting to her because at eleven in the morning there was no one better.

'Probably,' she said.

'You here with a girlfriend?'

'No. No girlfriend.'

There was no reason why she should be telling him this other than defiance. She had come away in defiance, even if Bob didn't know it.

'Would you like to come on my boat? I will take you on the sea. On the ocean.'

Kate allowed herself to smile. She had thought the flattery was because he was interested in her. Instead, he was selling package trips.

'No thank you.'

'She is a lovely boat. You will enjoy. Here it is hot, out there, it is cool.'

'No thank you. I don't want to go on a boat trip.'

She picked up her bag and got to her feet.

'You go already?' said Nero.

He stood up with her. His feet were bare on the hot flagstones, his legs muscular and hairy. They were about the same height.

'Yes.'

'Will you come back?'

The question made her pause. She liked the bar and the harbour.

'Probably.'

'Perhaps I see you later?'

'Perhaps,' she said.

Kate turned and walked away. By noon the sun would be too hot to do anything but lie by the pool. By the time she reached the steps of the Italian restaurant, she had already forgotten Nero.

The next morning, he was there again. Soon after she sat at a table in the shade of an umbrella, he appeared further along the harbourside, walking towards her as if he had been waiting for her arrival.

He sat at the same table as her without asking permission. They were the only customers. He spoke to the waiter in Maltese.

'You would like coffee?' he asked her.

'Yes.'

He ordered and the waiter went away.

'You did not come back,' he said.

'I had other things to do.'

'Alone?' He tutted and shook his head. 'You should not be alone.'

'I like being alone.'

He smiled, a wide smile that showed large white teeth. 'Beautiful women should never be alone.'

Did he think she was so gullible that she would fall for such a line? Perhaps he thought she looked desperate enough to believe him.

Desperate? She supposed she still was a little desperate, although not for false flattery.

'I still don't want to go on a boat trip,' she said.

'But the boat is beautiful and the ocean is beautiful. The sky and the sea become one. You would enjoy.'

'I can't afford a boat trip.'

If she made it clear she had no intention of becoming a customer he might try elsewhere.

The waiter returned with her coffee and a bottle of Seven-Up that was still frosted from the refrigerator. It made her wish she had ordered a cold drink instead of coffee.

When the waiter had gone, Nero leaned forward across the table and said. 'You do not understand, Kate. I would not take money from you.' He shook his head as if she had upset him. 'You are a guest in my country. I offered hospitality.'

Kate was momentarily at a loss. Upon his first approach, she had suspected him of sexual motives, then of commercial motives. Now she felt guilty at misjudging him.

'I'm sorry,' she said. Her face flushed in embarrassment. 'I thought . . .'

He smiled and touched the back of her hand in reassurance.

'That's all right. I have thick skin. Sometimes, I don't make myself understood good.'

She laughed at his fractured English. They talked more freely. He asked her which hotel she was staying at and about her fellow guests. He said he was a fisherman who no longer fished. He owned several boats and took a percentage of the profits and also had a tour boat moored at Sliema. He stayed away from work, he said. He paid others to work. He preferred to choose his own passengers.

He again invited her to take a trip and again she refused.

'You are safe with me,' he said. 'I am gentleman with ladies.'

'I'm sure you are.'

'Then you will come?'

'No. Thank you very much but no.'

'But you are on holiday. You should enjoy. You should not be alone.'

'I'm not alone.' He looked puzzled and she picked up a book from the bag that was by her feet. 'I have a book.' It was a novel by Danielle Steel. 'While I have a book to read I am not alone.'

He reached out and she allowed him to take the book. He looked at the cover and flipped the pages. Without warning, he got to his feet and walked to the edge of the harbour and held the book over the water.

'If I drop her and she drowns?' he said. 'Would you take a trip?'

'Nero! Don't you dare.'

It was the first time she had used his name and he grinned and came back to the table. He gave her back the book.

'You can bring her, too,' he said.

'I'm going to Mdina today. I've hired a car.'

'Then tomorrow. Come tomorrow. I'll be here at the same time. I'll show you Gozo and Comino, the islands to the north. You can swim in bays where no tourists go. The best day of your holiday. I promise.'

She smiled but shook her head.

'I don't think so.'

'They made *Popeye*, the movie, here in Malta. Built a town for him.' He stuck his chin out. 'I think maybe I'm like Popeye. I never take no. You make your mind up. Tomorrow I'll be here and the boat, she will be ready. I hope you will be ready.'

Kate already knew she would not even be at the harbour the next day. That, she thought, would be the best way to avoid an embarrassing scene. She had never been good with embarrassing scenes or at convincing anyone that she meant it when she said no. This was another situation from which she would walk away.

But that was before dinner in the hotel. Before the elderly couple from Barnet tried to take her into their protective custody to ensure she had a good time and did not feel left out.

There was a difference, she wanted to tell them, between being alone and being lonely. But, of course, she didn't. She tolerated them with her usual patience because they were full of good intentions and she did not wish to upset them.

Never mind her feelings, she had to be careful of theirs, until, eventually, she had to make a stand when they insisted she go with them to Valetta the next day.

They would look after her, they said. It was the last straw. But once again her defiance was less than sweeping.

'You're very kind but I'm afraid I can't. I'm going on a boat trip to Gozo.'

Chapter 10

Kate wondered if she had made a mistake. If so, it was too late to change her mind. The boat had left the harbour of St Julian's Bay and was lifting in the swell of the Mediterranean as it rounded Dragonara Point.

She was leaving safety behind on the sun terraces of the hotels and beneath the orange umbrellas of the Reef Club. She had accepted a trip with a man who was almost a stranger.

Even when she had gone to the harbour, her intention had been to have morning coffee before retiring to the seclusion of the Reef Club to avoid the couple from Barnet. At the club, she could swim, sunbathe, read and have lunch and wait until it was safe to return to the hotel.

After all, she'd have to be out of her mind to accept Nero's invitation.

Yet she had been unable to refuse when he met her with effusive greetings as if it had all been agreed. He had ushered her on board a thirty-foot motor yacht and she had been impressed by the comfort of the craft. The bridge was above the cabin. The stern was open and fitted with soft cushioned seating around its sides.

He had food in the larder and wine chilling in an ice box. Before she knew it, he had cast off and was guiding the boat from its moorings and between the red, green, yellow and blue fishing boats and out of the harbour.

Kate wore a cotton dress and sandals. Her hair, as usual, was tied in a bun and pinned at the back of her head. She had a swimsuit and towel in her bag for her visit to the Reef Club.

Nero looked at home on the boat and at sea. As they headed up the coast he pulled off his shirt and stood at the wheel on the bridge. She joined him and he pointed to the coastline and told her its history. Madliena Tower, Ghallis Rocks, Salina Bay and, eventually, round the point to St Paul's Bay.

He was right. She was enjoying herself. The blues of sea and sky melted into each other on the horizon. The breeze was a delight.

'Bugibba,' he said, pointing. 'A village once. Now big tourist centre.' He pointed ahead at two small islands. 'St Paul's Islands. Many years ago, St Paul was ship-wrecked on the islands. He landed in the bay and was thirsty. He struck the rock and a spring opened up. A miracle.' He laughed. 'Now the British and the Italians and the Germans strike a rock, and a bar opens.'

He shook his head, still laughing.

'All tourists now,' he said.

Kate felt she should apologise because she was a tourist.

'I suppose people come because your island is beauti-ful,' she said.

'No. Not beautiful. Too dry, too arid. We are too close to the Sahara. People visit Malta to become beetroots. Because the wine is cheap.'

He laughed and she smiled in sympathy.

They went leisurely along the north-west coast. From this perspective, the island was beautiful, but she also knew from her day exploring by car that it was, as Nero said, extremely dry.

'You should change,' he said. 'You should wear bikini.' He grinned with his teeth. 'No clothes, if you like. Very private here.'

His laugh diffused the suggestion. But he was right again. She should be wearing her swimsuit to take full advantage of the sun.

'I'll change,' she said.

Kate climbed down the short ladder into the stern of the boat and stepped into the cabin. The sides were glass and the roof had been slid open. Nero was above her and out of sight but she hesitated before undressing. His polo shirt lay crumpled on the bench seat bunk. She felt vulnerable and wondered again at the wisdom of accepting his offer.

But she *had* accepted it and, in so doing, had accepted the consequences. She did not think the man was a rapist but if he was, all she could do was endure it. It was a long swim to shore and no one would hear her if she screamed. The fact that she had actually run the scenario briefly through her mind caused her to smile at her foolishness.

Always unsure, always worried in case she said or did the wrong thing. Now The Little Woman was worried in case she provoked her own rape. Chance would be a fine thing.

Kate undressed, feeling daring as she slipped off the frock and stood in the cabin in her underwear. Safe white cotton bra and panties. Nothing much had changed. She had worn white cotton when she had gone swimming at Uncle Toby's.

The memory, sudden and hot, caused her to close her eyes. It had been a long time ago. She had learned since not to think thoughts that heated her senses and she had stopped, long ago, those secret touchings that had once given her so much pleasure.

Had they given her pleasure or was that a figment of the memory? The past always seemed better than the present. The joy and delirium always sweeter back then.

'You okay?'

His voice gave her a start. She opened her eyes and saw him leaning round the side of the cabin from the ladder. It took all her composure to stop herself from trying to cover her body with her hands.

'I'm fine.' She forced a smile. 'Won't be a minute.'

He grinned and disappeared back up the ladder.

If he had been contemplating an attack, perhaps her underwear had put him off. It was so plain and girlish it would tempt no one. Last week in Safeways car park, she had been more embarrassed by her underwear than sucking a prick.

Kate flushed. Where had that come from? It was a memory to bury. A dream sequence that had not happened. Language she did not use.

She took off the bra and pants and pulled on the one-piece black swimsuit. Now she hesitated before leaving the cabin and climbing back up to the bridge. Always hesitating. That was how she had approached life, with hesitation.

Deep breaths. She smiled. It was a line from a book. Yeth and I'm only fifteen. She had been sixteen, all those years ago.

Her breasts were bigger now, but not much. They were still firm. Childbirth had not caused them to sag because Bob had not wanted children. Once again she felt the surge of thankfulness that she had not had a child. Not with him anyway.

Perhaps her body suited the girlish cotton underwear. Perhaps she had never grown up.

Kate left the cabin and climbed up to the bridge.

'Beautiful,' Nero said, but his teeth grinned and she did not take him seriously.

They went past Mellieha Bay and Ahrax Point and across the channel to the small island of Comino. He pointed and talked, and she listened. They left Comino behind and headed towards Gozo.

'Here,' he said. 'You steer.'

'No, I couldn't.'

'Of course.' He was standing, leaning against a fixed high chair. He let go of the wheel and spread his hands. 'The boat, she is yours.'

'I've never . . .'

She was flustered and hovered. Taking the wheel would be a thrill but Nero had not moved. She would have to brush against him.

'It's easy. Come. I show you.'

Kate stepped in front of him and took hold of the wheel. He put his arms around her, his hands upon her hands. His body was hard against her back. She found it difficult to concentrate.

'See?' he said. 'Easy. Yes?'

His face was close to hers. She could smell his sweat, feel the hair of his chest against her back where the swimsuit scooped. Feel his muscular thighs against hers. Feel something else, too, hard and long. It fitted into the groove of her bottom.

Nero reached to one side, flicked a switch, pulled a lever and the boat surged forward. She squealed and lay hard back against him with the thrust of power. He laughed and his stance became firmer on the deck, his hips moved and the iron rod in his shorts dug against her softness.

'You like?' he said.

Kate was flustered and trapped. Images from the past threatened her senses. He reduced power and she broke away from the past and the present and moved to the other side of the bridge.

She put her face into the wind. Perhaps he would think the flush was caused by the sun.

He said, 'Gozo is a dangerous place.' His grin was wide. 'Ulysses stayed here seven years. He was...' he waved a hand to help him think of the right word '...seduced, yes, seduced, by the siren Calypso. Seven years he stayed.' He shook his head. 'Seven years of sex.'

Nero anchored in a deserted cove on the north side of Gozo that was protected by cliffs and swooping birds.

'You swim and I make lunch,' he said.

'Let me help you.'

'It's not a difficult lunch. You swim. It won't take long.'

Kate removed the pins in her hair until it hung around her shoulders. She dived off the boat into clear waters that were cool and refreshing. She swam with the fish that darted in silvery shoals. She twisted and dived, kicked and angled her body towards the sun and broke the surface of the water like a dolphin.

Had she once been a dolphin? A sixteen-year-old dolphin trapped in a swimming pool?

Nero interrupted her thoughts.

'The food is ready,' he shouted.

She swam back to the boat and climbed aboard using the stern ladder. He had erected an awning for shade. The aroma of the cooking teased her appetite.

'It smells delicious. What is it?'

He had set a table with a bowl of salad that glistened with oil, bread rolls and an open bottle of white wine. From the small galley he carried two plates that contained white fish on beds of rice.

'Lampuka,' he said. 'Malta's own fish.'

They ate.

'It's delicious,' Kate said.

'I know.' Nero grinned. 'Beautiful.'

He poured wine and she accepted a glass, although she drank rarely and never at lunchtime. Correction, she drank on Sunday lunchtimes at The Red Lion to her husband's direction.

'A pint?' George Mellish would say to Bob.

'Lovely.'

'And the little woman?'

'Kate will have a half.' He would smile at her without really seeing her. 'You like your half of bitter on a Sunday, don't you, dear?'

'Yes, dear.'

Kate hated bitter. She hated Sundays and she hated The Red Lion. My God, how could she even think of the place on a day like this when everything was perfection? A deserted cove, blue skies and an endless sea that murmured sleepily against the side of the boat, and a meal of delicacy and delicious flavour.

'Your hair,' Nero said. 'Better like that. Make you more beautiful.'

She laughed. But perhaps it did look better around her shoulders than piled upon her head like a Victorian schoolmarm.

Afterwards, Nero insisted she swim again while he cleared the dishes.

'Private place,' he said. 'No one to see. Swim naked. It's okay.'

The wine had relaxed her and his pronunciation saved her from blushing.

'I don't think so, Nero. I haven't swum naked since . . . oh, since I was a girl.'

'You're still a girl. Enjoy. Swimming naked best.'

'I'll take your word for it.'

Kate dived in and swam and sunk and floated and became a dolphin. Passive and gentle.

'Hey! You okay?'

Splashing nearby caused her to twist from her back and tread water. Nero was swimming towards her. His grin reminded her of a friendly shark.

'Great,' she said. 'The best day of the holiday.'

'I told you.'

He dived, grabbed her ankle and pulling her below the surface. She kicked away, resurfaced and took a deep breath. He was laughing nearby. She dived and went for his ankle in return. She took hold and pulled, and as he sank she realised he wore no shorts.

Kate swam away, shocked but not really surprised. His genitals had not looked threatening. They looked like they belonged on a statue. A limp appendage above a small package. She broke the surface but couldn't see him. Her leg was tugged and she went under again.

When she came up for air she could hear his laughter from a distance away. He was swimming back to the boat. She watched him climb out of the water, at ease with his nudity. But he didn't flaunt it. When he was aboard, he tied a towel around his waist and lifted a bottle of wine.

'Another drink?' he shouted.

Kate felt as if she were caught in a series of events over which she no longer had control. It was a familiar feeling, one with which she was comfortable and frightened of at the same time. She swam to the boat and climbed the ladder.

The wine was chilled and delicious. Nero had moved the awning and placed the seat cushions on the stern deck to make a sunbed. They did not talk much but enjoyed the sounds of nature and the heat and she felt the sea drying on her skin. She rolled onto her stomach and let the sun caress her and the movement of the boat lull her into sleep.

Nero woke her up gently.

'Too much sun,' he said.

'What?'

'I think too much. Your back is red.'

She sat up and felt the tautness of her skin. He placed a glass of cold wine in her hand. She was thirsty and drank it all.

'Maybe time to sit in the shade,' he said, and she agreed.

Kate went into the cabin and sat on the bunk seat but when her back touched the cushion it felt tender. He gave her another glass of wine. It was really very nice wine. Cold and very relaxing.

'Your back needs cream,' he said.

'It's okay.'

'No. I have cream. It soothes. Makes better.'

'Makes better?'

'Makes you okay.'

Kate drank more wine. Maybe it would be nice to have her back soothed. She could lie down again.

'Here,' he said. 'Lie down.'

She did as she was told and lay along the bunk seat on her stomach. It was cooler here and the boat still lulled her with its movement. She closed her eyes.

'Okay?' he said.

'Okay.'

She shuddered and gave a groan when he poured something cold onto her shoulders. His hands gently rubbed it in. He had spoken the truth. It was soothing. He poured more and spread it. His hands were good, his fingers probed pleasantly. Her skin cooled and her

106

stomach quivered. The heat was moving elsewhere in her body.

His hands continued their work and she lay with closed eyes and did not object when he slipped the straps of the swimsuit from her shoulders. They had been hurting and now the hurt was gone.

'Turn over,' he said.

She obeyed. She lay on her back, her eyes still closed, her arms by her side. The heat was moving down her body towards the apex of her thighs.

He pulled the straps further down her arms and it was good to be rid of the material that had been so constricting. The swimsuit was at her waist now and he moved her arms from the straps. He smoothed cooling cream into her shoulders. His oiled hands slid down her chest and she found it difficult to breathe.

The hands left her and she sighed deeply, then caught her breath as they returned, freshly lubricated, cupping her breasts and spreading the slickness over them. The hands caressed her breasts as if they were new discoveries. They manipulated them, squeezed them and rubbed the nipples.

How old was she? Where was she?

She sensed his face was close to hers and opened her eyes as his mouth descended and kissed her. His tongue pushed between her lips; big, like a demanding fish. She closed her eyes but the illusion had gone. He climbed upon the bunk seat and lay against her. The towel had gone and he was naked.

The genitals she had seen beneath the water had undergone a transformation. The small, limp appendage had become large and fierce. It had become the iron rod she had felt against her buttocks earlier that morning.

Kate struggled and broke away from the kiss.

'No,' she gasped.

She pushed him with her hands but the bunk was restricting and he was heavily built and strong.

'Is all right,' he said. 'Beautiful Kate, is all right.' His mouth slobbered over hers again until she twisted her mouth clear. His hands had become more demanding upon her breasts. 'Is all right. No one come here. We fuck now. We fuck all afternoon.'

'No,' she said. 'Get off me.'

'Silly girl,' he said. 'You nervous. You feel better when we fuck. I make you come. Many times I make you come.'

Kate twisted away from him and he moved off the bunk but only to pull the swimsuit from her buttocks and down her legs. He held her face downwards with one hand in the small of her back while he pulled the costume from her feet. She tried kicking but banged her foot.

He climbed back onto the bunk behind her. The iron rod was against her bottom. It slid into the groove between the cheeks of her buttocks, the groove that seemed to be made for the purpose. He raised his hips slightly and she felt more cream or oil being poured onto her flesh. He smoothed it in and his fingers slid along the groove and followed it between her legs.

Kate screamed as they slid over her anus causing her insides to spasm. His hand forced its way between her thighs, his finger rubbing and delving against her vagina. The lips of her sex parted and his finger went inside with ease.

Her treacherous vagina was wet. It had been lubricated by fantasy and the past. He pushed two fingers inside her.

'No,' she pleaded, tears on her cheeks.

'Kate, beautiful Kate. You want it. You know you want it. Say so. Say you want it.'

'No. Don't.'

His hand left her sex and he rolled against her. The iron rod slid in the groove with the movement of his hips and his hands slid beneath her and caressed her breasts. He licked her shoulder and she shuddered.

'Tell me, Kate,' he said. 'Tell me you want fucking.'

He slid the iron rod against her, hot as a poker, as hot as her insides.

'Tell me, Kate.' His hands squeezed her breasts, his thumbs rubbed her nipples. 'You do, don't you?' His groin lifted and thrust, the poker slid in the oil. 'Don't you?'

Her resistance had been weakened by the wine. There was no point in resistance. No one would disturb them in this deserted cove. No one would know. She had no alternative but to obey, as she had always obeyed.

She had no choice.

No one would know.

'You want fucking, don't you?' he insisted.

'Yes,' she whispered.

'Tell me?'

'Yes.'

He sighed with satisfaction.

'Tell me what you want.'

It was a command. An instruction and she had been born to obey.

'I want you to do it.'

'To do what?'

'To fuck me.'

'What do you want, Kate?'

The poker moved again. She moved against it.

'Fucking,' she said. 'I want fucking.'

Chapter 11

Nero turned her onto her back. He lay against her side on the narrow bunk, his hot manhood against her thigh. He held her face and his mouth descended again and he kissed her. Kate closed her eyes.

What happened would be inevitable. She would allow it to happen and she would obey.

He kissed her, his lips opening hers, his tongue digging into her mouth. How long had it been since she had been kissed? Tears prickled her eyelids. It had been years. It had been so long ago that she had forgotten.

His lips were wet, his tongue forced her tongue to react. They exchanged saliva. Unbelievably, she was kissing him back. She had to. It was a required response.

Nero's hand moved down her body. It squeezed her breasts before sliding lower, over her stomach. His fingers slid through her pubic hair and she moaned into his mouth, in despair rather than in passion. If things had been different, if she had met someone other than Bob, perhaps making love would have been like this.

Her only protection was to keep her eyes closed and think of another time, another place.

His mouth went over a breast and he sucked. His fingers went between her legs and parted the swollen lips of her vagina. Two fingers held the lips apart before their tips moved in a circular motion towards the pleasure spot Uncle Toby had called her rosebud.

It had been neglected a long time. She doubted if Bob knew of its existence and she had forsaken it ever since . . . But this was no time to remember. Nero's fingers found it and rolled it and she gasped. His fingers released a thousand sparks to course through her veins.

Kate rolled her head and groaned. This was not her fault. She was not stealing pleasure as she had stolen it in her bedroom as a girl. She had no control over what Nero did. She had to obey and respond and her body was responding to his fingers.

They flicked and rolled and her hips bucked.

Oh my God! She had forgotten! How could she have forgotten this pleasure?

She tensed and came, her legs rigid her breath wheezing from her throat. Kate shook. Her left foot rapped against wood panelling in rhythm to her shudders. Slowly her senses reluctantly coalesced and she became aware of her surroundings.

Nero licked her neck and face. His tongue pushed into her mouth again and licked her teeth.

He said. 'You like that?'

'Yes,' she whispered.

'I know you like that.' He pushed the two fingers into her vagina and she groaned. 'You like this, too?'

'Yes.'

He moved them in and out, building up speed and

lubrication until they squelched. Her hips moved to the rhythm.

His mouth went to her ear. He licked it and whispered, 'You want my cock?'

Kate knew her role. Knew what was required of her. 'Yes.'

'Say so.'

'I want your cock.'

He manoeuvred and slid over her body, pushing apart her legs with his knees. She could feel his erection against her stomach.

'You want fuck?'

'Yes.'

'Ask me.'

'Please.' Her hips moved. Her vagina twisted to try to rub against his weapon. Her treacherous vagina. 'Please fuck me.'

He knelt up and guided the head of his weapon into the mouth of her sex. He held it there, rubbing it backwards and forwards between the lips.

'You want it?' He was excited. 'You want it?'

'Yes.'

Was that her voice? It sounded desperate.

'Ask me.' Her hips twisted and thrust against it, capturing an inch before he pulled it back. 'Ask me, English lady.'

'Fuck me. Please, Nero. Fuck me!'

He thrust inside her and she screamed. His poker dug deeply, scorching through the layers of membranes to become embedded in the sleeve of her sex. He held it there, as if pinning her like a trophy.

'You like it?' he said. 'You like it, English lady?'

Kate was beyond speech. The barrier of obedience and automatic response had been breached. She was his trophy, to do with as he willed. He began to fuck her with long and measured strokes. They were joined only at their genitals, for he held himself above her. She felt him staring at her and opened her eyes for the first time.

He was smiling. The smile of a shark and predator at feast.

'Good, huh?' he said.

Her mouth was open, her eyes wide but she still could not speak. She moaned and his smile broadened.

'You need the fuck,' he said. 'I could tell. You need the fuck.'

He lowered himself upon her, his hairs scratchy against her breasts. He kissed her neck and licked her face. When his lips moved over her chin, her mouth opened and sought his. His hand caressed a breast, then went lower. He held her hips with both hands and dug beneath her to feel her buttocks.

Nero increased the speed of his strokes and she raised her legs, wrapping them around his back. Their mouths broke apart and he began to batter into her and the pounding caused them both to gasp and pant. His groin slapped against her, the piston was firing her for a second time.

His face went out of focus above her and she felt her senses slipping. The noises she made were those of a stranger, inarticulate, guttural, demanding. She closed her eyes again and heard someone scream and then she came. Her vaginal muscles contracted, her heels dug into his buttocks and her fingernails scrabbled for a grip upon his hairy back.

Kate shuddered again and, as the scream died, realised it was her scream. She was adrift, high on the tidal wave she had once loved and then forgotten, and still Nero pounded into her and his piston kept her riding the wave, kept her on the brink, half swooning, half aware.

'Fuck me!' she shouted. 'Fuck me!'

Nero's orgasm was violent, his heavy body crushing her, and the spasms of his groin threw her into another climax.

Kate passed out. She drifted so far she imagined she was back in the sea, floating like seaweed, floating on her back, lifeless and close to drowning. But a fish was nibbling between her legs and making her squirm in fear.

She opened her eyes and reality rushed in. She was lying on the cushions on the stern deck. The awning was above her, as blue as the sky. And Nero was between her legs lapping at her sex.

He held her vagina open and was licking at her clitoris, her rosebud, and the unnatural act was making her squirm and moan. She reached down and tried to push his head away.

'No,' she said.

Nero stopped licking and her spirits sank at the removal of such pleasure. He slid up her body, holding her wrists in his hands. He lay upon her. His penis was heavy but not erect and it lay between her thighs, nudging against the portals of her sex. He raised himself above her, his broad shoulders filling her vision, the gold glinting at his throat.

He stared at her with a serious expression, no smiles and no friendliness. It was an expression she recognised from long ago. It was lust, an emotion that she remembered was stronger even than love and fidelity.

'No more "no",' he said. 'Stop pretending. We fuck till I've finished. You do as I say. Everything. No more "no". You understand?'

Kate's hips moved against his penis.

'I understand,' she whispered.

Her will had been removed. She was to be submissive. Without control, without guilt.

Nero slid back down her body and licked again. She groaned and closed her eyes, thrusting her vagina against his face. She came, suddenly and gloriously, and he clamped his mouth to her sex mouth, and fucked her with his tongue.

There was no time for Kate to recover. Nero lay alongside her and put her hands upon his penis. It stiffened as she held it and it slid greasily in her hands. He took hold of her head and pushed it downwards.

'Suck,' he said.

She resisted the pressure of his hand.

'No.' His expression darkened and she felt shame. Tears puckered her face. 'I don't know how.'

A slight smile played on his lips.

'You don't know how?' he said, incredulously.

'No.'

'You never suck a prick?'

'Once,' she said, and shook her head. 'Twice. They just pushed it in my mouth and came. I'm sorry. I don't know how.'

He stroked her cheek.

'That's all right. I show you how.'

This time she did not resist when he pushed her head down to his groin. His penis had stiffened even more in her hand as they talked. She stared at it from close range. It was five or six inches in length, thick and coloured an angry dark red at its head where folds of skin encircled it. The vein that ran its length was heavy and throbbed.

He took hold of it and moved the sheath of skin that surrounded it up and down. The head of the glans slid into sight.

'Kiss it, Kate.'

She pursed her lips and kissed the glans as softly as a butterfly. He groaned.

'Lick it.'

Her tongue delicately touched the tip and his hips shook and the penis jumped in his hand. She felt a warm glow of achievement. She licked again, with more certainty. He moaned. She licked the glans and along the vein.

'Open your mouth,' he said. 'Put it in your mouth.'

Kate obeyed and slid her lips around the glans and partway down the length. He lay still without moving. Juices began to flow in her mouth and she sucked. He groaned loudly.

'That's good,' he said.

She kept sucking and salivated around it.

'No,' he said, touching the side of her face. 'No teeth. Your lips. Your tongue. Suck and lick.'

Kate held it around its base and sucked and licked. Because there was no pressure on her to perform an act she did not understand, she discovered the techniques in her own way and at her own pace. Nero lay back and let her. His groans let her know when she had done something that was particularly sensitive and effective.

After a while, he touched her face and said, 'Your mouth. Pretend it is your sex. Use it like your sex. Fuck my prick.'

She moved her head up and down upon his erection, rubbing its length with her lips, taking it in until the glans touched the back of her throat. It had been this action that had frightened her so much when her husband had attempted it that one and only occasion at the beginning of their marriage. His roughness had made her think she was choking.

Nero lay back moaning softly and she gained in confidence. She enjoyed mastering what had once been a mystery.

He rolled onto his side and crouched around her head. He cupped his hand at the back of her neck to hold her in position.

'Now I fuck you,' he said.

His hips moved and his penis went in and out of her mouth in simulation of sexual intercourse. He had assumed control and her nervousness returned because he was directing the depth and force of the thrusts. Panic began to rise because the glans pushed into her throat but he stopped abruptly and it slid from her lips.

'You are good,' he said, and stroked her hair. She looked up at him, her lips wet with saliva and juices, grateful for the praise. 'You do it again later. Now, I want to fuck you. Turn over.'

Kate lay on her stomach and he lay upon her back. His iron rod fitted sweetly into the groove between the cheeks of her bottom, so sweetly that it recharged a dim memory. He moved her thighs apart and the rod slipped between her legs. He raised himself upon her buttocks, manoeuvred, and found the entry. The iron rod slid between her sex lips.

Her husband used her from the rear but not like this. Her husband might as well be using an inflatable doll, for his mind was always elsewhere. His hands seldom fondled her, his lips never touched her skin, except occasionally to deliver an absent-minded kiss on the back of her neck when he had finished.

A kiss on the neck in reward. Presumably instead of an orgasm.

Nero fucked her with a lazy enthusiasm. His body moulded into hers, he handled her flesh with desire and enjoyment. Kate thought of Martini, the other woman. The letters she had written had been enthusiastic. For the first time, it occurred to her that her husband must have been good at sex with his lover. He must have known where to find her rosebud, how to make her come.

Bastard!

Her body was only good enough for an anonymous Sunday morning fuck but the damn Martini woman was having orgasms anytime, anywhere.

She moaned with frustration, twisting beneath Nero, and he reacted by fucking her harder. He held her hips and squashed her buttocks flat beneath his hairy groin. The piston stoked her insides afresh.

'Fuck me!' she said, desperate to forget, desperate to affirm her own identity. 'Fuck me!'

He pulled her onto her knees and pushed her head forward so that her back was a ski slope. He knelt upright behind her and gained even greater penetration. They sweated in the heat and with the exertion and their bodies taunted each other.

Nero withdrew and flipped her onto her back. She was amazed at his strength. He remained on his knees, sitting back on his haunches, and he hauled her onto his lap. He guided his penis and her vagina sank upon it. They sat clutching each other close, bodies slippery, their movements natural as if they had practised for years.

Now he pushed her from him so that she lay upon her back. He lifted her legs above her head and her vagina had never felt so exposed. He knelt above her and his penis slid into her. He lay over her, holding her ankles, and she shouted at the depth he was reaching, shouted with fear and pain and lust.

Lust, the emotion that took no prisoners had taken her. She was immersed in it. Her body ached from it. She existed in its haze.

He let go of her legs and she lay on her back again. He lay on top of her, still embedded within her, still fucking her, and they rolled on the cushions to attain different angles of attack. Her breath was shortening and she knew her orgasm was not far away.

'Yes,' she murmured, to herself as much as to Nero. 'Yes, yes.'

Kate began to come and, as she did so, his fingers slid beneath her, over her buttocks and down the groove.

They slid in the grease and juices as she bucked and groaned and, as the orgasm began to ebb, he touched her anus with the tip of one finger.

She moaned lightly at the sky and he fucked her harder still, his finger penetrating her and she was lost once more, writhing into higher ecstacy.

He allowed her time to recover. He lay next to her, stroking his penis, waiting until her breathing had become normal, until she looked at him with inquiring eyes.

'I want your mouth,' he said. 'I want to come in your mouth.'

Kate looked at how fierce his penis was. Red and angry. She remembered how flaccid and inoffensive it had been when she had seen him swimming naked. How swiftly the penis of the man in the car had became small after she had sucked him.

'Suck,' he commanded and she obeyed.

She moved down into his lap and took hold of his manhood at its base. Her lips cushioned the glans before her mouth opened and she accepted it inside. She tongued and sucked it. Moved her head up and down as he had taught her, as if she were fucking it with her mouth.

Nero began groaning deeply. His hips began to match the movement of her head. Without warning, he rolled over her, straddling her face. One knee was beneath her armpit, the other by the side of her head. He was partly sitting upon her breasts, his penis deep in her mouth.

Kate knew what to expect and abandoned herself, for she could do nothing but accept his final assault. She spread her arms, another sacrifice, another victim, and he held her head in the cradle of his hands and fucked her mouth.

She closed her eyes and she salivated, she endured. She submitted to sex and lust. She didn't choke and his excitement transferred itself to her. The tremors in his thighs made her shake and when he came, as violently as the first time, she swallowed and gasped and his sperm slid down her throat.

He fell away and lay gasping on his back, his penis limp and shrivelling. She watched him, amazed that she was the cause of his condition, that she had drained his strength. That she had created his desire and then slaked it.

Perhaps she really was beautiful.

Perhaps she was desirable and sexual.

Kate stood up and enjoyed the breeze on her naked body. She went into the cabin and poured herself another glass of wine. She could no longer blame intoxication. They had fucked each other dry of alcohol. She drank the wine, topped up the glass and took it back to Nero who was now sitting up.

'Beautiful English lady,' he said. 'English ladies always know how to fuck. English men?'

He made a rude and dismissive sound and she laughed and gave him the glass of wine. He drank it and got up.

'Now we swim,' he said. 'We swim nak-ed. After we swim, we fuck again. You want to fuck again?'

'Yes,' said Kate. 'I want to fuck again.'

Like Ulysses, she had succumbed to the siren call of the island.

Chapter 12

Kate lay on the bed in her hotel room with the lights out and the curtains drawn. Her body ached pleasurably. She drifted in and out of sleep. At times, she thought the afternoon had been a dream. The aches reminded her it had not.

Her sex life had been non-existent for years and now the Pandora's Box she had opened had led her into encounters that were unexpected, unlikely and unbelievable.

Sex had been something people talked about or wrote about and, she supposed, something in which a few of them actually indulged. It had been a concept, not a reality. An act that belonged in the movies because it was an illusion. Every bit as much a fantasy as fat girls who looked with longing at the photographs of thin models, or housewives trapped by drudgery who dreamed of emulating the imagined lives of glamorous Hollywood film stars.

Her experiences as a teenager had been wicked indulgences that had to stop. Sex was for marriage, it was sacrosanct, it was given in exchange for the love of a good man.

Unfortunately, her husband had never been a good man. He had been available and he had proposed and, at that particular time, she had wanted an escape and a penance. If she had known how to go about it, perhaps she would have entered a convent. Instead, she entered a marriage.

Her penance had been served in full. Her awakening, through anger and bizarre circumstance, had made her reassess all that she had forgotten. It made her reassess her marriage. It could have been different. Bob could have made it different, but he had been selfish and inexperienced and had not tried.

He was an adherent of her mother's code of behaviour. An embodiment of her logo for life. Sex was an afterthought. It was an act between husband and wife that was a sometimes necessity and reward, and he rewarded her on Sunday mornings.

It hadn't been clear until now, and even now it was not fully clear, but she was beginning to realise she had married Bob because the marriage would fulfil her mother's expectations. Her mother had not wanted happiness for Kate; she had wanted revenge.

All those years of wedlock, Kate had suppressed her sexuality until she had believed it to be dead. Could she blame her husband when she had also made no effort, when she had considered her underwear to be so unexciting it might have deterred a rapist? When she had been so unexciting?

Now she realised her sexuality had not died but had been dormant, waiting to be reawakened. The years in between had been as barren as the Sahara. Their tedium had made her doubt the intensity of those teenage experiences, had made her reject them as the imaginings of a hysterical girl at an awkward age.

But back then she had considered herself in the same category as the seventeeth-century nuns of Loudun. They had declared themselves possessed by the devil who required them to perform lewd acts and engage in sinful behaviour. Historians had concluded they were more likely to have been affected by sexual repression and used the excuse of possession as an escape.

Kate did not see the difference. Sex and the devil were the same. They had been the victims of possession which they should have resisted. So had Kate, and she should have resisted but she had not. She had been weak and had embraced the possession and wickedly wallowed in it. Her marriage had been deserved.

Is that how she had reasoned all those years ago? Is that how it had happened? How she had married Bob?

Bob: a man of nicknames, a man who had a place for everything and liked everything in its place. A man with models in the loft and half-naked models in dirty magazines in the garage. A man with a mistress who sent him obscene love letters.

Her husband might be successful at his job but he was a failure as a human being. He hid his weaknesses with bluster, he was insensitive and shallow, his personality depended upon the size of his car and the appreciation of his cronies. He had built his life out of cardboard and did not know it.

If he ever lost his job, she knew he would fall apart. She wondered what he would do when he lost his marriage? She wondered what his reaction would be if he knew what had occurred on a boat in the Mediterranean that afternoon?

Perhaps she would tell him in a letter. A sort of love letter.

But the memory of love letters was too uncomfortable. Sex was safer. Kate felt on the verge of release but was still unsure of how to proceed, still needed direction. The sex that afternoon had been good but did it compare to the first time? The day she lost her virginity. The day that might have spoiled the next thirteen years of her life?

Toby married her mother in September. He became Toby to Kate after the wedding because the prefix uncle seemed inappropriate. He and her mother separated a year later. But it was a night in late August that she remembered so vividly.

Her mother was at the hotel, supervising a Rotary dinner. Kate was in the house alone. She had showered and, because it was hot, wore only a white T-shirt and panties. The massage sessions with Uncle Toby had ended before the wedding and she was surprised at how normal their relationship had become.

Of course, she still remembered what they had done and she relived the memories alone in her bed, when her fingers went between her legs and relieved her tensions as he had taught her. But that was a secret she kept for the night. She never seduced herself during the day.

The massage room had once more become a guest

room and the rubber sheet had gone. Her bedroom was at the other side of the house.

Kate was bored and the heat made her uncomfortable, despite her lack of clothes. She wandered the house and found herself in the master bedroom. She had seldom been in this room and had avoided it. This was the room that knew her mother's sexual secrets and it made her uncomfortable.

A shirt of his lay on the floor where he had thrown it. Its untidiness looked out of place when everything else was no neat. She picked it up, intending to put it in the laundry basket, but she held it against her breasts and dipped her face towards its folds and smelled his aroma, that special mixture of his sweat and aftershave.

She opened a wardrobe and touched his clothes. His shirts, trousers, suits. In drawers she found underwear. She stroked the cotton shorts but did not pick them up. In her mind, she saw him wearing them.

A feeling of wickedness crept over her. She should not be here, even though she was doing no wrong. The wrong was in her mind. The wickedness made her stomach tingle and she opened other drawers. These contained her mother's underwear. It was a disappointment.

There were no secrets here, no lacy hints and promises. There were pantyhose and flowered cotton pants and brassieres like armour plating.

Kate closed the drawers and, still holding the discarded shirt, lay on the bed. She spread it over her face so that it lay like a soft shroud and inhaled her own memories and imagined this was her bed and Uncle Toby her husband.

He would caress her breasts like this, squeeze them and maul them and make the nipples hard.

Her hands went beneath the material and she rubbed the tips erect.

Toby would stroke her stomach and touch her buttocks. His hands would slide inside the panties and feel the softness they contained.

Kate groaned and felt her bottom.

Then he would touch her here, in that sensitive area he had taught her to worship with her fingers.

Her right hand slid over her pubic hair and down into the valley that waited to be explored and touched the gash that waited to be opened. It opened and her fingers delved for moisture.

He would manipulate her senses with his finger on her rosebud. He would make her hips writhe and her breath shorten and he would lay upon her and push his prick inside her and he would fuck her.

Kate made a penis with two fingers of her left hand and thrust them inside herself. She moved them rhythmically in and out while using the fingers of her right hand upon her clitoris. She writhed upon the bed, immersed in the soft smells of the shirt and her fantasy.

She came loudly, the freedom of the empty house to exploit, and subsided with a sigh.

The lull of peace that swept over her in the aftermath of the climax drifted close to sleep but she could not sleep here. She pulled the shirt from her face and sat up.

Toby was standing in the doorway.

His face was taut. Hers flushed. She gulped and got

off the bed. She lay the shirt upon the quilt. It was no longer hers to touch.

They said nothing to each other and she went past him and along the corridor, embarrassed at being caught trespassing, at displaying her covetousness. Embarrassed at having him watch her masturbate and spoil the memory of the ritual.

She went downstairs and sat on a couch to watch television. When she put her hand to her face she could smell her fingers. The shame intensified. How much had he seen? What had she done?

He came into the room. He wore the shirt and cords in which he had been out. He stood behind her, behind the couch and placed his hands upon her shoulders. His hands massaged her gently through the cotton, making her shudder again.

They moved down over her front and palmed her breasts. He held them, as she had held them. He mauled them, as she had mauled them. He kissed the top of her head.

'Oh, Kate,' he said.

'No.'

Kate pulled away from him and got off the couch. It was her fault that she had displayed herself so thoughtlessly, so provokingly. The best thing to do was to leave him alone and go to her room.

She moved towards the door but he was there first. He grabbed her and she struggled to get past him and they rolled into the corridor. There were no lights on in the corridor. It was a passageway of gloom. The glow of a lamp in the living room showed like a beacon for lost souls but she could not go back.

He held her wrists and forced her back against the wall. His body pressed against hers and she fought because she desired him so much. He tried to kiss her but she moved her head from side to side. He licked her neck and his tongue snaked into her ear. She wailed.

Toby let go of her hands and held her face. His mouth covered hers and he kissed her with infinite tenderness. Her arms remained pinned by unseen powers against the wall. Her lips parted and admitted his tongue. Her tongue made love with it.

Possession took her over. The tenderness went. She felt it leaving them both as if dragged from them by the devil's breath. His mouth still covered hers but the urgency was paramount. His hands gripped the T-shirt at her neck and he ripped it apart down the front.

His hands grabbed and mauled her breasts and she writhed against him, squirming her hips and trying to climb around him with parted thighs. Her fingers became claws that clung to his shirt.

He ripped the T-shirt again until it parted and his head went down over her breasts, sucking and biting. His hands pulled at her panties and they ripped too, the cotton shredding. He dropped to his knees and pulled the remnants down her legs and her upper body fell over him.

The panties were tugged from her feet and flung away. Toby buried his face between her thighs and she screamed. The power of his mouth flattened her back against the wall, arms and legs spread as if crucified. His fingers parted her vagina and his tongue dug inside and she came.

Kate shook and wailed, hanging on the wall by invisible nails, the pleasure sweeping through her body to make even her fingertips quiver.

Her eyes were wide and staring, her mouth slack, and when he stood up his mouth covered hers and she could taste herself. His clothes were unfastened and she felt his nakedness between her legs. The erection she had only ever felt between her buttocks was now between her thighs, hot and stiff and palpitating.

His features were heavy and contorted. She imagined hers were the same. They had become two strangers. Two people who used to know each other in a different life. Now they were consumed with the need to fuck.

He pushed the head of his prick between the open lips of her vagina. She had never felt so wet. She imagined juices running down her legs.

She parted her legs wider and stood on the tips of her toes to try to make it fit. He pulled her left leg higher and the hardness went in part of the way. She yelped. Already it felt big, already she felt full.

But she knew there was much more and she wanted it all. She wanted it to be buried inside her.

'Please,' she murmured, almost coherently. 'Please! Please!'

He held her thighs and lifted her, his hands beneath her, taking her weight. He was panting and shaking. It slid in another inch and met slight resistance.

She screamed.

'Go on! Go on!' she yelled.

He thrust and his prick stabbed her to the hilt. She hung upon him, her back against the wall, her thighs in his hands, her head limp upon his shoulder and the fire spread from her vagina and consumed her.

For long seconds he remained still. She lifted her face and felt her hair sticking to her forehead. She couldn't see him properly because sweat was in her eyes, but she could see his mouth was open. They kissed, lewdly, obscenely, their mouths slipping over each other's faces, their tongues licking and teeth biting.

Then he began to fuck her.

His first withdrawal and stroke made her shout. Each subsequent stroke brought noises that she didn't recognize. He had entered her with amazing ease and the more he fucked her the more lubricated she became. His pace increased and the noises she made became one continuous groan as she felt herself being overcome by orgasm.

'Now! Now! Now!' she screamed, her head back and eyes closed, lost in the dark corridor of emotions.

He did not come but continued his assault, his hands sliding further beneath her the better to hold her upon his erection. The tips of his fingers slid into the mouth of her vagina as he lifted her up and down on him and it felt as if she were being attacked by a phalanx of pricks.

Kate came again, more fiercely than before, and he shouted as he climaxed. His body trembled and, as he shot long agonising spurts deep inside her, she passed out.

Her senses were jumbled when she came round. She was being carried upstairs. What had happened? Then she remembered. Had the pleasure really been that strong?

He took her into the bathroom and she stroked his face.

'I'm all right,' she said.

They were still in darkness. Darkness suited them better.

Toby set her upon her feet and she stood against him. They held each other gently, only now the awareness of what they had done settling upon her. She raised her face to him and saw the regret in his eyes. He kissed her with tenderness, then shook his head.

'If only,' he said.

He let go of her and left the room. She heard him go downstairs and a door slammed. The engine of the Range Rover started and she listened to it fade as it went down the long drive.

If only.

Kate stepped into the shower. There was a little blood on her inner thighs mixed with juices and wetness. Now the passion had gone she felt remarkably clear-headed. Her virginity had not been much of a barrier. She supposed because of the horse riding.

The sex had been wonderful and she didn't care if she had been possessed. It had been an experience she believed would never be matched again. She knew there would be regrets but she did not want to think of them now.

Toby had been unable to resist her. A good man whom she had tempted too far. A man she had desired and with whom she had had her way. The lust had possessed them both and turned them into animals who had desired only one thing.

Had it been as good for him?

Of course it had. She had felt it in his body and seen it in his face. She had seduced him into making her a woman. It had been inevitable but they had not known it. If only.

Chapter 13

Hunger roused her. She laughed to herself, still self-conscious about her behaviour but realising she had discovered a truth: sex made you hungry.

Kate had nothing glamorous to wear for dinner and she viewed her underwear once again with despair. But these were parts of her life that could be changed. She wore a plain blue cotton dress that at least showed off her tan.

The sun had bleached her hair a shade lighter and she left it down. It really needed styling and cutting but she did the best she could by pinning two strands behind her ears so that the rest fell naturally onto her shoulders.

A touch of lipstick and she looked at herself in the mirror.

There was an improvement that had nothing to do with clothes or leaving her hair down. It showed in her eyes, if not a new confidence then a new hope. Or was it just a good fucking?

Kate took a paperback book with her as protection but went into the bar before dinner, something she had not done before. She breathed a sigh of relief that the elderly couple from Barnet were not there.

She glanced around a little unsure of herself. It had not been confidence after all, she had seen in the mirror. A couple in their thirties whom she had seen around the hotel waved. The man left their table and approached her.

'By yourself?' he said.

'Yes.'

'Why not join us?'

Her usual response to any such invitation began to surface but she stalled it. They were a good-looking couple and their smiles were friendly. They might also be better protection than a paperback book against the advances of the duo from Barnet.

They introduced themselves and Kate accepted a glass of white wine. They were Peter and Lorna Gregg, both in their mid-thirties. He was medium height and medium build, with regular features, dark hair and a moustache. He wore a grey Lacoste polo shirt and slacks. Lorna was slim and blonde and attractively made-up. Her dress was simple and of white brushed cotton that was fitted to the waist and had a full skirt to the knee.

The cut emphasised her hips and she wore it with high-heeled sandals. She made Kate feel dowdy.

They talked about the island and the weather and exchanged minimal personal details.

'I'm convalescing,' Kate said, wondering where the lie had come from. 'A week of total relaxation.'

Lorna said, 'Not a serious illness?'

'No, just generally run down. The weather at home didn't help.'

'I know what you mean.'

Peter said, 'Your husband doesn't mind?'

'He's very understanding, actually.' She smiled. 'He believes that we deserve our own space, from time to time.'

'Not me,' said Peter. He touched his wife's hand. 'I wouldn't let her out of my sight. God knows what she'd get up to.'

Lorna laughed.

'I'd tell you about it, afterwards.'

'I'd rather be there.'

Kate felt she was intruding, but they sensed they were being exclusive and made the conversation less intimate. They had another glass of wine and she began to feel at ease with them. When Lorna suggested Kate join them for dinner at a restaurant away from the hotel, she readily agreed.

The evening was a success. The restaurant had entertainment and dancing and Kate consumed more wine than she should have. She even accepted Peter's invitation to dance and enjoyed being in the arms of a handsome man. By the time they returned to the hotel, she felt they were old friends.

They sat in the bar for a nightcap and the couple from Barnet gave Kate a severe smile as they left.

'I think I've just been reprimanded,' she said.

'What?'

'They tried to take me under their wing but I declined.'

Lorna glanced at the backs of the departing couple.

'I think you had a lucky escape,' she said.

Peter said, 'They're probably white slavers looking for women alone.'

Kate liked his choice of words. A woman alone. It

sounded stronger than a woman on her own, which implied that she had lost somebody.

'They would have a job selling me,' Kate said.

'Top price,' Peter said.

He sat them at a table and went to the bar. Lorna looked at her.

'You've got a real down on yourself, Kate. What on earth for?'

'I suppose it's a role I'm used to.' She shrugged. 'I know I'm ordinary so why pretend?'

'Who said you were ordinary?'

'Come off it, Lorna. I know my limitations.'

'You don't, you know. If you think you are ordinary, you're way off the mark.'

Kate stared at the woman, looking for signs of false flattery.

'Then what am I?'

'A woman who's been taken for granted for too long.'

'What does that mean?'

'You're a lovely looking woman, Kate, without even trying. God, I wish my legs were as long as yours. I wish my boobs were half the size.'

Kate laughed. 'But you, you're beautiful. You make me feel dowdy.'

'I make the most of what I've got, but anybody can use paint and a sexy dress.'

'I can't.'

'Of course you can.'

'I wouldn't know how.'

Peter returned with two drinks which he placed on the table.

'Would you mind, Peter?' Lorna said. 'Women's talk.'

He held up his hands to show he didn't wish to intrude. 'I'll have mine at the bar.'

Lorna said, 'Are you really here convalescing?'

It had been such a good lie and so transparent. Kate saw no reason to be dishonest any more.

'No. I'm getting away from my husband. I'm divorcing him.'

'I'm sorry. How long have you been married?'

'Ten years. Ten wasted years.'

'You sound bitter.'

'I am. You're right. He *has* taken me for granted. But worse than that, he took my personality. I'd forgotten I had one until I got away.'

'How old are you, Kate?'

'Thirty.'

'You look younger. And you have the rest of your life to look forward to. You're going to make some man . . .' she grinned '. . . or men, very happy.'

'It's a nice thought but I'm out of practice.'

'How's your sex life been?'

'Non-existent.'

'Then you should rectify it as soon as possible.'

Kate smiled and was tempted to mention Nero, but that was too close. She felt far safer talking about her much more personal problems with her husband because they were so far away.

'Despite what you say, I wouldn't know how to go about finding a man.'

'You won't have to. they'll come chasing you.'

'Like this?'

139

'I told you. You can add the refinements.'

'But I don't know how.'

'I'll help you.'

'You will?'

'Of course. It'll be fun.'

'Like one of those make-overs on television. New hair, new face, new outfit?'

'Why not?' Lorna said. 'We could go shopping tomorrow?'

'Oh, I can't.' Kate was disappointed. 'I've arranged to go on a boat trip tomorrow.'

Again she was tempted to confess what had happened but resisted. Her disappointment was mitigated by the thought of another day of sea and sex, so far from anyone's prying eyes she could pretend it had never happened.

'The shops are open until seven,' Lorna said. 'If you're back in time we could do some shopping before they close.'

'Okay.'

'If not, the next day.'

Kate realised the week was rushing by.

'Definitely the next day.'

Nero was not even a man to whom she was attracted but he served a purpose. He was simply a man who had placed her in a position where she could submit to sex or be raped. Maybe she had known that all the time. Maybe she had wanted the lack of choice. She now knew that she had wanted sex. Uncomplicated sex without explanations or recriminations.

Tomorrow she would go with Nero on his boat and

have more sex. It had been a long time since she had had a prick that had been aroused by her and not the thought of a mistress. Nero wanted her as she was, but that was because he was probably using her as she was using him.

But afterwards, after Lorna had helped her discover a new identity, Nero would become another memory. Afterwards, perhaps she would find a real-life man who would fit her dreams and expectations.

Everything was possible, she felt. But that was because she had Pandora's hope.

Chapter 14

Nero kissed her hand as he helped her aboard the boat. Kate supposed he thought it was romantic but she wasn't interested in romance. She glanced back at the harbourside and hoped no one from the hotel had seen him greet her.

Their relationship was strictly physical and it would end today. She didn't think he would be heartbroken. He would soon be looking for another target in the bars of St Julian's and St George's bays and Sliema.

They sailed up the coast and she slipped off her cotton sundress in the cabin. Today she had worn her swimsuit beneath it. They drank cold white wine. Kate had three swift glasses to relieve her tensions. She still needed the buffer of intoxication to help her shed the inhibitions of ten wasted years.

Kate stood alongside him on the bridge and when he offered to let her steer, she lay back against him and felt his erection grow in the baggy blue shorts.

There was a *frisson* between them this morning. A sexual hangover from the day before, as if they wanted to touch each other but felt they should wait until they had reached seclusion.

Until they got there, she moved her buttocks against him and sensed his anticipation as she drank more wine.

They did not go as far as Gozo. After they passed St Paul's Islands he headed towards land. He took the craft into a small bay that was protected by cliffs. There was a strip of sandy beach and a cave. Another location stolen from paradise.

He stopped the engines, dropped anchor and shed his shorts. His penis was heavy against his leg but not erect. He pushed the strap of her swimsuit from her shoulder.

'Na-ked,' he said.

'Yes,' she said, her mouth dry with excitement. 'Naked.'

She removed the swimsuit, aware of his eyes upon her. As she stepped from it she saw that his penis had become erect. He stepped towards her but she laughed and jumped over the side into the clear water.

Her nudity felt natural. Her senses were opening, expanding for what lay ahead. Here in this bay, she was free to behave in total abandonment. There were no witnesses and therefore no one could judge her. There were no rules.

Kate swam to the beach. He followed but did not try to catch her. She stepped onto the sand and shook the water from her hair. The seclusion was complete. She dipped her head and entered the cave.

It was about the size of a small house and it was dry, the floor being part sand and part rock. The roof was domed and she was able to stand in the middle. It was cool after the heat of the sun. A shadow at the entrance made her turn.

Nero was watching. Waiting. His shape was dark against the sun. He rested one hand on the rock above his head and leaned forward to stare inside. With his stocky build, he looked like a hunchback with a phallus. A fertility symbol, a spirit of sexuality.

Kate licked her top lip. He looked like Punch.

He entered the cave and came for her.

'No,' she said.

She wanted to resist, to fight. To be taken.

He grabbed her wrists and their bodies pushed against each other as they struggled. The tip of his prick seared a hot trail across her belly. He licked her neck and twisted her arms behind her back, his body now hard against hers. Nero held both her wrists in one hand and with the other held her face. He kissed her, his lips slobbering upon hers, his tongue an invasion in her mouth.

Her body arched and she twisted her hips, keeping her sex away from the fierceness that sprouted from his groin. His free hand dropped to her buttocks, his fingers digging into the soft flesh, and he pulled her against him. His prick was stiff and hot and rubbed against her stomach.

She flung back her head.

'No!' she said, taunting him.

His fingers moved round her hip and dipped over her mons, prising their way between her thighs. They pushed and probed, and the lips of her sex opened, releasing her wetness and destroying her pretence. He pushed a finger inside her harshly and she yelled and was forced onto her toes.

145

Nero released one arm and turned her round with the other. He forced her onto her knees on the cool sand in the darkness of the cave and knelt behind her, between her legs. She was open and could not protect herself and that hot poker was rubbing in the damp valley of her sex. He pushed her face down, so that she had to spread her arms for balance, fingered her open and thrust his prick inside.

'You really want!' he said, then withdrew and thrust fiercely again. 'You want, English lady? You want?'

He thrust again and again, causing her to cry out, and then paused, waiting for a reply.

'You want fuck?' he said, his voice a hiss.

'Yes,' she said, her body limp, his hands clamped like irons upon her hips. 'I want.'

'Ask.'

'Fuck me, Nero. Fuck me.'

'Beg.'

'Please, Nero. Please fuck me.'

Saying the words was cathartic. Expressing the desire and the lust was a way of shedding a decade of repression.

He fucked her. His prick was a pummel that liquidised her insides. She yelled at the attack and her voice echoed and came back in distortion to incite her further. Kate yelled louder until the cave was a chamber of passionate noise and her senses drowned and she came.

Nero released her and she lay on the floor of the cave. When her body regained its spirit, she leaned up on one arm and stared at him silhouetted once more in the entrance. He had not come and the carved phallus still rose from the groin of Mr Punch.

He walked onto the beach and she got up and followed him, out of the cave and into the sunshine. She stopped abruptly. A small fishing boat was entering the bay under sail, its timbers painted red, yellow and green. Their seclusion had ended and she was naked. She shivered with a sudden chill. Perhaps this boat would not stop.

But its sail came down and, with its shallow draught, it glided closer to the beach. She backed into the shadows of the cave once more. The boat had a crew of two and one dropped an anchor overboard. The second man waved and Nero waved back.

'Who are they?' said Kate.

'My cousins,' he said. He smiled at her. 'They like to fuck, too.'

His words were like a blow in the stomach. She glanced at the cliffs and saw there was no way out of the bay except by boat. She was trapped, by her own gullibility and lust. Her body tensed in fear and expectation.

Nero was watching her reaction. His smile was threatening, his erection stiffened.

How many times had he executed this plan? How many other women had been lured to lonely bays and coves for the pleasure of himself and his cousins?

There was nothing she could do about it but submit. At least they would not harm her. Nero would take her back to St Julian's Bay when they had finished with her. Her life was not in danger and they would not wish to mark her body.

If they hurt her she might complain to the authorities.

But if she was able to return safely to her hotel, who would believe her? And would she want the embarrassment of an investigation?

The two men jumped over the side of the boat and waded ashore. They wore only shorts and were both tanned and almost black. One was in his fifties, with a bald head and grizzled grey hair at his temples. His belly was big and his shorts sagged below it.

His companion was in his twenties and had an arrogant swing to his shoulders. He was tall and sleekly muscular and knew he was good-looking. His black hair was long and wavy and he kept it from his face with a blue bandana that was tied around his forehead. He would have no trouble attracting English girls on holiday, but perhaps he liked rape better.

Nero spoke to them in Maltese and they laughed.

'The fat one is Rafel,' he said. 'The young one is Gianni. I told them I fuck you already. Make you ready for them.'

'You bastard.'

His good humour went.

'You be careful. You belong to us now.'

The two new arrivals removed their shorts. Gianni had an erection already, but Rafel's penis was limp. The three of them talked in Maltese, stared at Kate and laughed.

She was isolated by language. A victim like Ulysses, tempted here by the siren promise of secret sex. Her eyes went from man to man. Their faces had become masks. They wore smiles that meant nothing. They were wondering how she would react, whether she would submit or if they would have to take her by force.

Gianni looked as if he would prefer to take her by force, as Nero had done a short time ago. She was still wet, her stomach still bubbled from the way he had aroused her, and bubbled fiercer now with the edge of fear.

How would she react? She didn't know herself.

Her mouth was dry and she licked her lips. Yesterday she had been forcefully seduced because she had wanted to be. Today she had come looking for sex without complications. The only doubt in her mind being whether Nero would be able to maintain the intensity of their coupling. That doubt no longer applied.

No option. She had no option. Her ability to make decisions had been removed. She would have to submit to whatever they desired. A vessel for their pleasure. A vessel they could fill with sperm and fluids. And because she would be compelled there would be no guilt.

Her personality had been fragile after life with Bob. He had taken it away from her, she told Lorna. Now she felt it draining away again, as if she had become her own shadow and was standing alongside, watching like a voyeur.

The men also lost their individuality. They were simply men with appendages they would soon bury in her body. It did not matter who they were or how many they were. The old feeling swept over her: she had been born to submit.

Gianni stepped forward and her body reacted. She dodged past him and ran into the sea. The men shouted behind her and followed. She swam towards the power boat but without any clear thoughts. She did not know how to start its engine, raise its anchor or steer it. But from the beach it had looked like a refuge.

Excitement now mingled with the fear and her adrenalin pumped. Her heart beat faster and her senses were wide open. The water felt as if it were gushing through her as she swam, her energy unbounded. She reached the boat and climbed the stern ladder.

Now she had attained her objective she was at a loss what to do next. The men were approaching, Gianni in the lead. She stood on the deck and looked for a weapon. Why? She knew the ending.

The young man reached the stern and began to climb the ladder. She hit him with one of the cushions. He laughed and fended off the blow. The cushion fell back into the boat. She grappled with him and his balance was unsteady. He gripped her wrists and fell backwards, pulling her with him into the water.

They went under but he still held her wrists. She fought, at first to escape him and then for breath, but he held her down. Her eyes bulged and she stared at him, pleading silently. He kicked and they broke the surface. She gasped for air. The other men reached them and she was surrounded. Hands touched her but at least she could breathe.

She was pushed towards the boat and she grabbed the steel rungs of the stern ladder, but before she could climb aboard she was gripped at the hips. Gianni pushed against her in the water and opened her legs with his knees. His penis rubbed against her vagina.

Kate could do nothing but hold onto the bottom rung of the ladder, for she was holding their combined weight and if she let go they would sink and he might not let her up so quickly next time. He held her with one arm around her waist and used his other hand to probe between her legs, opening the lips of her sex.

This wasn't possible, she thought. Not in the sea?

But he made it possible. He guided his penis between the folds of flesh and pushed it inside. She gasped and clung tighter to the ladder. He was bigger than Nero and filled her more completely.

She hung suspended between two worlds. Blue sky above, blue sea below. She floated like a dolphin that had been caught on a hunter's spear. The spear dug into her, again and again, and re-ignited her wound. Kate gasped and let go of the rung and they slid beneath the surface.

The young man kept his grip around her waist and continued to thrust into her as their bodies sank, twisting idly in the current. She was molten and could not understand why the shoals of small fish that swam past them did not scurry to avoid her heat.

This time she did not care if she surfaced or not. She was consumed and her senses were overloading with pleasure as the oxygen left her body. She was close to drowning again as she had drowned in the cave, only more completely this time, with the sounds of the ocean in her head. Then her lover-rapist kicked his feet and they arched towards the sunlight.

They broke surface like mating mammals amidst spray that sparkled and dazzled. He was still inside her as he rolled backwards and she had no choice but to roll with him. They twisted and were back at the boat. Hands grabbed her arms.

Rafel, the fat man, and Nero were leaning over the

side of the boat. They held her and hauled her upwards. She grunted in protest as Gianni's spear slid from her wound.

Kate was lifted effortlessly by the two men and held down on the stern deck amidst scattered cushions. Gianni climbed the ladder and joined them. She lay on her back, captured and gashed with desire between her legs. The shadows of the three men moved over her, cutting out the sun. Her own shadow had gone. Was it hiding in the cave until they had finished?

The men's eyes were bright with the chase. She dropped her gaze. Their pricks were hard and erect. Now there would be no more escape. Now there would be only submission.

Chapter 15

They held her down, arms and legs spread, while Gianni climbed upon her. He inserted himself into her vagina without ceremony and began to thrust. His body was beaded with sea water and his hair was slick and shiny. His hand moved over her breasts and her skin felt rubbery from the water.

He fucked her. There was no other description for it. He performed the sex act without regard for her or her pleasure. All the time he was pumping in and out of her, he stared into her face and she stared back. It seemed important that she should concentrate on everything that happened.

Gianni gripped her hips, reared over her and came. Only as his prick spurted did she regain feeling in her vagina. She guessed she must have been in a delayed shock because she had felt detached from her body throughout the intercourse.

Even sounds had been muted and now they returned to add to the grasping, slithering reality. The men grunted and wheezed, she gasped and moaned. The boat moved as they turned her over and she lay on her stomach.

Nero held her arms and Rafel, the fat one, knelt behind her.

He pulled at her hips, raising her bottom onto his penis. It was not as large a weapon as the younger man's, but it was firm and penetrative from behind. His belly slapped against her and he exhaled deeply. He adjusted his position, moving closer between and beneath her thighs so that she was almost sitting in his lap.

Rafel said something she didn't understand and Nero laughed. The fat man moved his hips and developed a fast rhythm. He also moved her up and down upon him. He began to shout, curses or perhaps obscenities, and Nero shouted back, urging him on. He bent over her and came and her vagina felt flooded.

Kate was turned onto her back once more. Nero straddled her body, pinning her down with his weight, his genitals resting on her breasts, his penis pointing upwards like a cannon. He tied her wrists together with a length of rope. He threw the end to Gianni and the young man made it secure by looping it through a strut on the rail.

Nero moved down her body and knelt between her legs. He stroked his penis and stared into her face, smiling as if she were a prize he had won.

'What you want?' he said, in mockery of before.

She was helpless. She had to reply.

'Fucking,' she said.

'Ask.'

'Fuck me.'

'Beg.'

'Please.'

He grinned and twisted a nipple. She winced.

'Beg more.'

'Please, Nero. Fuck me. Please fuck me.'

Her submission was a fact. She acknowledged it.

His grin widened and she was aware that the other two, lying back among the cushions, were watching and listening. She guessed they understood the word fuck.

Nero placed the end of his penis into the apex of her vagina so that it rubbed against her clitoris. She groaned. He dropped its angle of attack a fraction and it slid into her saturated vagina. It squelched and the noise was a delicious obscenity.

He removed it and rubbed it once more against her clitoris.

'You want this?' he teased.

She knew she must answer.

'Yes.'

'You want my prick?'

'Yes.'

'Ask.'

'I want your prick. I want it inside me. I want fucking.'

He was taking delight in the situation but she could also feel his excitement. Perhaps that was why he was staying out of the cauldron of her sex. He was unable to stand the heat.

Her words and her subjugation had aroused him too much to make it last long. He realigned the angle and again pushed it deep inside her. Kate tensed herself around it and raised her hips to meet his thrust.

'Fuck me!' she urged, staring into his face, seeing the veins begin to rise on his forehead. 'Fuck me!'

The words were the catalyst and he orgasmed, holding

himself above her on outstretched arms, staring into her eyes as he ejaculated in long bursts.

Kate had been mauled and used. The three men had emptied themselves into her and, she had no doubt, would do so again. They had aroused her but she had not come. She did not feel it would be appropriate to orgasm. The fear had yet to subside; the fear of the situation and of her own desires.

They erected a canopy over the stern deck and arranged the cushions to make the sunbed she had used the day before. Nero unfastened the rope from her wrists. They knew she would not try to escape again for there was no escape.

'Obey!' he warned.

She sat on the sunbed and waited to be told what to do. Her mind was still disembodied, she realised. She watched the men's erections become heavier as they drank wine and talked. They made her drink and she accepted gladly. Alcohol had helped release her shackles yesterday.

A short while ago, she had been a sexual object. Now she was sitting in the shade drinking wine, wondering whether it would enflame her passion. This period in between felt so normal it dulled both the fear and the desire. It enabled her to look at the men differently, to imagine and rationalise their lives.

Madness, she thought. She would be excusing their behaviour next, maybe offering them a tip when they took her back to St Julian's Bay. The wine was obviously having a greater effect than she had realised. It must be causing an imbalance in her mind.

Thought was the trouble. Her mind was the trouble. She shouldn't be thinking, she should be reacting.

Nero brought from the cabin a large bottle of baby oil. He spoke to the men and they laughed, nodding in agreement. They took the glass from her, lay her down and knelt around her. Nero poured oil over her shoulders and breasts and Gianni smoothed it into her skin.

More oil was poured over her stomach and thighs and Rafel spread it. The oil matted her pubic hair and trickled between her legs. His fingers followed it and stroked the open lips of her vagina.

Kate closed her eyes. Her mind and her senses drifted in a haze of heat and alcohol. The fingers between her legs were knowledgeable. They touched her rosebud and rolled it in oil. Her hips moved and she sighed. The fingers rolled it more firmly and rhythmically and she gasped.

Rafel spoke terse, serious words and Nero grunted.

She was turned over and Gianni sat on the cushions in front of her, rubbing his penis in her face.

Nero said, 'I tell him how good you are. How you like to suck.'

Kate took hold of the penis and put it in her mouth. She sucked and Gianni exhaled with contentment. Behind her, oil was poured onto her bottom. Hands smoothed it in and followed the rivulets that ran into her secret creases.

Her mouth was being used, her breasts were being felt and fingers were making deft sorties between her legs, moving slickly from her vagina to her anus. At last she was losing her identity and sensing only her body.

There had been no one to watch and judge what happened but herself, but now even that spectre was dissolving, its power weakened by the hands that touched and the smells and tastes in which she was beginning to wallow.

Gianni shuffled on the cushions and he held her head more firmly. His demands were taking on an urgency. She was raised onto her knees and a fat belly brushed her buttocks and she knew Rafel was behind her.

The tip of his penis slid the length of the crease between her buttocks. It dipped into her sex and was as quickly removed, slid backwards a fraction, and pressed against her smaller orifice.

Kate tensed and hands gripped her. She could not move and she could not complain. Rafel held his penis in his right hand and she could feel the backs of his fingers against her thighs. He pushed again and the tip gained a small entry.

In a different situation her body might have tried to reject what she would have considered an unthinkable possibility. But her body had been abandoned by her mind. All she had to do was react and submit and nothing was impossible.

Rafel pushed and it went deeper. It hurt and she moaned. The moan excited Gianni. It excited Kate, as well. The fat man pushed again and his penis sank into her and she was on fire with the new sensation. She tightened her grip on the base of the young man's prick and groaned loudly.

Her groan, which was evidence of her successful

sodomisation, tipped him over the edge and he came a second time. His paroxysm dislodged his penis and, after the first spurting into her mouth, it slipped from between her lips and she caressed it against her face as it jettisoned the remainder of his juices onto her neck.

Gianni lay slumped against the side of the boat, his interest drained with his coming. She nestled her head in his groin, immersed in the smell of his sex. Her narrow passage amazingly began to adjust to the wedge of flesh the fatman had inserted.

She lay on a plateau of new experience, not fully aware of how she got there, and not really sure of what would happen next, but hoping the experience would intensify.

Rafel leaned over her back and she trembled when he flexed his penis inside her. He moved it slowly, small withdrawals and reinsertions, and the hurt began to recede. Her emotions were stretched and words made no sense in her head. Only feelings were real.

He moved more rhythmically, creating fire in another part of her body. She was lost and in need of relief but knew she would not achieve it this way. The man gasped and thrust harder, grabbing at her flesh. He held her hips and mauled her breasts. Her legs gave way and she lay with him upon her back, his groin flattening her buttocks. The movement constricted her passage and made his prick fit tighter than ever.

The fat man grunted and held it deep inside her as he shuddered into a climax that removed control from his limbs and caused his full weight to shake upon her.

Kate was relieved when he rolled away. For a moment it had been like drowning again. She ached and was tired with the exertions and the wine, but she was turned onto her back once more and Nero leaned over her, smiling smugly into her face.

'English ladies like to fuck,' he said, as if making conversation.

He spread her legs and knelt between them. Kate had to concentrate to be certain he had entered her. Her body was stressed in so many areas and her vagina had been so well used it was difficult to tell.

'You like, yes?' he said.

Her mind was gone. There was no focus, only haze.

'You like fucking?'

He shook her shoulders and she groaned. He pulled at her breasts, twisting her nipples, and she gasped in pain as a shred of reality came back.

She had to obey.

'You like it?'

He was moving in and out of her as strong as ever.

'Yes,' she said.

His fingers touched her neck and scooped up the sticky juices spilt by Gianni. He laughed.

'You look good in pearls,' he said.

He put the sticky fingers to her mouth and she sucked them clean.

'A good fucking,' he said. He was muttering to himself, lost in his fantasy, pulsing in and out of her with greater vigour, riding closer to the edge. 'Beautiful English,' he said. 'Beautiful fuck.'

He fell upon her as he was overcome by the orgasm and discharged into her vagina. Kate felt his shakes gently subside and thought it was like dying. She was a

vampire who drank the life force of men and left them
spent and useless and without direction. She turned
them into zombies with lethargic limbs and disinterested
eyes.

Nero rolled away and her body was at peace. The haze
descended and she fell asleep.

The smell of cooking woke her. When she sat up, they
smiled and nodded to her, as if this had been a regular
pleasure cruise around the island. Her mouth was dry
and she wanted a drink of water but she was unsure of
her status. Nero had said obey, he had not given her
leave to make requests.

'You okay, English lady?' he said.

'I'm thirsty. Could I have a drink of water, please?'

He gave her a bottle of water from a cold box and
she drank deeply. Its recuperative effects surprised her.
It also seemed to reactivate the wine she had consumed
because she felt light-headed. Light-headed and hungry.

Sex and hunger. That was the discovery she had made
yesterday. Had it only been yesterday?

Gianni gave her a plate of fish and rice and she ate it
ravenously. It tasted delicious.

'Good?' the young man asked.

'Good.' She nodded enthusiastically and he beamed.

'Me cook,' he said, pointing to his chest.

'Beautiful,' she said, and continued eating.

Rafel, the fat man, moved to the stern seats and, as
he passed her, he stroked her hair. He sat down, his legs
spread, his genitalia hanging between his thighs like a
small bunch of exotic fruit. He said something in Maltese
to Nero and smiled at Kate.

Nero said, 'He say you are good fuck. A beautiful fuck. He say we do it again later.'

The fat man smiled and nodded at her and Kate smiled back, unsure whether she would ever find reality again and, if she did, whether she would recognise it.

When they finished eating they swam. The threat and the fear and anxiety had gone. The water soothed the aches of her body. Gianni swam with her and touched her. His legs brushed against hers. He caressed her bottom. The truce was ending.

The other two swam closer and they touched her as they wished. Kate felt a different ache return. The ache of frustration and the need for release. No one was watching except the birds. Not even herself anymore.

As she walked onto the small beach, Nero pulled her down into the shallow water. He rolled with her and she felt his prick hard again. He lay upon her and kissed her: her first kiss since the arrival of the men he had said were his cousins. She responded.

Gianni said something and Nero stopped kissing her. They exchanged words. Nero got to his feet and held out his hand to Kate. She took it and he pulled her to her feet. He took her in his arms again and kissed her, his erection pushing hot against her stomach, and she closed her eyes.

Another stiff penis pushed against her bottom. Gianni had stepped behind her and was pressing it into the groove between her buttocks. He licked and kissed her neck. Two pairs of hands roamed her body.

Kate had become a simple recipient. She was empty of reason and waited only to be filled with pricks and pleasure. Her libido had at last been fully released and she squirmed between them, turning her head when Nero stopped kissing her, to offer her mouth to Gianni's lips.

Rafel, the fat one, shouted and broke her gathering momentum. Nero let go of her and replied. Gianni still held her from behind, still pushed his penis against her softness, still kissed her mouth. More words were shouted and he reluctantly stopped what he was doing and let her go. Kate felt abandoned.

Nero said to her, 'We go back to the boat now. We finish the fuck.'

Rafel had already started on the return swim and they followed, the two younger men flanking Kate. No one spoke anymore. They pulled themselves through the water with purpose and set faces.

On board the boat, they dried themselves with towels. Rafel had remade the sunbed on the stern deck beneath the awning. Kate stood next to it, the three men standing around her. Rafel produced a cloth and he put it around her eyes and tied it in a knot behind her head.

They had rendered her blind. Vision, the last distraction, had been removed. Hands touched her and she whimpered. Bodies brushed against her, hot pricks probed her softness. Oil was poured over her breasts and shoulders, her buttocks and stomach. They began by using their hands but, as the slickness spread, bodies took over the intimate massage.

Mouths covered hers in rotation and she kissed and fought with tongues. As one open mouth slid from her lips and licked her cheek, it was replaced by another.

163

Her breasts were sucked, her nipples nibbled and tormented, and hard maleness slithered like rampant snakes around her bottom and her hips and the curve of her stomach.

Kate was edging to delirium when they lay her on the cushions of the sunbed. She did not try to differentiate between the bodies and the hands, the mouths and the pricks. She was being devoured by a many-limbed sex beast. Her body was open and available. It waited to be taken.

A penis slid into her, a hard male stomach pushed against her soft belly. More stiff masculinity pushed at her from behind. She rolled between them on her side. Mouths still kissed her and sucked her flesh. The fucking began and she came.

The release blanked her mind. She let herself go without reserve and her limbs spasmed and jerked and groans were shaken from her throat. As one orgasm subsided, she slipped into another. She was riding waves of pleasure so intense her sense of being became extinct.

Kate did not know how long the four of them coupled and heaved. Her orgasmic reaction intensified their attentions. Pricks pierced her vagina and her anus and she kept on coming, groaning into the mouths that covered hers.

Identity returned slowly when her body was finally alone and at peace. She was somewhere between sleep and exhaustion. The blindfold that was still around her eyes was an aid to acceptance: that it had happened, that she had responded, that it was over.

The engine of the boat throbbed and they rode different waves. She lay naked and unmoving and waited for her mind to reassert its authority, although she knew she would never be the same again and that part of her would forever remain in a lost cove in a lost land where fantasy came true.

Chapter 16

The magic began to seep away as they arrived at St Julian's Bay. She had put the dress on but the intimate parts of her body ached too much for her to don underwear.

After the solitude of the sea, the boats and activity of the harbour confused her. The people who walked on the busy road were aliens with ordered concepts that made them wear holiday clothes. They were freshly bathed and normal.

Kate had nothing in common with them. She was an outsider from another world.

Nero tied up against the harbour wall. They had not spoken on the entire voyage back. He picked up her bag and jumped onto the quay. He waited and held his hand out for her but she hesitated.

A landau went by on the road above her, heading towards Balluta Bay. A brightly painted bus came in the other direction, heading for the chaos of the narrow road that wound up towards the area of restaurants and hotels.

Did she know anyone on the bus?

Faces were white and blank behind the windows. It

could have been filled with her fellow guests at the hotel but she would not have known them. She no longer belonged. She no longer knew anyone. Illusions and delusions had been shattered. Social facades had been destroyed and were no longer relevant but she had nothing with which to replace them.

Nero waited, his hand extended. She had to leave the boat, leave that part of herself in that hidden cove to which she would never return. She accepted his hand and stepped onto dry land. The journey was at an end.

He guided her with a hand upon her elbow and they climbed the steps to the road. Kate had no sense of direction or purpose. She allowed him to take her across the road and put her into the back of a taxi at the rank. He spoke to the driver and gave him money. He looked at her and smiled.

Was there a hint of guilt in the smile?

'Goodbye, English lady,' he said.

He closed the door and the taxi wheezed into the traffic. Like most of the cars of Malta, it was old and rattled.

Kate did not look back and she took no notice of the people they passed or where they were going. The journey did not take long and when the vehicle stopped she turned her head and stared at the hotel.

The driver spoke to her. What was he saying? He was telling her she was here. That she should get out. She did so and the driver shook his head and drove away.

People were entering and leaving the hotel. Some of them were familiar and they smiled and said hello. She smiled automatically in response but when a middle-aged woman asked her a question she did not understand it and did not reply.

Her behaviour was wrong. She knew she appeared odd but was incapable of correcting how she acted. She had forgotten how to behave.

A man leaving the hotel held the door open for her and so she entered. A key. She needed a key and then she could attain the safety of a room. She went to reception but had forgotten what she should ask for. The young woman recognised her and smiled and gave her a key without her having to say anything.

The young woman asked something about having a good day.

'Thank you,' Kate said.

Kate went to the lift and remembered she should press the button marked three. Good. Responses were returning. She didn't like being in limbo. The doors opened on the third floor and she stepped into a carpeted corridor. She went left. Trays containing dirty plates and stainless steel coffee pots were outside some doors.

She turned the corner and continued walking. A room door on her left opened and startled her. A woman was at the door, looking back into the room and talking to someone in Italian. Beyond the woman, a suntanned man in shorts sat eating sandwiches. A slice from someone else's life. But where was her own? In a room down here?

A woman approached her with a smile. A woman with blonde hair and a neat figure.

'Have a good day?' she said. The woman's face changed. 'Kate? What's wrong?'

169

'Lorna?'

Kate felt immense relief that she had found someone she knew. She dropped the bag and put her arms around her. Lorna held her. Someone else's body, someone else's smell. Lorna smelled of perfume and cleanliness.

'Here.'

Lorna took the key from her, picked up her bag and, keeping an arm around her waist, led her further down the corridor. She unlocked a door and they went into a room whose shades had been drawn against the sun. Kate had reached her haven.

She lay on the bed and rolled onto her back. Lorna sat alongside her and brushed the hair from her face.

'You're all right now,' she murmured. She kissed her forehead gently. 'You're safe now.'

Kate began to cry, although she did not know why. Lorna lay alongside her and held her in her arms. The tears stopped as suddenly as they had started and Kate sighed.

'What happened, Kate?' Lorna said.

'I'm tired.'

'You'd be better off in bed.'

Lorna unfastened the buttons down the front of the dress and paused when she opened it and found Kate was wearing no brassiere. She stared at the marks on her breasts. She rolled Kate onto her stomach and eased the dress from shoulders and arms, then rolled her back and slipped it over her bottom and down her thighs.

Again she paused when she saw she was wearing no panties. Her nose twitched as she smelled her body. She dropped the dress onto the floor.

'Do you want to talk about it?' she said.

Of course she did. Why hadn't she thought of that?

'Yes.' Kate stared into Lorna's face, a pretty face that was full of concern. 'Hold me.'

Lorna held her. Her perfume was delicious. Her body was exquisitely soft after all the male hardness she had endured.

'What happened?' Lorna said softly.

'I went on a boat. A beautiful boat, a beautiful day. We swam in a bay. High cliffs. Clear water.' She remembered being a dolphin and moved against the young woman. She remembered being caught. 'There were three of them. They fucked me.'

Kate felt the tremor that ran through Lorna. The woman stroked her face again and held her closer. She kissed her cheek and her forehead. Kate looked into her eyes. The concern was still there but she had not been mistaken about the tremor. There was excitement as well.

'Oh, Kate. I'm sorry.' She held her tighter and Kate could feel the softness of her breasts. 'So sorry.'

'I'm not,' Kate whispered.

Lorna stopped rocking her in her arms. They looked into each others faces.

'You're not sorry?' Lorna said.

'No.'

The sexual tide that had washed her up on the harbour at St Julian's was reclaiming her. Her senses were becoming activated once more.

'What do you mean?'

The blonde woman's delicately painted lips quivered as she asked the question.

171

'It was glorious.'

'Glorious?'

'I enjoyed it, Lorna. They fucked me into oblivion and I enjoyed it.'

Lorna gulped and she moistened her lips with the tip of her pink tongue.

'What did they do?'

'They raped me. They subdued me. They sodomised me. They came in my mouth. They abused me until I lost my mind.'

'You enjoyed it?'

'They fucked away the fear. The pretence. They fucked away ten years.' She smiled and raised her head from the pillow, kissing Lorna on the lips. 'It was marvellous.'

Lorna's features had subtly changed and Kate's smile became more assured. She recognised the look in Lorna's face, she recognised the lust. She could feel it in her friend's body. Even last night she would not have understood the small signs but now her comprehension was automatic. What was more, the possibilities inherent in what she had deduced didn't frighten or embarrass Kate.

For the first time, she felt free to explore her own sexuality, and even that was not a conscious decision. It was a truth that was self-evident. Kate had never kissed a woman before, had never allowed herself to be attracted to a member of her own sex. But her shackles were broken and the urges that surged within her no longer recognised differentials. They recognised only sex.

She put her arms around Lorna and pulled her head down. Their lips met. Lorna was shaking but she did not attempt to pull away. Kate began the kiss and parted

Lorna's lips with her own. Her tongue made the first invasion. Lorna shuddered and her tongue fought back. The kiss was enjoined. The possibilities began.

When their mouths parted, Kate pulled at Lorna's dress.

'Take it off,' she said.

Lorna hesitated and Kate's fingers found the zip that ran down the back of the dress. She unfastened the hook at the top and pulled down the zipper.

'Smell me,' she whispered. 'I'm covered with their smells.' Lorna shuddered and Kate pushed the dress from her shoulders. 'Take it off.'

Lorna reached behind her and completed unfastening the dress, pushing it over her hips. She kicked it from her feet and it fell to the floor. Kate's hands were already on her breasts, feeling the small mounds beneath the silken bra.

'And this,' she said.

The blonde woman again reached behind her and unclipped the bra, pulled it from her breasts and threw it away. Without being prompted, she pushed her panties off. Her shoes fell from the end of the bed, one after the other.

They lay together, the curves of their bodies in soft complement in the darkness of the room. Kate slowly allowed her hand to slide down the arch of her companion's back, into the downy valley and up again over the lush rise of her bottom.

The woman was in perfect proportion. Her breasts were small globes that dangled above Kate. The nipples were hard and pointed and scorched her flesh when she moved them across Kate's bosom.

'You're beautiful,' Kate whispered.

They had called her beautiful. A beautiful fuck. Beautiful would never mean the same again.

They kissed, long and fulfilling. When their mouths parted they gasped for air.

Lorna said, 'I've never felt like this before.' Her eyes bored into Kate's. 'I have no resistance. What have you done to me?'

'Touched you.' she stroked her face. 'Shown you the power.'

'The power?'

'In my eyes.' Their eyes locked and Kate felt as if she could pluck out the woman's soul with the penetration of her gaze. 'I wallowed in sex. Now sex wallows in me. I can do anything.'

They kissed and the power surged between them. Kate felt herself to be irresistible. She was generating the lust they both shared. The kiss became wilder and their hands moved over each other's bodies. The softness was incredible.

Kate pushed Lorna's hand between her legs.

'There, there,' she said, directing her fingers. 'Feel them. Feel their stains. Feel where they pushed their pricks. Where they came.'

Lorna's fingers went inside Kate and she gasped. Her vagina opened immediately and her juices flooded. She arched around the hand and climaxed, gasping against her friend's shoulder.

The orgasm was not followed by a pacifying lull. It made Kate want more. She rolled over, pushing Lorna onto her back, and lay upon her. Now her larger breasts hung down and she raked the woman with her nipples. She knelt up and rubbed them across her face. Lorna's open mouth sought them and she licked and sucked.

Kate slid down her body. Their legs parted and they rubbed themselves against each other's thighs. Lorna's vagina slid wetly against her.

For the first time, Kate was in control of a sexual situation. She was bigger than Lorna and could dominate with her strength. It was not better than submission, it was different, another variation in the pursuit and attainment of pleasure.

She moved down her body and sucked Lorna's breasts, rasping her tongue across those hard little nipples to elicit a gentle moan. Kate captured a nipple in her teeth and nipped and nibbled, and Lorna moaned louder at the incitement of the pleasure and pain.

Kate's hand lay over the blonde woman's mons. Her fingers scratched distractedly in the pubic curls. Lorna squirmed. Her hips were asking Kate to touch her between her legs but she delayed.

Lower she went, and her tongue dipped into Lorna's navel, before trailing down into the soft forest of dark blonde curls. She had not yet touched the woman in her secret place but they had aroused each other so much that Kate could smell Lorna's desire.

She slid lower, trapping one of Lorna's legs between her thighs so that she could rub her own sodden vagina against her ankle. Her head bent to the aromatic valley and she combed apart the curls with her fingers.

Lorna's sex was open. The lips swollen and apart, and

moisture like dew shone in the pink grotto. The vision was so beautiful, Kate forgot to breathe.

Beautiful and sex. The two words were now indelibly linked.

Kate exhaled slowly, her breath caressing the open flower of the woman's sex. It was so beautiful. The petals of sensitive flesh begged to be kissed. The clitoris was as hard as a penis and demanded attention.

This was taking sacrament. This was the true worship of one woman for another and for every woman.

She dipped her head and ran her tongue along the length of Lorna's vagina. It slipped into the small crushed cavern and she tasted her for the first time. Beautiful. Her tongue continued its lazy journey and circumnavigated the clitoris.

Lorna moaned from deep in her throat and Kate squirmed her own sex against the trapped ankle between her thighs. She pushed a finger into the cave and watched it become swallowed in the sensitive flesh. She withdrew it and pushed in two fingers. Lorna moved against them.

Kate twisted the fingers as she moved them in and out and the young woman's moan became continuous. She lowered her head again, sucking upon the clitoris, and Lorna bucked as if touched by a live electric wire.

The current of sex was surging through her and her fists were clenched. Kate licked her clitoris, pistoned her fingers and felt Lorna on the verge of orgasm. As she tumbled into it, with shaking limbs, Kate removed her fingers and pushed her face into the wet cavern, digging deeply inside with her tongue. The fingers, slick with secretions, slid beneath the curve of her bottom and prodded at that other rosebud.

Lorna soared from one peak to another and the orgasms ran into each other. It was as if she was connected to the source and Kate knew that she was the source. She stopped licking and probing and the young woman subsided, temporarily replete.

Kate moved back up the bed and lay upon Lorna, the mounds of their sex touching. They kissed so that Kate could share the intimacy of her first fellation. Lorna looked up at her with suddenly timid eyes.

'How did this happen?' she said.

'Because I wanted it to happen. Because you did, too.' After being empty of reason, Kate's mind was now filled with new knowledge and understanding. 'You did want to, didn't you, Lorna?'

'I don't know.'

Kate kissed her and stared into her eyes.

'Be honest, Lorna. I said fuck and rape and you wanted sex. Didn't you?'

'Yes.'

'The words revolted and excited you.'

'Yes.'

'You imagined what had happened. How I'd been fucked. You could smell me, smell them upon me. Couldn't you?'

'Yes.'

'And when I said I enjoyed it, I freed you from the guilt. Without guilt, without revulsion there was only lust and sex.' She kissed her again. 'And I wanted you, Lorna. You had no choice.'

Lorna shook her head.

'I don't understand. Tell me what happened?'

Kate felt sorry for Lorna because she felt the experience she had been through in the cove had been so total it had imbued her with insight and purpose. It was only to be expected that Lorna would not understand and would be confused.

Even telling her what had happened would not explain her rebirth. If she sincerely tried to put it into words, it would sound mystical and idiotic, as if she had become unbalanced by what she had endured.

Her reasoning sounded unbalanced even to herself, an assessment developed under the influence of drugs, which, in a way, it had been, for among the many discoveries she had made was how powerful a drug sex could be.

Three men had desired her and had taken her not once, but many times. The more she had submitted, the freer she had become. Had they seen her sexuality begin to burn? Had she exuded a lust they had been unable to resist?

That last time aboard the boat, when she had been blindfolded and they had slithered around her like eels, had been beyond rape, love or sexual intercourse. She knew they had all felt it, all expired a little. They had all left something behind in that deserted cove.

Kate remembered the look on Nero's face when he put her in the taxi. She had thought, through the haze that had enveloped her, that it might be a look of guilt. It might also have been a look of uncertainty. That he had known he had changed her irrevocably and he was unsure what she had become.

She kissed Lorna and explored the cavities of her mouth with her tongue.

'You want to know what happened?' she said.

'Yes.'

'You want to know how they fucked me?'

Lorna groaned and squirmed her sex against her.

'Yes.'

'Ask me.'

Kate squirmed back and they both breathed heavily with arousal. It was her turn for games.

'Tell me what they did.'

Lorna licked her neck and her tongue dipped into Kate's ear.

'You mean how did they fuck me?'

The word worked its sex magic and Lorna groaned, moving beneath her.

'Yes.'

'Ask me. Use the word.'

'How did they fuck you?'

'They fucked me every way they could.'

'And you let them?'

'I had no choice. I couldn't escape. I had to submit. I had to let them do what they wanted.'

'No choice?'

Kate trailed her tongue across Lorna's cheek and into her mouth.

'It was a freedom. Like I freed you from guilt.'

'Were you frightened?'

'At first.'

'And later?'

'Later . . . later there was no fear, no meaning. Later there was only sex.

Kate told Lorna in detail what had happened during the

two days she had been with Nero. Lorna sighed, squirmed and began to lose herself in the revelations. She came several times during the telling, on her own fingers and at Kate's hands.

Finally, Kate made her go down on her and taste the dried sperm that was still between her thighs and lap at her vagina until she came one last time.

They lay together in silent exhaustion for a while.

Eventually, Lorna said, 'Peter will wonder where I am.'

'Where does he think you are?'

'Shopping with you.'

Kate was tired now and wanted to sleep. She knew Lorna wanted an excuse to leave.

'Can we do that tomorrow?' she said. 'Shopping?'

'Of course.'

The darkness of the room had intensified as night had fallen beyond the shades.

'You'd better go,' said Kate.

'Are you all right?'

'Of course. I'm a new woman.' She squeezed Lorna's hand and laughed lightly. 'A seducer.'

'I still don't understand.'

'Neither do I anymore.'

Lorna got off the bed and opened the curtains a little rather than switch on the light. Her body gleamed in the moonlight, ethereal and lovely.

'You really are beautiful, Lorna.'

'So are you. Perhaps now you realise how beautiful?'

She began to put on her clothes in the shadows.

'Have you ever done it with another woman before?' Kate said.

The hesitation was only slight before she replied.

'Yes.'

Kate felt disappointed, as if someone had blown out the candles on her birthday cake. She had deluded herself that she had been in charge and had seduced the young woman into a sexual first. Her mystical experience had been put into perspective.

Lorna said, 'It was a long time ago.'

'How did this rate?'

Kate regretted the question as soon as she had said it for she had been unable to hide the edge in her voice. She had sounded petulant.

'This was incredible.'

The words comforted her. She had thought it incredible, too. She wanted to ask more about Lorna's experiences with women but realised she did not know her well enough. They had engaged in thrilling sex but were not yet friends.

'You don't regret it?' Kate said.

'No. Do you?'

'No.'

'Was this your first time?' Lorna asked. 'With a woman?'

'Yes.'

Lorna stepped into her dress. She paused with it around her waist and stared towards Kate, even though they had become only shadows.

'That makes it special. Was it good?'

'It was very special.'

Lorna zipped up the dress and looked for her shoes. She found them and put them on. She stood at the end of the bed.

'What will you do tonight?'

'Sleep.'

'You don't want to come out with us?'

'It's a kind offer, but no. I ache too much to walk.'

The young woman came and sat next to her on the bed. She held her hand.

'Is it true?' she said. 'What you said?'

'Yes. It was all true.'

'And you have no regrets? About what they did?'

'I think I was looking for it. I found it with Nero, after all, the first day. I mean, why else would he have asked me to go with him on his boat? It had to be because he wanted to have sex with me. Seduce me. Deep down, I knew that and I still went.

'Today, I expected the same. I shouldn't have been surprised when his cousins turned up. Now I'm glad they did. I wouldn't recommend the experience to everybody, but it worked for me. But then I think I was a special case in need of special treatment.

Lorna laughed softly.

'You make it sound as if you spent the day on a psychiatrist's couch.'

'In a way I did. You might say it was a brutal form of regression but it worked. It really was glorious.'

'Do you think I should try it?'

'I don't think Peter would let you.'

Lorna squeezed her hand.

'You'd be surprised what Peter would let me do.'

'Would he let you make love with me?'

'The idea would send him wild.'

Kate smiled in the darkness.

'Then send him wild. Tell him.'

'There could be consequences.'

'Consequences is a good game to play.'

'I have to go.'

Kate held onto her hand.

'That other time? Who was it with?'

'A girlfriend at school.'

'Will you tell me sometime?'

'If you like. But now I have to go.'

She leaned down and kissed Kate on the lips. She walked to the door.

'Goodnight, Kate.'

'Goodnight, Lorna.'

'Tomorrow we'll go shopping.'

'Good.'

Lorna let herself out and Kate stared at the dark ceiling. Two weeks ago, the highlight of her week had been two half-days in the Oxfam shop.

Today had been eventful and tomorrow there would be shopping and consequences. And all because of two love letters and a set of polaroid photographs.

Thank God her husband had had an affair. Thank God she had discovered the letters. Thank God she had rediscovered her life.

Chapter 17

The morning brought yet a new perspective. Nothing seemed so certain. Kate lay in bed and wondered how she should feel. The previous day could have been a nightmare but she had turned it into a fantasy. She had used it as a battering ram against the restraints of the past.

She smiled at the analogy. The smile reassured her: she still had a sense of humour.

It would be necessary to adopt a veneer of normality again, so that she could re-enter polite society. But if she did, would that jeopardise her new-found freedom?

Kate had been without freedom for so long and, she now realised, without a sense of humour for so long, that she saw normality as a bigger threat than three men in a boat. She laughed again, this time at herself.

There was no way she could ever return to being The Little Woman. No pressure of society would be able to make her conform to any role she did not wish to play. Last night, the aftermath of the previous day had left her awash with half-mystical philosophy about the meaning of life. She wondered if she had frightened Lorna.

Not with the sex but with what she'd said.

Now she could assess her experience in a more measured fashion and the bottom line was she had needed a good fucking. She had needed to shed her inhibitions and had not known how. They had been ripped from her because she had had no choice and she was grateful she had emerged without mental or physical scars.

Nero and his cousins needed shooting, or perhaps something more painful. She could think of several interesting things to do with fish hooks. They had been calculating seducers praying on a foolish woman. Maybe she would return one day and pay them back. Surprisingly, she felt capable of doing just such a thing.

Her renewal was not imagined. After being drained of identity the day before, she was now filled with strength and curiosity. That, she guessed, was her missing personality. She wondered if she would like herself.

She wondered if Lorna would like her.

Making love with Lorna had been a natural conclusion to an unreal day. It had also helped make the transfer from a fantasy encounter in a distant cove to a hotel room and a woman she would see again today.

A bridge had been built that ensured her sexual progress would continue. Lorna had threatened consequences. With both her and Peter? The thought was appealing.

The new perspective was no longer frightening. Social facades were essential to move through the day, but she would never lose her inner self again and never let it be subjugated to someone else's code.

Behind her facades she would nurture her knowledge and her sexuality and indulge herself whenever the opportunity arose.

Kate stretched and realised she was hungry. She lifted the sheets to climb out of bed and smelled herself. Sex and hunger. But on this occasion they did not go together.

She called room service and ordered breakfast but had a shower before it arrived.

Kate found Peter and Lorna sunbathing by the hotel swimming pool. He was reading a paperback book and Lorna was dozing behind sunglasses.

'Hi!' Kate said.

Peter lowered the book and he smiled. She recognised the optimism in his look.

'Hello,' he said.

Lorna removed the sunglasses and grinned, a little sheepishly.

'Did you sleep well?' she said.

'Like a baby.'

Peter got off the lounger he had been occupying and pulled another one closer.

'Here,' he said to Kate.

Kate wore her hair in a simple ponytail. The sun had bleached it further and her skin was golden brown. She wore no make-up, but when she had inspected herself in the mirror her green eyes had sparkled and she had been pleased with the way she looked.

She dropped a towel on the floor and slipped off the beach robe.

187

'Very nice,' said Lorna.

'I bought it at the hotel shop this morning.'

The new swimsuit was black, had a deeply scooped back and was low in front and cut high at the sides to reveal her buttocks.

Lorna said, 'I don't think you'll need me this afternoon.'

'Oh yes I will.' Kate sat on the lounger in between husband and wife. 'You can't back out.'

'I don't intend to.'

Peter had put down the book and was sitting sideways on the lounger facing the two women.

Kate said to him, 'Has Lorna told you?'

He blushed and coughed. 'Erm?'

'About going shopping in Valetta?'

'Oh, that? Yes. It's a good idea.'

'Do you think she can make me beautiful?'

He looked embarrassed. 'You are beautiful, Kate.'

Her smile was one of contentment. She was beginning to believe it.

Kate said to Lorna, 'What did you do last night?'

'We went to the barbecue at The Hilton.'

'A good time?'

'Great. Good food, sea breezes and a nice band.'

Kate glanced at Peter before turning back to his wife. 'Did you tell him?'

Lorna's cheeks flushed and she put her sunglasses back on.

'Is this the place?' she said.

'Why not?' Kate grinned and looked at Peter. 'Did she tell you?'

He coughed again, still embarrassed.

'Yes. She told me.'

'Everything?'

'I don't know. Everything about what?'

Kate said to Lorna, 'What did you tell him?'

'About us.'

'Not about what happened earlier?'

'No. Not that. I didn't know if you would want me to tell him that.'

Kate smiled and nodded. They had started as lovers and now the friendship was developing. She could be trusted with secrets.

She looked at Peter.

'Lorna said it would send you wild. Did it?'

He coughed and looked at the swimming pool.

'It was quite stimulating.'

'But did it send you wild?'

Lorna said, 'It sent him wild. All night and this morning, it send him wild.'

Kate laughed.

'If I can spread a little happiness as I go on my way,' she murmured.

Peter said, 'I thought she was joking. Then I thought she was making it up to get me going.' He licked his lips. 'I still wasn't sure. Have you made this up or is it true?'

'It's true. We made love.'

He shuddered and his reaction excited her. She had not thought she would be able to respond so soon after all that had happened in the previous two days. It was a delicious discovery to realise she could.

189

Her voice dropped and became intimate, even though there was no one else near who might overhear.

She said, 'We fucked each other, Peter. It was great.'

'Jeez . . .' Peter said.

He got up, walked to the swimming pool and fell in without attempting a dive.

Lorna said, 'Are you becoming a tease?'

'I thought we were playing consequences?'

The two women stared at each other. Lorna removed the sunglasses so they could make proper eye contact.

'The change is incredible,' she said.

Kate knew she meant not the swimsuit but her attitude and the sexual aggression she had just displayed.

'I have a lot of catching up to do.' She thought she saw concern in Lorna's eyes. Who for? 'But I may get over-anxious. Am I an intrusion? Between you and Peter?'

'No.'

'I don't want to be a threat, Lorna.' Lorna smiled and held her hand. 'I don't want you to think of me as a threat. I'm still a novice and I need help.'

'Do you find Peter attractive?'

'Yes.'

'Would you like him to make love to you?'

'No.'

Lorna raised her eyebrows in surprise.

Kate added, 'But I'd like him to fuck me.'

'That would be nice.'

'You wouldn't mind?'

'It would send me wild.'

Kate glanced at the swimming pool. Peter was doing lazy lengths.

'Have you two done this sort of thing before?'

'Occasionally.'

'No hang-ups afterwards? No problems?'

'Not if you do it right.'

'And you love each other? I can tell that. You love each other.'

'Oh yes, we love each other. That's what makes it so much more exciting.'

'It does?'

'Sex is one of life's great experiences. Love is another. Combine the two and they are both better.'

'So why involve someone else?'

Lorna said, 'It's impossible to maintain the same intensity. You'll find that, after yesterday. What we do is add the spice of a third party from time to time. We have love, sex and jealousy. It's a cocktail, if you like. It can be very potent.'

Kate was reconsidering her own role in all this which seemed to have been devalued.

'The third party could be anybody?'

'Certainly not. We do this very occasionally. When we find the right person. They have to be special, like last night was special.'

Kate smiled ruefully.

'You make me feel like an outsider, but I suppose I must be.'

'In this, you must. But a special outsider.' Lorna sat up on the lounger and turned to sit sideways to face Kate. 'You asked me to explain and I've been honest. Love makes itself felt in different ways. Last night, when we made love, I loved you. I still do, because of what we shared, but it's a different love to that I have for Peter.'

Now she looked at the swimming pool and at her husband.

'Love is a peculiar emotion. It sometimes gets itself confused with desire. With wanting to fuck someone. Like when you were at school, perhaps, and you had a crush on some bloke. The love lasted right up until he fucked you. But not afterwards.'

She looked back at Kate.

'Am I making any sense?'

'Some. But love is hard to understand after the last ten years.'

'Did you ever love your husband?'

'No.'

'Have you ever loved anyone, Kate?'

It was the question she had been avoiding for years and now she felt there was no longer any need to.

'Yes, I think I did. A long time ago.'

'Did you make love?'

'We fucked. Violently. But it was also making love. We both lost control.'

'Was it good?'

'It was the most amazing experience I had ever had.'

'Did you still love him afterwards?'

'I think I've always loved him. I think that may have been the problem.'

'But you didn't marry him?'

'He was already married.'

'Did you see him again?'

'I saw him but not as the same person. Neither of us could be the same people, not the way we had been that night. We never made love again. We never touched again. I closed a door and walked away.'

'You make it sound like a tragedy.'

'In a way, it was.' Kate stopped remembering and smiled at Lorna. 'But it was a long time ago and there is no going back. I'd rather play consequences.'

'With me and Peter?'

'I can think of nothing nicer.'

Chapter 18

The two women took a taxi into the island's capital of Valletta at three-thirty. Peter remained at the hotel.

Kate had some ideas about how she wanted to look and a Visa Gold Card. Bob had insisted she carry it as a symbol of his success but she had rarely used it. This was the first time that she was glad she had it and she fully intended to test its buying power.

The taxi dropped them at the Triton Fountain and they walked through the city gate. Republic Street stretched ahead of them, all the way down to Fort St Elmo at the top of the promontory. The streets were narrow and built on a grid system. There were few department stores but an abundance of boutiques and small shops.

Lorna said, 'There's plenty of fashion, if you don't mind the cost.'

'I don't mind the cost,' said Kate.

The credit card would take care of the cost and her husband would take care of the bill when it arrived, which would be after she had kicked him out. He could count it as a farewell present.

Kate had originally thought of the shopping expedition

as a necessity. Her clothes were dowdy, her underwear a bad joke. She needed to change her image and she had worried in case she picked the wrong new image, which was why she had been grateful for Lorna's offer of help.

Now she knew her image had already begun to change, in the way she felt and observed, in the way she walked and because of the new awareness of her body. There would be no mistake in what image she picked. Her confidence was high.

And instead of a necessity the shopping trip had become another exciting adventure, one she had never properly embarked upon before.

Lorna had booked an appointment for her at a hairdressing and beauty salon in Old Bakery Street that had the reputation of being the best in the city. They went straight there.

A slim young Maltese called David discussed styles with them. Lorna suggested a bob and for a time Kate was confused until she saw a photograph on the wall.

'That's what I want,' she said.

Her decision was so definite that it silenced Lorna. The hairdresser looked at the photograph and at Kate. He swept the hair from her face.

'Yes,' David said. 'That would be good.'

'A bit drastic?' said Lorna.

'It has to be,' said Kate.

'Not everyone can wear the hair so short,' David said, as he prepared her. 'The bone structure has to be right.' He touched her chin. 'You, madam, have perfect bone structure.'

Beyond him, Kate saw Lorna pull a face and pretend to be sick.

He washed, cut and styled her hair. The long unkempt locks fell around her. She was a butterfly emerging from a cocoon. More hair fell until her head felt bald. He dried it, snipped, and the scissors felt as if they were snipping her scalp.

Finally, he said, 'Yes.'

He held a mirror behind her and she was silent. For a moment she couldn't speak because the change was so dramatic.

Lorna said, 'Superb.'

'Thank you,' said David.

'I meant Kate.'

It was superb. An elfin cut that was wispy and fine and lightened her sun-bleached hair even more. Her features had never been so prominent. Were her eyes really that big and so green?

A beautician applied make-up and Kate watched and learned. With her good skin and golden tan, minimal make-up was necessary. The girl concentrated on her eyes and subtly highlighted her cheekbones. She applied lipstick and painted her nails.

The result was beyond her expectations. She had wanted to change her appearance but had not believed she could look this good.

Near the Palace Square they found a Marks and Spencers store. The underwear fascinated Kate. She bought matching sets in black and white, and stockings of different shades.

They had a coffee and a brandy at an open-air restaurant in Republic Square before exploring the arcades and covered walkways of the ancient buildings, where small shops offered everything from designer-labelled fashion to locally made shoes and jewellery.

When she tried dresses on, Lorna joined her in small cubicles and they enjoyed the intimacy. They did not touch each other on purpose, but when they brushed against each other their breath quickened at the thought of what the night might bring.

The collection of bags they had accumulated was getting bigger.

'Don't you think you have enough?' Lorna said.

'I'm sorry.' Kate laughed. 'I didn't know it was such fun. Is it getting late?'

'It's not the time, it's the amount of stuff we have to carry.'

'Okay. Have we missed anything?'

'I doubt it. Make-up, hair, underwear, shoes, dresses, perfume, string of pearls, earrings. Anything else?'

'Actually, I wouldn't mind a new watch. I've had this one since school.'

Lorna sighed.

'Jeweller's. Over there.'

'Oh, look!'

Next to the jeweller's was a small boutique with a window display of underwear far more risqué than anything they had seen in Marks and Spencers. They entered and found it a haven from the bustle outside. They inspected garter belts and basques and Kate made more purchases.

Eventually they went next door to the jewellery store and sat in chairs while a man in a grey suit attended them. Lorna admired a Gucci but Kate picked a discreet gold Rolex and produced her Visa Gold Card. Gold for gold seemed appropriate. The man smiled.

'Could you also get us a taxi?' Kate asked.

'But of course, madam.'

He made a telephone call and Lorna waited by the door while Kate went with him to pay. The taxi was a large and venerable Mercedes and it arrived with a honking of its horn up the narrow street. The man in the grey suit helped them load it with their parcels.

'Another half-hour and we would have needed a trailer,' Lorna said.

Kate laughed and held her hand.

'Indulge me. It happens once in a blue moon.'

At the hotel, they filled the small lift so that other passengers had to wait. They joked as they carried the parcels and bags down the corridors of the third floor to Kate's room. Lorna went inside with her.

They dumped everything on the bed and Kate opened the mini-bar.

'You deserve a drink. What will it be?'

'Gin and tonic.'

Kate poured two large gin and tonics. Lorna opened the drapes to let in the sunlight but left the window closed. Outside it was still hot, inside was air conditioned. They toasted each other with the glasses.

'A successful day,' said Lorna.

'And maybe a night of consequence.'

They unpacked, admired the items and put them away. Kate removed from the wardrobe and drawers most of her old clothes.

'These are to go,' she said, putting them into the now empty shopping bags.

The final package she opened was a miniature carrier bag in embossed gold that came from the jewellery shop. She took from it the Rolex in its box, which she opened and lay on the dressing table.

Lorna said, 'Rather nice.'

'So is this,' said Kate.

She took from the gold carrier bag a long green box. She opened it and handed it to Lorna. It was the Gucci watch she had admired.

'What's this?' said Lorna.

'A present for being so good.'

'I couldn't. I mean, Kate. This is too much.'

'Not for what you did. For the friend you've become.'

'No, Kate. It's too expensive.'

'Believe me, it's not. It's yours.'

The two women embraced as friends, rather than lovers. When they parted, Lorna was still embarrassed.

'I think I need another drink.'

Kate flopped on the bed, and pushed the pillows up behind her head.

'Me too. Same again, please.'

Lorna got the drinks and Kate moved up so she could join her in half sitting and half lying on the bed in companionable silence.

'Who was the girl?' Kate said.

'The girl?'

'Don't be coy. You said I wasn't the first. Who was?'

'Caroline Bell. We were on a school trip. We shared a room. It just happened.'

'It just happened?'

'We were in Belgium on some kind of cultural trip. One of the boys obtained a magazine. He gave it to

Caroline. I suppose he hoped it would enflame her passion. I suppose it did.'

'Caroline preferred you to the boy?'

'Not really. The boy wasn't available, we were two highly sexed sixteen-year-olds and we were sharing the same bed so we could look at the magazine together. It seemed natural that it happened.'

'What happened?'

'We touched each other. Made each other come.'

'Like last night?'

Kate was no longer jealous, just teasing.

'No, not like last night. We were both fairly innocent. We used our fingers and we rubbed ourselves against each other.'

'Mmm,' said Kate. 'Sexy little sixteen-year-old.'

'Isn't everybody at that age?'

Kate said, 'Does Peter know about this?'

'It's his favourite bedtime story.'

'How long have you been married?'

'To Peter? Eight years.'

'You were married before?'

'Yes.'

'What happened?'

'It didn't work. But I got to meet Peter.'

'Was Peter the reason you got divorced?'

'No. I met Peter at a sex party, only I didn't know that's what it was when I went. My first husband, Brian, took me.'

'Did he know what sort of party it was?'

'Brian? I think he suspected. I think he wanted to see how far things would go.'

'I've never been to a sex party.' Did yesterday count

as a sex party? she wondered. 'How many people were there?'

'Five men, including Brian. And me.'

Chapter 19

Kate's insides lurched. She was no longer thirsty and put the drink on the bedside table. Their conversation had been light and amusing. All of a sudden it wasn't anymore. She turned on her side to look at Lorna.

'Is this a story?'

'It's true.' Lorna sipped the gin and tonic and looked at Kate. 'Do you want to hear about it?'

'Of course I want to hear about it.'

Lorna smiled. 'Turned on?'

Kate's voice had become suddenly husky. 'Yes,' she said.

Lorna put her drink on the table at the other side of the bed, turned back and went into Kate's arms. They kissed, lying facing each other. Kate's body was tingling with tension again, that beautifully wicked tension she had come to know so well. But they restricted their contact to the kiss, and their hands held each other softly or stroked a cheek.

'You want all the details?' Lorna said.

'Yes. Educate me.'

Lorna smiled.

'I was twenty-six,' she said. 'I'd been married to Brian for three years. It was an okay marriage. He was about ten years older than me. The night it happened, we'd been out to dinner and he'd bumped into an old business associate. A man who was very successful. Very rich. That always impressed Brian. Being rich.

'After we'd finished dinner, Brian said we'd been invited to a party at this chap's house. A few late drinks on the way home. I had no objections. I quite like parties. What I didn't know was that this chap had a reputation. But Brian obviously knew.'

Kate put her arm around Lorna's shoulders. She stroked her hair as she talked.

'When we arrived I felt the atmosphere was wrong. It was a big house in its own grounds. The only other people there were Eric, who had invited us, and three young men who worked for him. Alan, Philip and Peter.'

'Your Peter?'

'My Peter. The first time I saw him.' She licked her lips. 'Eric said there had been a change of plan. The others hadn't been able to come, but he insisted we have a drink anyway. The drinks were large ones, of course. I suppose to get me in the mood. The atmosphere was charged, you know what I mean? I was aware I was the only woman there, but I was with my husband.

'I was actually thinking that when we got home the sex might be good. I was sure he could sense it, too, and we would pretend. But we didn't have to pretend.'

Lorna's voice had changed and she nestled against Kate. Their faces were close together and Kate inhaled the whispered confession as it was told.

'We were in a big room that Eric called the den. Sofas and big chairs, a TV and stereo. Music was playing and Philip, one of the younger men, asked me to dance. I laughed and said I wasn't in the mood but he insisted. I looked at my husband and he just grinned and said, "Go on. Have a dance." So I did.

'Brian's grin was lopsided, as if it might slip off his face. I could see his tension. He knew what was going on. Anyway, I danced with Philip, a slow dance, and he held me close. I could feel him get big in his trousers.'

Lorna smiled.

'That pleased me. That I had made him big. He was married and I knew his wife slightly. She was an attractive girl but snooty, you know? Looked down on me. Well, I had made her husband's prick go stiff and I was pleased with myself. Stupid, really.

'The record ended and another drink was put in my hand and, for some reason, I had the impression we would be going soon and that I had to drink it quickly. The music started again and this time Alan wanted a dance. I could hardly refuse. We danced, slow again, and I felt another prick go stiff.

'Each time we turned in the dance, I looked for my husband. He was by the door with Eric. His face had got tighter. I knew what he was thinking, what he was imagining. I thought, when we get home we'll have one hell of a fuck. Eric laughed and said something to my husband and then he flicked a light switch and half the lights went out.

' "Save the last dance for me," he shouted. Then he led my husband out of the room. As soon as they had gone, Alan began to touch me. His hands slid over my bottom and he pushed his prick harder against me. I have to admit, I was aroused. I had been looking forward to good sex when we got home and I had enjoyed getting Alan stiff as a sort of prelude. You know? But now he was getting a bit too pushy.

'When the music ends, I thought, I'll stop it then. The music stopped but he held on to me. Philip came and stood behind me and said it was his dance next. Alan laughed and said this wasn't an "excuse-me." They were standing against me, one at the front and one at the back, and I could feel both their pricks. They were talking as if this was a big joke but they were making no secret about their pricks.

'The music started and they both began dancing with me. Not really dancing, just swaying to the music. It was hot in the room and I'd had too much to drink and wondered where my husband was. They touched my breasts and kissed my neck but I wouldn't let them kiss my mouth. I was on fire, Kate. I knew this was wrong and I wanted to go home and fuck my husband but I was on fire.

'All this time, Peter was sitting in a chair, just watching. He took no part in it, just watched. Then my husband came back and stood in the doorway, watching the three of us pretending to dance. Eric came into the room and poured more drinks and took one to my husband.

'He said something crass like, I was a lovely mover, and laughed suggestively. He asked my husband if I was a lovely mover and Brian smiled. And all the time, Brian's eyes never left me and I wondered when he would say, that's enough, we're going home, but he didn't.

'Eric said, "Nice legs," and something stupid about how long they were. He asked Brian, loud enough for us to hear, whether I was wearing stockings and Brian said yes. Always. Eric gave a mock groan, as if it was still all a game, and he called across the room. He said, "Come on boys, give us a show."

'They pulled my skirt up. It was a tight skirt, black silk. They pulled it up and I couldn't have stopped them if I'd wanted to. I felt it get higher, felt it reach the tops of my stockings. They paused with it around my thighs. I looked at my husband, still standing in the doorway as if he didn't belong in the room, still watching, the same silly damn smile on his face that wasn't a smile.

'He liked the way I dressed. I'd posed for him before we went out. He liked the black stockings and the black garter belt. He liked them now, staring at them in public. So did Eric.

' "Higher," Eric said, and they pulled my skirt up until it was around my waist. I looked at my husband. I wanted guidance, wanted to know what I should do, but he wouldn't look at my face, he wouldn't meet my eyes. He just looked at my legs and at the hands that were touching my thighs above the stockings, that were touching my bottom.'

She sighed and Kate cuddled her and kissed her forehead, not because Lorna was in distress, but as encouragement to continue.

'The rest was inevitable. One of them kissed me and his tongue went down my throat and they stopped pre-

207

tending. They took me to a wide sofa. I looked towards the door as my panties were removed. My husband had switched off the hall light and stepped back into the shadows as if he wasn't there but he was, and he still watched.'

Kate leaned forward and they kissed. Both women tremored in excitement but refrained from touching each other intimately.

'What did they do?' Kate said.

'They fucked me. One after the other. Then Eric fucked me and my husband fucked me. They left me on the sofa and I don't know where Eric and my husband went. I think there was a snooker room. I was alone with Peter. He pulled my dress down and asked if he could take me home.'

Lorna smiled.

'As if we'd been to a dance, or something. He drove me home and we didn't speak very much on the journey. When we got home he kissed me. A lovely kiss. He said I should get rid of my husband and marry him.' Lorna smiled again. 'Eventually, I did.'

They held each other and Kate wanted to make love to her but knew they should wait until later, that it would be unfair to exclude Peter again.

She said, 'Why should that story excite me?'

'Why not?' said Lorna. 'It excited me. I came each time I was fucked.'

'You did?'

'It was my husband's fantasy and he put me into it. He let it come true. There should be no real pain in fantasy. Only pleasure. So I took my pleasure. I came four times.'

'But you fell out of love with your husband?'

'We were never *in* love. It was an okay marriage but I always knew something was missing. Peter provided that. He provided tenderness. He provided real love.'

Kate shook her head slightly.

'There's a contradiction here somewhere, but I can't find it.'

'Sex is full of contradiction. You shouldn't try to understand it, you should concentrate on enjoying it.'

'Perhaps you're right.'

They kissed again, but this time the urgency had receded and they were able to enjoy the kiss without requiring that it lead on to something more.

Kate said, 'I would have thought that experience would have put you off. Especially as you met Peter.'

'Put me off?'

'Experimenting.'

'You mean because we fell in love?'

'Yes.'

'If you believe love is a happy-ever-after sort of thing, then maybe. But I don't. I believe it needs spicing up from time to time. Besides, that evening was also something of a revelation.'

'Because you enjoyed it?'

'Enjoy is the wrong word, but it's close enough. What I mean is I would never have suggested doing anything like that. My husband was responsible for it happening. Afterwards, I think he was scared by it. Scared by my reaction.

'You see, it's my experience that men quite often like the idea of playing out a fantasy and that women need persuading. But once they try it, it's men who have regrets and want it to stop, and their wives who want it to continue.

'Once the barriers have been removed, women are by far the more adventurous sex.'

Kate thought of her own situation. Her appetite had been whetted and she wanted more. Men, like Nero and his cousins, like the small fat man in Safeway's car park, were two-dimensional. She was beginning to realise they were predictable in their desires because they were usually penis-driven.

For them sex shot out of the end of their pricks. It was a physical discharge rather than an emotional experience.

'I think you're right,' Kate said. 'I think I feel sorry for men. They really don't understand, do they?'

Lorna said, 'Don't put them all down, Kate. There are good ones about. I think I've got one of the good ones.'

'The love of a good man,' Kate said.

'What?'

'Nothing.'

Lorna gave her a parting kiss and said, 'I'd better go.'

'Where are we dining?'

'Here in the hotel.'

'What should I wear?'

'Something simple.' She kissed her on the lips and got off the bed. 'We'll meet you in the bar at seven-thirty.' She smiled. 'You can make an entrance.'

'I wouldn't know how.'

'I think it will come easy.'

Lorna left and Kate remained lying on the bed, wondering at the contradictions of sex. Lorna's first husband had been a brute to have placed his young wife in such a situation, and yet the situation had excited everybody present, including Lorna. Everybody except Peter? She must ask him.

The situation had also excited Kate. Was it because she still had the desire to be dominated? The submissive teenager and housewife? Perhaps, a little domination in its place might still be pleasant. But there were other conundrums amongst the contradictions of sex that she wished to explore first.

And before she attempted to investigate any of them she had to plan for an entrance. How did one make an entrance?

Chapter 20

Kate wore a simple knee-length black dress, black stockings and high heels. When she had dressed in the underwear and shoes she looked at her reflection in the mirror and compared herself with the polaroid photographs of her husband's mistress.

No contest. No bloody contest.

The straps of the garter belt felt like a harness. When she walked they made her aware of her thighs and the tautness of the stockings. They made her aware that she was dressed for sex, and the knowledge aroused her.

Her final accessory was a string of pearls around her throat. Pearls suited her. Nero had said so. She was still smiling at the thought when she went into the bar and paused in the doorway to look for Lorna and Peter.

This is what Lorna had meant. Kate realised she had made an entrance.

The bar was crowded with people having a drink before dinner and most heads turned to look in her direction. There was even a perceptible lull in the conversation and Kate had to stop her smile from widening into a grin.

Making an entrance was something she had read about in books or seen in films, but actually making one herself was almost as good as sex. Almost.

Peter and Lorna had a table near the windows that led out onto the wide wooden terrace with its view over the swimming pool and the Mediterranean. Peter stood up and raised a hand and she walked towards them. Heads turned and followed her progress. Her body had never felt so good.

'Am I late?' she asked, rather facetiously.

Lorna said, 'Perfect timing.'

Peter said, 'You look absolutely stunning, Kate.'

'Thank you,' she said, accepting the chair he pulled out for her.

A waiter was at the table almost before she sat down and took her order for a gin and tonic with lots of ice. She wondered what the reaction would be in The Red Lion on a Sunday lunchtime.

Lorna was elegant in a dark blue dress. Peter wore white trousers, a white silk shirt buttoned to the neck, and a navy blue single-breasted blazer.

They made a group that seemed to be familiar to Kate and she laughed.

'I think I've seen us before,' she said. 'In the Sunday supplements. We look like an advertisement for something sophisticated.'

'Like martini?' said Peter.

'No. Not martini.'

She wondered what her husband was up to and hoped it was an activity that would aid her divorce.

Lorna said, 'Tongues are already beginning to wag.

214

Before the evening is over we could be the object of rumour, speculation and gossip.'

'How nice,' said Kate. 'I've never been the object of speculation before.'

The elderly couple from Barnet who had attempted to befriend her had been sitting outside on the terrace and now came in on their way to the restaurant. She wore a cardigan over a brown dress and he wore a military tie with grey flannels.

'Hello,' she said as they passed.

The woman smiled quizzically and the man nodded formally, saying gruffly, 'Good evening,' but they did not stop. They had not recognised her.

'To think,' Kate said, 'instead of boat rides and you two, I could have taken the tour to boredom and religious interest with them.'

Peter said, 'You win some and lose some.'

They dined in the restaurant and returned to the bar afterwards. A trio was playing dance music and the atmosphere was convivial.

'I'm in a dilemma,' Peter said. 'Two beautiful women. Who do I ask to dance first?'

Lorna said, 'You must dance with Kate. She's our guest.'

Kate did not argue.

'Be gentle with me,' she said as they walked to the dance floor.

'All you have to do is move to the rhythm,' he replied as they faced each other.

'I'll bet you say that to all the girls.'

They laughed and moved into each other's arms and

215

danced fluidly together. Their thighs brushed and their groins moved against each other. The action was not blatant but it was a pleasant precursor of things to come.

There was no need for conversation. They had talked through dinner and at the table over drinks. This was another ritual, she realised, Like flamingoes rubbing legs, or peacocks preening. It was a very civilised ritual that allowed fully clothed men and women to simulate intercourse in public and she was enjoying it.

Peter danced with Lorna and they rested and continued to chat over drinks.

Lorna said to her, 'You have a brace of admirers.'

'Really?'

'Two men at the bar. They've been watching you for the last half-hour.'

'They're probably watching you,' Kate said.

'Just as long as it's not me they're interested in,' said Peter.

Lorna took his hand.

'Dance with me,' she said. 'We'll leave the field clear and see what happens.'

Kate wanted to stop them. She didn't want to know what might happen. She was safe with them and looking forward to an intimate and uncomplicated evening.

God, were these the thoughts of the original Little Woman? Had she progressed so far that an evening of three-way sex was uncomplicated? And maybe she was assuming too much?

She and Lorna had talked of sex and consequences but nothing specific had been said or suggested. Perhaps it couldn't be. Perhaps planning in advance might spoil the spontaneity. But she had assumed they would eventually retire to a bedroom and engage in a three-way affair.

Lorna and Peter danced closely. They looked good together and Kate felt a tinge of jealousy because she was alone. But there was a difference between being alone and being lonely, she reminded herself.

'Excuse me? But would you like to dance?'

The man was tall and his skin darkly tanned. His hair was thick and black and combed straight back. He wore a light-coloured linen suit and an open-necked shirt. He was aged close to forty, his accent not English, and he was very good-looking.

Kate subdued a blush.

'Thank you, but I'm with friends.'

'They are dancing.'

'They will be coming back.'

His smile was crooked. It suited him.

'Only a dance,' he said. 'I will bring you straight back.'

The hint that he might attempt something else made her laugh. What could he attempt? She had already been kidnapped.

'All right,' she said. 'Thank you.'

They went onto the dance floor and he held her close but respectfully.

'My name is Gino Colletta. I am Italian and here on business. I want to thank you for making the trip worthwhile.'

'Me?'

He shrugged and moved her a little closer.

'The business was not so good. But at least I can say

I danced with the most beautiful woman on the island.'

Kate laughed aloud.

'Is that a line that usually works?'

He contrived to look hurt.

'This is no line. This is the truth. And I don't even know your name.'

'Kate.'

'Kate.' He murmured his approval. 'It is a name from Shakespeare. A very English name.'

'You speak English very well.'

'I visit England often. London and Manchester. I like England.'

'And English girls?'

'But of course English girls.'

He was holding her right hand with his left upon his shoulder as they danced and Kate looked pointedly at the gold ring on his wedding finger. He laughed.

'My wife and children are in Naples.'

'Is that another line that usually works?'

'A line?'

'Honesty.'

'But we are having a dance, nothing more. And afterwards I will return you to your friends. Unless . . .'

'Unless?'

'Unless you would like to spend some time with me? A lonely businessman with nothing to do but lavish you with attention.'

His crooked smile was almost a temptation.

'We're not talking about a long-term relationship here, are we?'

Kate was remarkably at ease. She had thought she

would feel threatened or gauche but she was enjoying the chess game of words and the flattery.

He laughed and shrugged.

'Two people far from home.' He glanced out of the windows at the sea and the night. 'The stars, the sea, the moon.' He kissed her fingers. 'Would you like to go outside and look at the moon?'

'No thank you, but you asked beautifully.'

The song began to reach its conclusion and he swirled her around him so that their limbs became entwined and she felt his hardness. She did not pull away from it. He remained holding her, an expectant look in his eye, when the music finished.

'Another dance?' he said.

'You are very sweet,' she said. How dare she call this tall, dark, handsome and sophisticated man sweet? 'But no thank you.'

He sighed and escorted her back to the table where Peter and Lorna had already resumed their seats. Peter stood up as they approached.

'Thank you again,' Kate said.

'May I buy you all a drink?' he said.

'No, really. This is a special occasion for us. A private celebration. I'm sure you understand.'

'But of course.'

He left them and Lorna said, 'A private celebration?'

Kate said, 'I'm going home tomorrow. This is my farewell party.'

'Perhaps we should have champagne.'

'I can think of something better.'

'What?'

'Making love with you.'

Kate was looking at Lorna when she said it. Now she looked at Peter.

'Would you like that, Peter? Would you like to watch?'

Peter unfastened the top button of his shirt.

'I would like that very much,' he said.

'And would you like to fuck me?'

He licked his lips and glanced at his wife before looking back to Kate.

'Very much.'

'We can have the champagne afterwards,' Kate said. She brushed at the elfin strands of hair that spiked her forehead. 'Has it suddenly become hot in here?'

'Just a bit,' Peter said.

'Perhaps we should take a walk by the pool.'

Kate looked from one to the other. Peter was ready to be led anywhere, but then he was a man. Lorna's face had tightened. Her eyes spoke of her desire.

They stood up and Peter led the way. He slid open the glass door and waited until they had stepped out onto the wide wooden terrace before he followed and closed it after him. Only one young couple were out here at a discreet table and probably for similar reasons to their own, Kate thought.

The lights were dim but the pool was lit. They went down the outside wooden staircase to the ground. The night was hot, the sky cloudless; black velvet infinity speckled with stars. The two wings of the hotel curved around the pool area. Lights were on in some of the rooms.

They linked arms, Peter in the middle, and walked

around the swimming pool to the path that dropped to the rock pools below and led to a short concrete jetty. There were only two or three dim lights down there. There were mainly shadows, alcoves in the rocks, and the hulls of two upturned boats.

Kate led the way.

'Careful,' Peter warned.

High heels, black stockings and a designer dress was not the most suitable attire for wandering a jetty. Unless ...

The Italian might have brought her down here to kiss and caress before he invited her back to his room. Perhaps on another occasion she might have said yes.

They were out of sight of the hotel, in a depression in the rocks, and leaned against an iron rail that lined the walkway. The lights of the casino glowed at the head of the Point but, otherwise, emptiness stretched before them and the only sound was the sea lapping gently at the land.

'It's beautiful,' said Lorna.

'So is this,' said Kate.

She turned Lorna so that the blonde had her back against the rail and took her in her arms, stroking the hair from her face. Peter stood close by and both of them were aware of how closely he was watching.

Kate parted her lips and touched the top one with her tongue. They kissed, mouths open, and their tongues found each other. They murmured and moaned, not for effect, but because they were aroused.

The kiss lasted a long time and their saliva became mingled. Their lips parted reluctantly and their tongues

221

still touched, still lapped at each other.

Kate half turned to Peter and reached out with an arm which she put around his neck. She kissed him, while Lorna watched, her face inches away. Kate's thighs rubbed against Lorna's vagina and Peter's groin. She turned to face Lorna again, but pulled Peter behind her.

The two women kissed while Peter lay his head upon Kate's shoulder and watched. His penis pressed against her bottom. She could feel its heat through his trousers and her dress as it lay in the groove between her buttocks. That ready groove.

'Do you like this?' she whispered to him.

Her tongue played with that of his wife. He kissed Kate's ear.

'Oh yes,' he said, his voice a little shaky.

He held his wife's head and stroked her hair as the two women kissed. When their mouths broke apart, Lorna smiled at him.

'Dreams do come true,' she said.

Peter groaned and rubbed himself against Kate's bottom.

Kate said, 'Fuck me, Peter. Here and now. While Lorna holds me. Fuck me now!'

Chapter 21

Peter reached down for her skirt and pulled it straight up to her waist. He was as impatient as her.

The air felt good around her limbs. His hands mauled her flesh above the stockings. His palms globed her buttocks before sliding around her hips. His fingers went between her legs and found her already wet. She felt as if she had been wet for days without end.

Kate and Lorna continued to kiss, their bodies pressed together. Softness at the front and hardness behind. The night air and the sound of the sea and a crowded hotel beyond the rock wall.

Another sacrifice. But a willing sacrifice. She had become an instigator and manipulator. No longer a victim.

Her panties were pulled down around her thighs and Peter fumbled with his clothing in his excitement. She tilted her head back, away from Lorna's lips and the blonde woman licked her neck.

This was all so desperate, so degenerate. They all groaned and gasped and thrust their bodies. Kate caught her breath as Lorna's fingers went inside her.

Peter was at last unleashed. His prick lay along the groove and he pressed her softness around it and it burned her flesh. He shifted his hips, she parted her thighs and it went between them and was enveloped in her heat.

Kate curved her bottom backwards to facilitate his entry and, as the head of his penis slithered at the mouth of her sex, she caught the whiff of tobacco and glanced towards the jetty. The Italian who had danced with her was silently watching, the red glow of a cigar visible against his ghostly outline in the linen suit.

An extra dimension, an extra barb to her pleasure.

'Fuck me! she said, loud enough for the Italian to hear.

Peter fed his prick inside and gasped as he pushed against her. He held her hips. She looked into Lorna's face and smiled. He thrust and pushed her against his wife and Kate gasped.

The women kissed again and held each other tightly while Peter fucked her. When their mouths finally broke apart, Kate turned Lorna's head so she could see the Italian. He stared back, his face impassive in the shadows.

Kate tilted her head back onto Peter's shoulder and he kissed her.

'We have an audience,' she whispered. 'Make it good.'

He thrust harder and grunted with effort. She yelped in response as she was pushed rhythmically against his wife. Lorna's fingers went back between them and touched her clitoris. Kate gasped loudly.

'Yes!' she said. 'Yes, oh yes!'

'I'm going to come,' Peter warned, his body beginning to shake.

Lorna's fingers played between her legs, strumming her on the edge of orgasm. Kate was in control: of her climax, the situation, the night, everything. It was a wonderful experience, to be totally in control for the first time.

'Yes!' she shouted.

Peter came and she rode his prick into her own orgasm and let her breath sigh out onto the warm night breeze.

Another performance, another conclusion, but this time she had been the diva and her companions waited for her lead. Peter slipped from her and stepped away and she turned to stare at the Italian. She held his gaze as she let the panties slide down her legs. When they were around her ankles, she stepped out of them, picked them up and held them casually in one hand. She pushed the skirt down from where it was bunched at her waist and it fell to cover her nakedness.

'I'm thirsty,' she said softly. 'Shall we have the champagne now?'

Again she led the way out of the darkness and onto the main jetty where the Italian still waited.

'Are you going?' he said.

'Yes.'

He licked his lips. His sophistication seemed a little ragged. Kate smiled up into his face. She put her panties into his top pocket, pushing the black silk inside with two fingers.

'Is that all?' he said.

'Perhaps.'

'Perhaps?'

The hope in his voice sounded juvenile.

'Perhaps a dance.'

Kate walked past him, and Lorna and Peter followed, once more composed. They laughed and linked arms again at the top of the steps above the rock wall and walked back the way they had come.

They climbed the wooden staircase to the terrace that looked, from below, like the deck of a ship. Kate was extremely wet between her legs. Across the terrace and through the windows of the bar, they could see respectable hotel guests dancing to respectable music. Did they also have respectable thoughts?

Kate wondered what she would find if she could peep into their minds. Would there be an undercurrent of lust beneath even the stuffiest jacket and demeanour? There had to be. Sex was a driving force, a motivator. Without it the human race would have become extinct.

Society had covered it in mystique and buried it beneath taboos. They had tried to make it an unsuitable pursuit except within marriage. Except for the love of a good man. But it refused to be browbeaten and hidden. It perpetually lurked in the psyche of everyman; clerics and judges, shop assistants and secretaries. Everybody was fascinated despite their denials. It waited in the most subjugated for release, as it had done in her.

There was no one so fervent as a convert. She smiled as they reached the glass door that led back into the bar. A convert who now wanted to be a missionary, who had the urge to announce to the respectable world that danced before her that she was wet between her legs.

How many would be shocked? How many would be aroused? How many envious?

Peter opened the door and Lorna stepped through. Kate glanced back. The Italian had followed and was at the top of the wooden staircase. He had removed the panties from his top pocket and was holding them to his face.

They ordered a bottle of Bollinger although they were already intoxicated from their adventure below the rocks. Their glances between each other, their touches and laughter, set them apart. They were outsiders. They had broken from the conventions of the normal dance to create a lambada of their own.

The three of them were close. Tonight they were inseparable, but at the back of her mind a cloud refused to evaporate because she knew that tomorrow Lorna would still have the love of a good man, while she would be alone.

For God's sake, she had been robbed of ten years of life because of a man. Did she want another? Did she need another? The idea went against her new-found principles of freedom. Her strength was solitary. If she shared her life she would have to share her strength.

And anyway, the events of the night had yet to run their course and the champagne had yet to be drunk.

The Italian approached their table. He did not look at anyone but Kate.

'A dance?' he said.

This time her smile was a little crooked, a little sophisticated. She got to her feet and allowed him to escort her to the floor. The evening was getting late and the lights had been dimmed. The music was slow and she went into his arms. His hold was no longer respectful but it was unsure. His erection was monstrous against her.

'Is this a game?' he said.

'No.'

She squirmed herself deliberately against his hardness and was rewarded with a gasp.

'Why do you do this?'

'Because it is my choice.'

He kissed her neck and she moved her head a little in disapproval.

'Why not me, Kate?' They were not moving their feet, merely swaying to the music. He rubbed himself against her. 'Why not me?'

'Because it is my choice,' she repeated.

'My room is close by.'

'I told you. Tonight is a special party with my friends.'

'Can't I come too?'

Kate moved her head so that she could gaze into his eyes.

'The only way you can come is here and now.'

He was puzzled.

'Here and now?'

She moved her hips and his eyes glazed momentarily at the friction.

'When this dance is over, my friends and I are leaving. We are going to fuck each other.' His eyes glazed again. 'You are not invited.'

'But . . .?'

'But this?'

He meant his prick. Her belly caressed it, her thighs rubbed against its base.

'Yes,' he gasped.

'Do it here. Now. Come while we dance.'

His eyes widened. His hand strayed lower over her hip. His mouth opened and closed as he gulped. His sophistication had abandoned him.

'You are a tease.'

'You have a choice.'

'Bitch!'

Kate took it as a compliment and smiled. The power she had over him was immensely satisfying.

'Sexy bitch,' she said.

She moved deliberately and rubbed herself against his erection. His head tilted slightly as if he was not completely in control.

'The music is nearly over. Do you want to come?'

He groaned and the bulk of his shoulders moved around her as he abandoned pretence and held her hips. She put her arms around his neck. They stood and swayed and he held her close with one hand in the small of her back. The other dropped over her buttocks and she did not care that other guests could see how blatant were his actions.

Surely they must be able to see what he was doing? How was their respectability standing up to such a show?

Kate licked his neck and he shuddered. He was attempting to be circumspect about his movements but there was no hiding the tensing rhythm of his groin and buttocks.

'The blonde woman?' she whispered. 'I'm going to

make love to her while her husband watches. I will go down between her legs and suck until she comes.'

He shuddered again, his control ready to break. His prick throbbed against her as if it possessed a heartbeat of its own.

'And then I shall suck Peter's cock.'

His hand gripped her soft flesh and he gasped into her hair.

'And he will come in my mouth.'

He cursed in Italian and she felt him begin to come, his body hunched around her, his sweat and the aftershave she had earlier thought discreet, now overpowering.

Kate swayed against him, drawing his passion from him, draining him of energy, absorbing it, thrilling at the spasms she had caused within his trousers.

His breath had become a rasp and he was making an effort to appear normal, even to continue to maintain the rhythm of the dance, but his shudders must have been unmistakable even to casual observers.

He sighed and shuddered as an aftermath tremor racked his body.

'I think,' she whispered wickedly, 'you may need to go and change your underwear.'

Kate broke from his grip which had become lethargic, as if he had been overcome with sudden fatigue. He stared at her, his eyes now dulled and beaten.

'Bitch,' he whispered.

'You're lucky. Your room is close by.'

She blew him kiss and left him on the dance floor, returning to the table by the window.

Lorna said, 'Did he do what I think he did?'

'Yes.'

Kate sat down. She imagined that she squelched upon the seat. She looked back at the dance floor but Gino had already gone.

'Whose idea was that?' Lorna said.

'Mine. He wanted me to go to his room. I said no. I said he could do it there if he wanted.' She smiled. 'He wanted.'

Lorna's eyes glinted. Her features were sharp with eagerness.

'Did you enjoy it?'

'So much I may have stained my dress.'

Peter poured the remainder of the champagne.

'A last toast?' he suggested.

Kate said, 'Are you eager to leave?'

He shrugged.

'Whenever you're ready.'

Her power knew no bounds. It was good to be in control. Gino had been easy to manipulate and Peter now waited for her decision. Even Lorna wanted to go. She could tell. She could also see that Lorna understood that the balance of power had shifted.

Maybe when Lorna and Peter had first seen her alone in the hotel, they had wondered whether she might be a subject for one of their sexual adventures. Perhaps after Kate's first day on the boat with Nero when she felt she had blossomed a little.

Had they seen her as a target?

If they had, she was not upset. She was grateful for the opportunity to expand her mind and knowledge.

231

being with them had been rewarding, physically and emotionally. And Kate was no longer a target.

She raised her glass and they followed her example. 'To sex,' she said.

Chapter 22

They went to Lorna and Peter's room. Again, it was Kate's choice. She wanted to be able to leave when she chose to.

'No lights,' Kate said.

Instead, Peter opened the curtains to allow the glow of the moon to tint them with its paleness. For a moment, the three of them stood apart, three separate entities that would soon be joined.

Kate reached behind her and unzipped the dress. She allowed it to fall from her shoulders and, holding it by its straps, stepped out of it and draped it over a chair. She unclipped her black brassiere, dropped it from her breasts and placed it upon the dress.

She smiled, at them and for herself. She stood on high heels, wearing only a string of pearls and a garter belt and stockings. She was sex personified and her body tingled. Slowly, she pushed the garter belt down and peeled the stockings from her legs.

Lorna followed her example, removing the blue dress and shedding her white underwear. This was the woman whom Kate had wanted to emulate. She had admired her looks and assurance when she had first seen her. She was a very attractive woman, with a slim but shapely figure, and small pointed breasts.

But Kate knew she had surpassed her, as she had surpassed her own hopes. Kate was taller, her breasts fuller. Kate knew she was beautiful. What she found hard to understand was how her beauty had been submerged for so many years.

Perhaps beauty came from within, like confidence. She had confidence, as well.

Kate said to Peter, 'Watch.'

She took Lorna in her arms and their softness melted together. For a while they simply swayed, body to body, holding each other gently. Peter slowly undressed until he was naked. He sat in a chair in a corner of the room, legs stretched before him, his right hand massaging his erection.

There was a full-length mirror in the wall near the entrance lobby. Kate moved Lorna so that they stood in front of it. They were sculptures cast by Michelangelo, pale and ghostly, their flesh curved marble. But these buttocks and thighs were too sensuous to be created by man. They quivered. Kate slid her hand from the small of Lorna's back and watched it caress the curve, felt its warmth, felt the contraction of Lorna's vagina as it moved against her own.

They kissed and their hands moved. Their tongues swam and fought together, their hands stroked breasts and buttocks, their hips moved like snakes. And Peter watched.

Kate liked having an audience. The presence of the

Italian had been a spur and so was Peter. It turned a wonderful act into a wonderful performance.

She moved Lorna to the bed and pushed her down upon it so that her feet were still upon the carpet. Her mouth slid down from Lorna's mouth, detouring from one small mound to the other to suckle her breasts and flick her nipples with a rasping tongue.

Lorna groaned, also performing for their audience, her husband, who still watched and waited his entrance, still stroked the hardness that grew from his groin.

Kate slid lower, so that she knelt on the carpet between Lorna's open legs. Her fingers combed the pubic curls and her lips made wet patterns on the softness of the blonde's inner thighs. Her fingers strayed close, so close, but stayed away from that sex mouth that already gaped.

Her lips stole closer but remained that inch away from providing the kiss of deliverance. Kate sighed as she inhaled the rich smell of sex that oozed from Lorna and her fingertip probed into the fold of flesh at the top of her thigh. Lorna moaned and writhed her hips.

The moonglow cast Lorna's limbs pale but her vagina was a pink oyster that lay at their conjunction and begged to be devoured. Kate stroked the lips wider apart with tender fingers and the blonde woman moaned again.

She dipped her face and blew hot breath and kisses into the pink folds of flesh and the hips writhed in torment. Her sex was beautiful and demanded to be worshipped. Kate opened her mouth, descended upon it and took communion.

Lorna's moans rose and her hips moved. Her arms

and legs were spread upon the bed. She had given herself up to the consummation of pleasure and Kate could tell ecstasy was not far away.

Kate felt it coming in the little twitches and contractions she sensed as her mouth and tongue worked in Lorna's vagina. She welded her mouth to the sex mouth and held her friend's buttocks, as if drinking from a chalice, and the orgasm arrived.

Lorna bucked as if in shock. Her thighs closed around Kate's head and cut out sight and sound. All Kate could feel was the intensity of the experience as it enveloped her. An experience for which she had been responsible.

The women slid apart and Kate crawled onto the bed alongside Lorna. They exchanged a long kiss that was wet and aromatic with sexual secretions. Lorna rolled Kate onto her back and her mouth trailed wetly down to her breasts.

As Lorna licked and sucked and used her hands between her legs, Kate watched Peter. He remained on the chair although he now sat up to watch, bent over the hardness that he held in his fist. A handsome naked man who waited for her call.

Lorna went between her legs and her mouth consumed her and all the juices there. Kate closed her eyes and rode the pleasure as it built with the lapping of her sex. She was almost there when she remembered Peter and opened her eyes to see him leaning even further forward in his eagerness, his hand moving rhythmically upon himself.

She reached a hand in invitation and he came swiftly to the bed. He lay alongside her and they kissed. She

236

lost concentration and her mouth sagged beneath his as the orgasm took her senses.

Limbs and bodies were rearranged, although Kate was not fully aware of what was happening until his penis penetrated her and drove away the gentle peace of aftermath and pushed her high again. His prick was big and urgent and pounded her. Lorna lay alongside them, the three of them embracing and sharing kisses, tongues and mouths a hydra of sensuality.

Peter shortened his stroke and Kate's eyes widened as she squirmed and concentrated to match him. He came and yelled as he discharged fiercely into her and she lost her breath and came again, Lorna giving her a kiss of life as she slid into the wondrous death of orgasm.

Kate was suddenly tired but Lorna was not. The blonde slid over her and her hips moved, her thigh rubbed between Kate's thigh. Her sex was wet and she rubbed it against Kate's sex which was sodden with discharges. They kissed and the tiredness fell away.

They rolled upon the bed, touching and rubbing, without hurry. Peter lay alongside them, an audience without willpower, an audience sapped of desire. They kissed and masturbated each other and Lorna groaned into another orgasm. Kate moved between Peter's legs, hairy and muscular and so male. She rubbed her breasts up his thighs and caressed his limp penis with their softness. He groaned and desire began to return.

She held the limp penis and felt life stirring within it. Her head dipped and she took it between her lips and sucked, and the small animal became large in her mouth. Kate concentrated on fellating him, images of the little fat man in the car and the way that Nero had forced her adding to her arousal.

If only her husband had known how to approach her, how to educate her. She sucked and slobbered deliciously, a child with a lollipop. She held Peter's pleasure in her hand and in her mouth. It was fierce in lust and yet such a small and insignificant creature once it had spat its venom.

Kate enjoyed the power she had over it and felt sorry that man was ruled by such a temperamental organ. One that could destroy common sense and, in its aftermath, leave embarrassment and chagrin. It was another indication that man did not understand sex and did not have the capacity to embrace it as a woman could.

Lorna's softness tempted her away from the freshly erect penis. She moved up the bed to embrace and kiss her and take sensuous pleasure from her curves. They lay face to face on their side and Peter manoeuvred behind his wife. As the two women kissed, he pushed between her legs. Lorna gasped as he entered her.

He moved against her and the sound of his rhythm was intoxicating to Kate. Sweating and wet flesh slid and suctioned, the hardness of his groin slapped against the softness of Lorna's buttocks. She kissed and licked Lorna's face and rubbed herself against those small sharp-pointed breasts.

The three of them were panting and Kate knew Peter would not rise again once this immediate mission was accomplished. She slithered around on the bed and licked her way down Lorna's belly. Their groans told her they approved of what she intended. Lorna parted Kate's thighs and her mouth went between them to lap again at the wetness there.

Kate parted the flesh at the apex of Lorna's vagina and stroked the erect clitoris. She watched Peter's prick slide in and out, listened to the slap of their coupling, and was almost overcome by the perfume of their lust. The moonlight made it unreal, a shadow show of eroticism.

But the smells and sounds and Lorna's mouth between her own thighs told her this was beyond reality. This was close to nirvana.

Her head dipped and she licked. Her tongue stroked the clitoris and caressed the length of the prick as it pistoned in and out. Sounds were muffled now because she was submerging in flesh and taste and a growing heat that was spreading from her vagina.

She put her arms around quivering thighs and held on; she licked and sucked and her hips began to shake. Peter's thighs tensed and he withdrew his penis. Kate could not see anything but she could feel it against her face as it lay in the folds of Lorna's sex. She mashed her mouth against it and shared its ejaculation.

He rolled away and it slid from between Lorna's wet thighs. Kate turned and lay face to face with her friend once more. They kissed and shared his life force, their tongues swimming in the sticky juices.

They lay awhile and Kate could not tell whether she or Lorna had orgasmed. The pleasure had been so intense it had been hard to tell. They kissed, their lips still sticky from their final intimacy, and she knew it was time to leave.

Kate climbed from the bed and pulled on the dress and her shoes. She carried her underwear and stockings in her hand. Peter and Lorna lay side by side on the bed, two silent moonglow portraits, with pale unmoving limbs, linked only by the holding of hands.

They watched her without speaking, the ghost of an adventure past that was preparing to take its leave. Again she felt the loneliness of being alone and again she subdued it. She stared into their faces and saw affection that would have been embarrassed by words.

The three of them had been bonded, but already it was past tense. She blew them a kiss and left the room.

Her own room was a floor above. The corridors were long and silent and dimly lit, the abandoned corridors of a ghost ship. She climbed the stairs and felt the silence of the night envelop her. These were the hours between lives. The hours of limbo when thoughts and fears had a habit of being unreasonable.

Kate reached her own room and entered it gratefully. She switched on the light and threw her underwear on the bed. She was tired but did not want to sleep, did not want to be part of the night.

It was three o'clock. She called reception and asked for an alarm call for six and a taxi for six-thirty to take her to Luqa Airport. Then she called room service and ordered a steak and salad and a pot of coffee. Sex and hunger. She wondered at the combination.

She was in the shower when the waiter knocked at the door, and she wrapped a towel around her and let him in. He was overweight and fifty and probably wondering why she wanted to eat at this time of night. He reminded her of Rafel, the fat one, from the boat. Had that been only yesterday?

He avoided staring too much at her in the towel and put the tray on the side table. She saw him notice the underwear on the bed and now he did look at her.

Did he know the secret of sex and hunger?

Kate picked up change from the desk, put it in his hand and he left. She dropped the towel and lifted the lid from the plate. The steak looked good and she was refreshed from the shower. She ate the food and drank the coffee and its caffeine fooled her into thinking she was wide awake.

She filled her cup and went to sit on the balcony. The casino was still lit at the end of Dragonara Point to her left and cars were parked along the road past the Reef Club which was dark and shut. Lights picked out the coast beyond the Hilton as far as St Julian's Point and along the road to Sliema.

Night sounds were gentle and the air warm. She sat naked on the balcony and was a ghost again, a ghost who had drifted into Malta and would drift out again tomorrow. She would be a memory in the minds of Nero, Gianni and Rafel. A bitch of a memory in the mind of the Italian: a sexy bitch of a memory.

And to Lorna and Peter? Particularly Lorna, the first woman she had loved, the first woman with whom she had shared so much in such a short time. To them she would be a recurring ghost whom they would conjure as a stimulant to love and sex. In what percentages? she wondered.

There had been love there, of a kind, but one that

could not last. A love that was intense because of the brevity of its duration, that knew it had to end to protect and safeguard Peter and Lorna's relationship.

Were relationships always two-way affairs? Did they always have to hurt when they ended?

Kate had learned a great deal about herself in a short time but knew there was more to discover. Was sex for its own sake a worthwhile pursuit or should it be bonded in love for a good man?

She gazed at the darkness of the Mediterranean. She had come a long way from Uncle Toby. Where was he now?

Chapter 23

Heathrow was an appropriate place to face up to the rest of her life. A crossroads of the world. But she was tired after the sleepless night, despite a fitful sleep on the aircraft.

To confront her past she had to be feeling at her best. Her confidence had to be high. Maybe there was a little cowardice among her reasoning but she delayed the decision she had been toying with and took the tube into London and caught a train home.

Home. It was still a misnomer and she did not want to go to the house in Maple Drive. Besides, her husband believed she was still in Malta.

Kate still did not know what she would do when she finally emerged from the station in the early afternoon. It was drizzling and she needed to make a swift decision. She hailed a cab and her destination came to her as if it had been waiting to pop out when asked.

'The George Hotel,' she said.

The George was a three-star hotel with pretensions. It stood in the middle of the High Street opposite the Norman Cross and had always seemed a little smug because of its black and white half-timbered frontage.

Kate had walked and driven past it but had never been inside. The only hotel she had been to was The Red Lion on a Sunday lunchtime which was further along the High Street by the river. The only other pub she had been in was The Grapes for the occasional chat and comfortable silence with Paul after rehearsals.

She obtained a room with a view of the High Street and unpacked. Kate had gone to Malta with one suitcase and had returned with two. She unpacked her new clothes and new identity and went to bed. The past week was finally catching up.

Uncle Toby and her mother were waiting to invade her mind in an unguarded moment but she did not want to listen to their excuses and accusations.

Toby had looked sad when he and her mother had called her into the study. A week had passed since her own explosive encounter with him. A week in which they had hardly exchanged a word.

Her mother had adopted her china face, all stern chalk and no expression. She could have been delivering a party political broadcast rather than announcing the end of her marriage.

'It has simply not worked out and we thought it only correct and proper that we tell you together.' Her mother's lips had pursed. 'There are no recriminations and we will still remain friends.'

The smile was a forced grimace that almost cracked the china mask.

'We are two adults who are too set in our ways. Perhaps in this modern world, it might have been more prudent to have lived together before we married, to see if we could make a go of it, but you know my views on that. There are certain things between a woman and a man that should always remain within wedlock.'

Uncle Toby had stared at a spot on the wall behind Kate. Kate had felt as if she was part of a stiff-upper-lip play.

'So we have decided to amicably go our separate ways and allow a divorce to follow in the natural order of things. Separations are never easy, Kate, but Toby is being a gentleman. He has agreed to leave the country for a while until I can sell the hotel.'

Kate had said, 'Sell the hotel?'

The spontaneous question had not been because she had great affection for it but because she could not imagine her mother doing anything else but running it. The hotel was her world where she was queen. It would also mean that if they moved she might not see Uncle Toby again.

'Yes, I know it will be hard, dear, but it will be for the best. People can be cruel, and although I can rise above idle gossip, I have to think of you. It will be best if we move.'

Kate had looked at Toby and said, 'Where will you go?'

His eyes had met hers for the first time. They were too sad to understand.

'Kenya. I have property there.'

'When will you come back?'

'When we have gone,' her mother had said.

Kate remembered and thought of all the questions she had never asked. She also remembered the details her mother had not disclosed. Uncle Toby had been generous in his divorce settlement. Her mother had bought another hotel in Bournemouth and Kate had never seen him again.

Under her mother's guidance and permanent frown, she had taken business studies so that she could help run the new hotel, although only in a capacity that remained behind the scenes. Mother had wanted no competition with her captive audience of guests.

Bob had been the son of an old school friend of her mother. He was, she said, a good prospect. He had seemed to be both a way of escaping her mother and accepting a penance. The only man in her life, she had believed, was Toby. She had been the victim of a doomed love affair that could never have been, so she might as well marry the first good prospect who came along.

Her mother still ran the hotel in Bournemouth. She and Bob visited once a year, the week before Christmas.

'Not Christmas, dear. We can't spare the rooms at Christmas. We're always fully booked for the festivities.'

Festivities? They would be as false as the plastic holly. Kate had often wondered who in their right mind would choose to spend Christmas with her mother and pay for the privilege. Now she knew.

People like Bob who needed his happiness constructed for him: an orderly life and an orderly wife. A cosy home, slippers and coffee, toy trains in the loft and a Little Woman to rely upon.

People like Bob would go to her mother's hotel and

believe they had found the spirit of Christmas because they had paid for it and it came with a carol service and housey housey.

This year, she thought, she would give the week before Christmas a miss. Without Bob there was no reason to pretend anymore. Perhaps her mother might even be grateful. They had never been friends and she could not remember a time of love.

All Kate could remember was her mother as her jailer and, after the split with Toby, her silent acrimony.

Not yet, mother. I'm not ready yet and perhaps I never will be.

Kate told the memory of her mother to go away and finally fell asleep.

At ten o'clock she was too late for dinner so had room service send her sandwiches. Her hunger was no longer so great. She watched television whilst lying in bed. The night had once more brought doubts. She comforted herself with the thought that she would be able to banish them with the dawn.

Rather than go down for breakfast, she had a cup of tea in her room. Without sex, maybe she would become anorexic? She laughed. In that case it would be necessary to ensure she regained her appetite.

Kate telephoned Stanley Bevan, Private Investigator, who seemed to think that ten o'clock in the morning was early but agreed to see her at noon. Yes, he said. They had the evidence she required.

Next was Martin Bell, solicitor. Mrs Who? was the

response from his secretary. Kate had obviously not
created a lasting impression. She would have to try
harder. Mr Bell was busy, it was difficult, but, if she
insisted . . .

Kate insisted with her newly acquired authority. His
secretary said he would squeeze her in at three o'clock.

Two appointments with two men who had taken her
for granted and been more interested in the photocopied
polaroid photographs of the other woman than they had
of her. The lack of concern had shown in their faces.
Their sympathies had been with the husband. She could
imagine them exchanging case notes.

I mean, can you blame him with that to come home
to?

The impression she made this time would be different.
She power dressed. But it was her own version of power
dressing that began with her underwear. Black and
wicked, with stockings to match. Shoes with an extrava-
gant heel and a black two-piece suit that hugged her
figure. She carried a shoulder bag that could double as
a briefcase.

There was an hour before she saw Flat Stanley Bevan,
private eye. There was time to go to the library.

The sun was shining but the temperature was cool in
comparison to Malta. But she was warmed by the
admiring glances she attracted as she went down the
High Street. As she waited at a pedestrian crossing, she
realised she could be classed as a danger to motoring.

Had she really changed so much in a week?

At the library, a woman assistant who had checked in
and checked out books from her on countless occasions
was behind the counter.

'Is Paul in?' she asked.

'Paul?'

The woman looked suspicious.

'Paul Hudson?'

He was the only Paul who worked in the library.

'Who shall I say wants to see him?'

Kate smiled. The woman had still not recognised her.

'Kate Adams.'

'Oh . . .?'

The reaction was worthwhile but Kate realised she had something else to get rid of: her husband's name.

Paul emerged hurriedly from a side office. He had obviously been warned by the assistant but his eyes widened and he glanced past her to see if there was anyone else waiting.

'Kate?'

His hair was still in need of a comb and probably styling, and the jumper and corduroy trousers he wore might not have had many takers on a jumble stall, but she was glad to see him and she grinned. She held her hands out as if taking a bow.

'What do you think?'

'Amazing.'

'Can I buy you a coffee?'

'Of course. I'll just tell Sheila.'

He disappeared into the office for a moment and reemerged holding his jacket and looking suspicious, as if she might have changed back into plain old Kate. They went to the tea shop above the confectioners and, for a short time, shared a silence.

His smile, that smile that was always slow to emerge,

as if he had all the time in the world, finally spread across his face.

'I don't believe the transformation,' he said.

'A haircut and new clothes.' She gave him a meaningful look. 'You should try it.'

'I don't mean that. The clothes are terrific and your hair, well, it suits you perfectly. What I meant was you. You have changed inside yourself. You are so full of . . . life. Confidence.'

Kate nodded.

'Hard to believe after what I was.'

His eyes widened to dispute her unspoken self-criticism.

'You were a lovely person. Are a lovely person.' He shook his head. 'You're confusing me, Kate.'

'I'm still me. At least, I hope I am. But I have changed. I'm not frightened anymore. I know my worth.'

'I'm not sure, but I think you frighten me a little,' he said.

Kate smiled and reached across the table to hold his hand.

'Tell me honestly. Which is better? Old or new?'

'I liked the old well enough.' He smiled sheepishly. 'I thought the old was beautiful.'

'And what about the new?'

'Maybe too beautiful for me.' He pulled a face. 'But I'm happy for you, Kate. It suits you.' He nodded. 'It is you.'

He really was a good man. A lot of what they had previously shared, stolen moments from amateur dramatics and library duties, comfortable silences in tea shops and The Grapes, now made sense to her.

'You did find me attractive, didn't you?' she said.

'Yes.'

'Did you think of maybe having an affair with me?'

'I thought about it. But I thought an affair wouldn't suit you.'

'Did you love me, Paul?'

'I still do.'

'Why didn't you tell me?'

'It was not an appropriate thing to tell you. You would have felt guilty. You would probably have stopped seeing me. I would have lost the little we had and you would have lost ... the theatre group, perhaps even the library.'

He was right and her loss would have been the greater. Without the theatre group, the library and Paul, the small portion of her life she had been able to steal for herself would have ended.

'I wish you had,' she said. 'I needed something to make me wake up. Even if it was dissatisfaction. Desolation.'

'I thought you'd found desolation when you found those letters.'

'I did, but thank God there was anger in there as well. And thank you for listening to me when I needed someone. For being there.'

'I'll always be here.'

He looked out of the window across the road towards the library, as if to say he was the one who was stagnating now, while she was on the verge of other things.

'For me?' she said.

'Always for you, Kate.'

He had got used to the change and was now looking

at her in the same old way she remembered. The way that made her feel good and worth being with. The look that had given her so much comfort.

'I'm going to see the private detective. The divorce will be sooner rather than later.'

'You don't see any difficulties?'

'There will be no difficulties.'

'Suddenly, you're so sure of yourself.'

'Aren't you sure of yourself, Paul?'

'In some things. In big things, I'm never sure. Life has a way of waiting for you round the corner to smack you in the face.'

'Only if you let it.'

He smiled and nodded.

'What happened in Malta?' he said.

'I found myself.'

'All I ever found in Malta were churches and the Blue Grotto.'

'You should go with me next time.'

He smiled but didn't answer. She could tell he thought the possibility to be unlikely.

'And now?' he said.

'Now I get my life back.'

'What will you do with it when you get it?'

Kate had pondered the same question.

'I don't know yet. There's someone I have to see first before I decide.'

They lapsed into another of their silences. He broke it by chuckling.

'What?' she said.

'Look at you. You are stunningly beautiful and I bring

you to a tea shop. It should have been champagne at
The Red Lion.'

'No, not The Red Lion. But you can buy me a drink
at The George tonight.'

'The George.'

'I'm staying there. Bob doesn't know I'm back. Will
you come?'

'Will I have to wear a suit?'

He said it with a smile.

'Wear what you want, Paul. You'll always be the same
to me.'

'What time?' he said.

'Seven-thirty? I'll buy you dinner.'

'Seven-thirty,' he said. 'And *I'll* buy dinner.'

Chapter 24

Flat Stanley Bevan was still sweating in his three-piece suit and the central heating in the office in the Bank Buildings. He had not sounded overly excited at the prospect of having Kate visit, but maybe that was because he remembered her differently.

'Hello,' he said when she entered, a smile further creasing his much-creased face. He even stood up.

'Hello, Mr Bevan.'

'And what can I do for you?'

It was a voice he could have used for offering sweeties to children.

'I'm your twelve o'clock appointment.'

'I'm sorry, but that's with ... Mrs Adams.'

Kate sat down in the chair opposite and watched him watch her cross her legs. It was amazing how fascinated he was with such a simple act. Perhaps it was because his legs were so fat he couldn't do it. Perhaps it was the stockings.

'What have you got for me?'

'What? Oh, yes. Of course.' He reached for a folder. She could see him wondering how he had ever got his first impressions of her. 'Evidence for the prosecution.'

'You have some?'

'Oh yes.' He grinned, his eyes not sure whether to look her in the face or the hemline. 'We've been quite successful.'

'You mean my husband has continued his affair?'

'With you out of the way, he became very indiscreet.'

'Tell me about it.'

'Your husband and the third party . . .'

'The third party?'

'The woman. Valerie Hudson.'

'Then call her Valerie Hudson. Third party makes it sound like he's been seeing an insurance agent.'

He coughed.

'Your husband and Valerie Hudson met every day while you were away. She accompanied him on a business trip to Liverpool where they spent the night at The Trials Hotel in Castle Street. A double room. Paid for by credit card. They checked in as Mr and Mrs Adams. He also spent one night at her flat.'

He looked over the report and smiled. A smug smile. He had something better to come.

'Two nights ago, we got what you really want. The third, sorry, Valerie Hudson spent the night at twenty-three Maple Drive. They were sexually intimate. In the living room and the bedroom.' He reached for and held up a video cassette. 'Full colour, full sound. Triple X rated.'

So he had been unable to resist and he had taken the bitch home. Anytime, anywhere including the marital bed of another woman.

'Show me,' she said.

He raised an eyebrow.

'You want to see this now?'

'Yes.'

He shrugged.

'All right. You're paying.'

He got up from his desk and took the cassette to a TV and video that were in the corner. He switched on, put the cassette in and found the right channel. Kate moved her chair to face the screen. Flat Stanley flopped onto a battered chaise longue and sat in a position that gave him a good view of both the screen and her legs.

It was a shock to recognise her living room and her furniture. It was a shock to see her husband in such a frivolous mood.

The woman was not as attractive as she had first thought. Rather mousy, in fact. Kate told herself to be objective rather than jealous. She stared hard. Even being objective, Valerie Hudson was mousy. But she was eager.

They had obviously arrived at the house after being out drinking. He pushed her onto the settee and tried to pull up her skirt and she laughingly fought him off.

'You dirty boy,' she said. 'Can't wait, can't wait.'

'Take them off,' he said.

'Here?'

She looked round the living room. Was that a sneer? Kate was angry even though she didn't like the damn living room either.

'Right here.'

The woman grinned and unzipped her dress. She stepped out of it and threw it across the room. The bra followed and then the panties. Her husband was out of camera angle and she could not see what he was doing but she could hear him gibbering like a demented monkey.

Finally the woman lay back upon the settee and spread her legs.

'Come on then, sex pig. But don't make mess. The Little Woman wouldn't like it.'

Her husband came into shot. His trousers were open and he was obviously masturbating.

'She wouldn't know what it was,' he said. 'She'd think it was modelling glue.'

They both laughed as he positioned himself upon her.

'Poor cow,' Valerie Hudson said.

Poor cow indeed. Kate was less angry than she had thought she would be. They would see who the poor cow turned out to be.

'Fast-forward it,' she said.

'But we're getting to the good bit.'

'You think she's a good bit?'

'Well. That's not what I meant.'

'Fast-forward. I want to see the bedroom.'

Flat Stanley fast-forwarded the video and her husband and the anytime girl were funnier than Laurel and Hardy. He stopped it when the background changed. They were naked and having sex on the bed.

They groaned a lot and her husband had a bigger belly than she had realised, but then she never saw him naked from the front. The patch of damp beneath the window showed up, even on the video. Again she was objective but again she came to the same conclusion. All Valerie Hudson had was an appetite for sex and black underwear.

Maybe she should not be so critical. Until last week, she had neither. Whose fault? She looked at her husband. He was as elegant as a beached walrus. His chin looked weaker without a collar and tie. The tie helped to differentiate between face, neck and body.

Kate smiled to herself. Now she was being bitchy. But she was entitled to. Thank God he had made no sexual demands other than once a Sunday facing the wall. Thank God he had a train set to keep him occupied and, latterly, the anytime girl.

Had he been semi-celibate for years like her? she wondered. Was his fervour because he had so much bottled-up sex to give?

'The inquiries you made,' she said. 'Did you find out how long this affair has been going on?'

'This one? Four months.'

'This one?'

'This is just hearsay, of course, and can't be used as evidence, but he has a reputation. He's supposed to have had a string of affairs over the years.'

On screen, they broke for air. The woman pulled at the covers and delved beneath the pillows.

'Where's the bedjacket?' she said. 'I wanted to wear it.'

He laughed.

'What do you want it for?'

'You can pretend I'm her.'

'No chance.'

'Why not?' She pretended to sulk.

'My cock would go limp. She's the biggest turn-off in the world.'

'Don't you ever fuck her?'

'Every other Sunday when she's not looking. I bang it in her from behind and think of you.'

'Think of England!'

'No, you. It keeps her happy. Lets her know I love her.'

He said I love her with heavy sarcasm.

'Poor cow,' said Valerie Hudson.

'What about me?' he said. 'I'm married to her.'

'Why don't you leave her?'

'I've told you. A divorce would be messy. Besides, what would she do without me?'

'You're all heart, you sex pig. What you mean is, it comes down to money.'

He grinned. 'Well, she does have a nice portfolio.'

'Try fucking her portfolio.'

'I have.' They both laughed. 'What do you think pays for your underwear?'

Kate had gone cold with fury. Flat Stanley Bevan watched her uncomfortably.

'I've seen enough,' she said.

'Your husband's mad. I mean, there's no comparison, Mrs Adams. What he said, don't take it seriously. He must be a mental defective.'

Her smile was calculated.

'I take it very seriously, Mr Bevan. Tell me, in your professional opinion, how would that dialogue effect a divorce settlement?'

'He hasn't got a leg to stand on. You can wipe him out, Mrs Adams.'

'That's what I intend to do.'

He pressed re-wind on the remote control.

'There are photographs and signed affidavits from me and my assistant. Three copies of the tape. Some of the photographs we took from the tape.' He smiled, still uncomfortable. 'They might amuse you.'

'Amuse me?'

'He wears her underwear.' Flat Stanley shrugged as if he couldn't understand the motivation. 'Stockings, the whole lot. He looks a right berk.'

It did amuse her. She could think of nothing funnier than her overweight walrus husband in stockings and a garter belt. What, she wondered, would George in The Red Lion think?

'All this stuff, Mrs Adams. The evidence. You've run up quite a bill. I mean Kevin, my assistant, had to go to Liverpool. And there's the rental of all the electronic gear. It has turned out to be quite expensive.'

'No doubt.'

Kate uncrossed her legs, moved slightly upon the seat, and crossed them again. His gaze was riveted.

'How do you wish to pay, Mrs Adams?'

His voice was wandering, his eyes still hopeful on the hemline. Perhaps he could see the top of a stocking, the hint of a garter strap.

'I think we should come to some arrangement, Mr Bevan.'

'An arrangement?'

'You give me the evidence, the affidavits, the photographs and the videos and a receipt saying that my account has been paid in full, and . . .'

'And?'

261

'I promise to give you the highest recommendation to all my friends.'

'Erm, I don't think . . .'

'And I'll fuck you.'

He went red and spluttered. The splutter became a cough.

'I'm sorry. I don't think I quite heard what you said.'

Kate got to her feet. She stood with her legs slightly apart, a sexual and aggressive pose. She stared into Flat Stanley's face with total composure and placed her palms on her hips. Ever so slowly, she slid the skirt up.

His breathing became laboured. His eyes became fixed.

The skirt reached the welt at the top of the stockings. She inched it higher. He would be able to see the black ruched silk of the garter straps by now. He licked his lips and gulped. She felt the hem of her skirt slip over the stockings. The flesh of her thighs would now be on show.

Kate stopped. She maintained the pose, her palms on her hips. He kept staring. He seemed incapable of doing anything but stare.

'Would you like to touch, Mr Bevan?'

'What?'

His voice was a croak.

'Would you like to touch? Would you like to put your hands up my skirt?'

'Oh my God.'

'Or how about my breasts? You could suck them, Mr Bevan.' His eyes came up to her face. He was totally bewildered. 'Or you could put them around your prick. Would you like me to suck you, Mr Bevan?'

He had been sweating when she arrived but now he was sweating even more profusely. He loosened his tie and unfastened his shirt collar. He shook his head and coughed again and stood up. He went to the television and removed the cassette from the video.

'This is a respectable business, Mrs . . .' he seemed to have forgotten her name '. . . Mrs Adams. I can't do business like that. The bill is extensive.'

He turned round and he seemed disappointed that she had dropped her skirt back into place.

'Write the bill off as a bad debt.'

'I can't do that.'

'It's your business. You can do anything you want.' She walked to the door and leaned her back against it. 'Does this lock?'

'Yes.'

'Then lock it.'

'I couldn't.'

'What would you like to do to me, Mr Bevan?'

Kate licked her top lip. The situation had taken her over. He was a fat man who sweated but the situation was sex. Its vibrations filled the room. If he did not agree to her terms she might be forced to fuck him for free simply for the relief she needed.

'Mrs Adams.' He shook his head. 'Kate . . .'

'Mrs Adams,' she corrected. 'Let's keep this business.'

She unbuttoned the bodice of the black suit. Three, four buttons, and opened it so that it gaped. Her breasts trembled in the black shelf of a bra.

'Do you want these, Mr Bevan? Do you want them round your prick?'

'Oh my God.'

His thinning hair was wet upon his forehead.

'What would you like to do to me, Mr Bevan? Fuck me? Suck me? Anything you want, Mr Bevan. Anything.'

'All right.'

He stepped towards her and his hands reached for her breasts.

Kate leaned back against the door.

'Two things,' she said softly. 'Lock the door ... and write a receipt.'

Flat Stanley Bevan this time reached for the key and locked the door. Kate moved away and stood in front of the chaise longue. He hesitated again and she pulled the skirt up to her waist. His eyes drank in the sight of her tanned thighs above the black stockings, the taut garter straps and the black triangle of silk, and he was lost.

He staggered to the desk and picked up a pen.

'What do you want me to write?'

'Do you have my account there?'

'Yes?'

'Then write across the bottom, paid in full, and sign it.'

He took a sheet of paper from the folder and wrote upon it.

'Show me,' she said.

He held it up so she could read it and she smiled with satisfaction.

'Please put it in my bag. And the folder and the photographs and the tapes.'

The fat private investigator followed her instructions. He put all the evidence and the receipt into her shoulder bag that was by the chair.

He turned and looked at her and she completed unfastening the bodice of the suit so that it hung open.

'I don't know what I'm going to tell Kevin,' he said.

'Tell him you had a good time.'

Chapter 25

Kate remembered her first visit to this office when he had been more interested in the photocopied polaroid photographs she had shown him of her husband's mistress. Now he only had eyes and thoughts for her. His eyes bulged and his thoughts were scrambled.

He moved slowly towards her across the office and she took hold of his shoulders and turned him so that the chaise longue was behind his legs.

'Sit down, Mr Bevan.'

Flat Stanley sat down. Kate stood in front of him, legs slightly apart. His breath rasped.

'Touch me, Mr Bevan.'

He raised his large hands and held them either side of her thighs without placing them upon her, hesitating in disbelief at what was about to occur. Her own desire tingled between her legs. Her hips swayed tantalisingly before his face.

'Touch me,' she whispered.

He touched her and exhaled deeply. His breath was a hot breeze on her silk-covered vagina. His palms caressed her nylon-covered legs. They slid higher, from stockings to flesh. His palms were behind her legs, his thumbs traced the black ruched garter straps.

His palms followed the curves of her buttocks and slid beneath the panties. He held her and pushed his face between her thighs and buried his nose in the aromatic silk.

For a big man he was surprisingly gentle. Kate rested her hands on his shoulders and moved herself against his face. His nose rubbed against her clitoris and she shuddered.

'Do whatever you want, Mr Bevan. Anything you want.'

He removed his hands from beneath the panties, reached up to the waistband and pulled them down her thighs. His thumbs parted the lips of her sex and his face burrowed back into the cleft beneath her belly. His tongue licked, his mouth covered her sex, his hands regained their grip upon her bottom and she came.

Flat Stanley Bevan was surprised that he had induced an orgasm. When she had subsided he looked up at her and his expression was quizzical.

'You have such a beautiful tongue, Mr Bevan. That was delicious.'

Kate took a step backwards and allowed the panties to drop down her legs. She stepped out of them and knelt in front of the fat man. The bra was front fastening and she unclipped it, releasing her breasts.

'Do you like them?'

She offered them in her hands.

His large hands pushed away her fingers and enveloped the soft globes. He stared at what he held in half-glazed eyes. She tried to unfasten his trousers but the belt and buttons were trapped beneath his stomach because he was sitting forward. She stroked his groin through the material and felt his stiffness. He let go of her breasts and slumped against the back of the chaise longue so she could release him.

Kate unfastened the belt and waistband of his trousers and unzipped him. She pulled apart the material and his shirt flaps and dug into a pair of baggy underpants. The underwear was worn and faded but his erection was fierce and new.

She looked up at him, at the confusion on his face, her eyes big beneath her lashes, and licked her lips.

'What do you want me to do, Mr Bevan?' she said.

He breathed heavily. He was beyond words.

Her tongue trailed across her top lip.

'Do you want me to put it in my mouth?'

Her fingers squeezed it around its base. A palm rubbed sensually over the head.

He nodded, unable to speak.

'Do you want me to put it between my breasts?'

He nodded again.

'Do you want to fuck my breasts?'

The fat man closed his eyes and sighed heavily.

'Do you want me to suck it?'

'Yes,' he groaned. 'All of it.'

Kate eased herself forward and enveloped the hot penis between her breasts. She held their softness around his stiffness and moved herself against it. He murmured unintelligible words and his hips moved in response.

'Do you like that, Mr Bevan?'

'Yes.'

His head was tilted back, his eyes closed, his hands limp by his side. Kate changed her position and dipped her head. She took the end of his penis into her mouth and sucked loudly and lasciviously.

The fat of his stomach quivered. His moan trilled as if someone was flicking his throat with a finger. Her control was total. She could finish him now or play him like a fish. Like a whale.

Kate moved her head up and down. She salivated around his prick and rubbed the shaft with sensitive fingers. She took the glans of his weapon deep into her throat. The noise he made changed. He grunted in time to her suctions.

Between her legs she had her own desire that made her squirm. This service she was rendering might be in payment, but it need not exclude her own pleasure.

She abandoned his penis and stood up. His eyes opened and he stared without comprehension. She pulled at his legs.

'Lie this way,' she ordered.

He moved. He obeyed. His legs hung over the end of the chaise longue and he lay flat on his back along its length. He lay waiting for her. She had said he could do anything he wished but he lay waiting for her. His desire had robbed him of decision. She had stolen his willpower.

'Do you like my taste, Mr Bevan?'

Kate stood alongside him, her skirt still around her waist, her breasts hanging free within the bodice of her suit. Her fingers stole across her pubic hair. He watched them disappear between her legs, watched them push inside herself, and he shuddered.

'You do, don't you?'

'Yes.'

Yes seemed to be the only word he could manage.

Kate parted her sex lips with the fingers of her left hand and pushed three fingers of her right hand deep into her vagina. For a moment she squirmed against them. His eyes never wavered as he stared at what she was doing. When she withdrew the fingers, she offered them to his mouth and his lips parted and he sucked them clean.

'You like that?' she said.

'Yes,' he whispered.

She put her left knee on the side of the chaise longue and swung her other leg over his face. She straddled him, holding herself above him. She faced his erection. His hands held her hips.

Kate leaned forward and took hold of his prick. She sucked it into her mouth and began to fellate him. She lowered herself and stifled his grunts with her vagina. His mouth covered her sex mouth and ate greedily.

His mouth and tongue were not enough. As she sucked, she squirmed upon his face. Her sex had become an open wound that itched and demanded salving. She rubbed it over his features and felt the salving and salvation near at hand.

He gripped her hips desperately and his mouth and tongue worked to give her pleasure but it was the fact she was using his whole face as an object of sexual fulfilment that made her so hot she felt she could ignite . . . and then she did.

Kate came and pushed down on the fat man's face. His prick slid from her mouth and she held it against her cheek like a talisman and her breath keened from her as she shuddered upon him.

Her awareness returned and she felt immediate concern. Her pleasure had been intense enough to smother him. She climbed from the chaise longue. Flat Stanley Bevan lay upon his back, his lips wet, his mouth open and useless, his face smeared with her juices. His breathing was ragged and his eyes had trouble focusing upon her. When they did his lips twitched. She realised he was attempting a smile.

'Your turn now, Mr Bevan,' she said. 'You want to fuck?'

His head moved slightly in an affirmative nod.

Kate stepped astride of his legs that hung over the end of the chaise longue. She faced away from him and turned from the waist, hands on her hips to hold up the skirt, and smiled at him. He was staring at her thighs and buttocks, poised above him.

Sitting back upon him, she reached between her legs for his prick. She guided it into her open sex and contracted when his heat met her heat. She sank lower and the folds of her inner flesh suctioned it inside and enveloped it. Her bottom pressed against his groin and she leaned back and held herself on extended arms.

'Is that good, Mr Bevan?'

Speech had again abandoned him. He grunted and wheezed and his hips twitched. She tilted her pelvis in gentle movements and her inner membranes milked him. It was the gentlest of fucks but that was all he needed.

Flat Stanley Bevan gasped, his penis quivered and he came. His stomach shook and she pushed down heavily upon him. The orgasm continued to pulse, vibration following vibration. Perhaps it had been a long time since his last one. By the amount of sperm he shed, she thought it might be a long time before he was capable of another.

Kate slipped from him. Her body glowed with achievement. She put her panties on and pushed the skirt down, fastened the bra and began buttoning the bodice of the suit. The fat man remained unmoving upon the chaise longue. His mouth was open, his eyes closed, his breathing shallow.

He was in that never-never land of aftermath, that perpetual silver lining, floating on goodness and comfort as content as a child.

'Thank you, Mr Bevan,' she said. 'It has been a pleasure doing business with you.'

His mouth twitched into a smile and his head rolled sideways to face her but he didn't open his eyes.

'Thank you, Mrs Adams. If there is anything else . . .?'

'I'll let you know.'

Kate shouldered her bag, unlocked the door and left.

Her appetite had returned and she walked along High Street towards The George intending to freshen up and have lunch. Heads continued to turn to follow her progress and cars slowed, making the usual congestion worse.

Kate wondered if she would meet anyone she knew. Where, for instance, was her husband or Valerie Hudson?

Her husband would probably be on the road, selling. No matter how he wrapped up his title, he was just a glorified sales representative who happened to earn a lot of money. And Valerie?

For a moment, she was tempted to go looking for Miss Hudson, spinster and insurance investment consultant, wearer of black stockings and a lady of insatiable appetites when it came to making love to a beached walrus.

Was Kate in a position to criticise after what had transpired in the Bank Buildings? Of course she was. Kate had transacted a most advantageous business deal and taken her pleasure at the same time. There had been no pretence at love or even compatability.

Sex with the detective had been all the hotter because there had been no emotion.

Maybe when she started her new career, Kate would become a lecturer and hold seminars on sexual behaviour. The seminars would provide endless opportunities for seduction and group activities. She smiled to herself. She knew just the hotel in Bournemouth where she could hold the first.

Kate showered and had lunch sent up to her room. Afterwards, she put on the black underwear with clean panties, the black suit and went to see the solicitor.

Chapter 26

The secretary was called Jennifer, Kate remembered. Thank you, Jennifer, he had said when she tottered into and out of his office in a tight skirt.

Jennifer wore another tight skirt and had a problem placing Kate until she introduced herself, even though they had last seen each other just over a week ago when Kate had delivered the photocopies of legal papers she had been asked to provide.

Even women took you for granted, Kate thought. Perhaps Jennifer had been conditioned by the male chauvinism of her employer.

Kate sat in a chair and waited but she knew her presence was making the secretary uncomfortable. Jennifer went into Martin Bell's office and when she returned, she held the door open for Kate.

'Mr Bell will see you now,' she said.

'How kind.'

Martin Bell was behind his desk, ostentatiously signing letters. Kate strode across the carpet and waited for a reaction. Jennifer waited for the letters. He finished signing.

'Thank you, Jennifer.'

He held the letters sideways and glanced up. His lips parted in surprise. He withdrew the letters. Jennifer, reaching for them, tottered over the desk.

'Mrs Adams?'

'That's right.' She glanced at the secretary. 'I hope I haven't come at a bad time.'

'What?' He remembered Jennifer and thrust the letters at her. 'No, of course not.' He stood up as his secretary left the room. This time he didn't watch her tight skirt, he held his hand out to Kate. She allowed her fingers to be squeezed and he said, 'Please, sit down.'

Kate sat and crossed her legs. Men, she thought. They were easier to read than books. Just like Flat Stanley Bevan, he had been unable to resist watching the manoeuvre.

'Have you made any progress?' she said.

Her question brought his mind back from up her skirt and into the real world. He pulled a file towards him and opened it.

'We certainly have.' He moved papers and checked a list of items with a finger before looking up at her. 'I take it you are of the same mind?'

'I am.'

'You want me to prepare papers for a divorce petition on the grounds of your husband's adultery?'

'I do.'

'Have you seen Mr Bevan?'

Kate opened her bag and took out an envelop that contained statements, photographs and a video. She uncrossed her legs, causing him to cough, and leaned forward to hand them to him.

'The evidence is all there.'

He held up the video cassette.

'Filmed together?'

'Yes.'

'Holding hands? Having dinner?'

'Fucking.'

He gulped. 'I beg your pardon?'

'The video is of my husband and Valerie Hudson fucking, Mr Bell. Fucking in many and various ways.'

He coughed and tried to look unaffected. He failed.

'I hope it was not obtained illegally.'

'It's perfectly legal. The cameras were in my house. I gave Mr Bevan permission to put them there.'

'Well, then.' He looked at the cassette in his hand. 'Sexually explicit, you say?'

'Totally explicit. There are stills from it in the envelope.'

He found the photographs and examined them thoroughly. There was also a transcript of what her husband and his mistress had said. He read it.

'It's open and shut, Mrs Adams.' His eyes kept dropping to her legs. She had deliberately crossed them high. 'And I have other good news for you.'

'You do?'

'When you married your husband, you had an inheritance.'

'That's right.'

'You used part of it as deposit on the house which you now share and you allowed him to invest the remainder?'

'That's correct.'

'According to the papers you provided, your husband invested only your money. He used none of his own.'

'He had none of his own.'

'Excellent.' The solicitor stared at the papers in front of him. Money, it appeared, was as appealing to him as sex. 'I am happy to say the investments have been very successful. Even allowing your husband a fee for administering the portfolio, the amount you could expect to liquidise, if you so wished, is substantial.'

'How substantial?'

'In the region of £180,000.'

Kate said, 'There is also the house?'

'Of course. There is the house.' He tapped the transcript. 'The normal division of property and assets will hardly apply for he has no case against the evidence he has himself provided.'

'Can the financial arrangements be agreed in advance?'

'That is always the best way.'

'What do you suggest?'

'Your inheritance was crucial in providing the joint home and the portfolio. The dividends from the portfolio have paid for the mortgage. I also suspect, from the evidence of these accounts and from what your husband has admitted on the tape, that he has used these dividends for purposes other than household expenses.'

'You mean on Valerie Hudson?'

'Quite.'

'So?'

'If you wish, I will prepare a document that it would be extremely wise for him to sign, relinquishing all claims. He will, of course, wish to consult a solicitor but the best legal advice he will be able to obtain will tell him to sign.' He shrugged. 'If we wanted to be awkward about it, we could allege malpractice or even fraud. I doubt if he would want that.'

'I'm sure he wouldn't.' She knew of other aspects he would wish to remain secret, as well. 'That all sounds satisfactory.'

He smiled at the praise.

'We aim to please.'

'When will the papers be ready?'

'Ah!' He gave a professional grimace. 'They will take some time, of course. Perhaps in two weeks?'

'I want them in two days.'

He laughed and then stopped laughing because he could see she was not joking.

'Impossible.'

'I want them for Sunday lunchtime. I want to deliver them myself.'

'Mrs Adams, we prepare the petition and lodge it with the court. It is the court's duty to send your husband a copy of the petition.'

'That's okay. You can do that Monday. I want to deliver my own copy to him on Sunday.'

'That is not the way it is done.'

'It's the way I wish to do it.'

'There is the financial agreement we need to negotiate.'

'I would prefer to do that myself.'

'But apart from the legal protocol, it is simply not possible. This is Friday afternoon. My staff couldn't possibly begin to prepare them until Monday at the earliest.'

Kate smiled, uncrossed her legs and crossed them again the other way.

'In the last week, I have discovered that most things

are possible, Mr Bell. It is a question of attitude. I see that you have a television and video. Why don't we review the evidence? Behind closed doors?'

'The evidence?'

'Put the tape on, Mr Bell. Let's see how strong a case I have.'

'I don't think that will be necessary, Mrs Adams.'

Kate uncrossed her legs extravagantly and his eyes widened. She stood up and picked the cassette from the desk and took it to the video machine. She bent over to slot it in and peeped round at him.

'Do you think you should lock the door, Mr Bell? This is extremely sensitive. Perhaps you wouldn't want Jennifer to see what happens?'

'No. Of course.'

He thumbed his intercom and said, 'Jennifer. I don't wish to be disturbed.'

Kate took the remote control and sat on a wide leather chesterfield settee. She patted the cushion next to her. On the screen, she was fast-forwarding the antics of her husband and Valerie Hudson. He left the safety of his desk, locked the door of his office, and joined her.

'This is unnecessary, Mrs Adams,' he said. 'Your case is unassailable. But I'm afraid we can't prepare the papers until next week. Perhaps by Wednesday?'

'I want them for Sunday lunchtime.'

'It's just not possible.'

Kate pressed a button and the couple on the television screen slowed to real time. Valerie Hudson was bending over the sofa while her husband had sex with her from behind.

'An opinion, Mr Bell?' she said. 'Sexual, not professional. How do I compare with Miss Hudson?'

'There is no comparison, Mrs Adams.'

'Call me Kate.'

'Kate.'

He could not quite drag his eyes from the screen where they were changing positions. Her husband lay back on the sofa and the woman began to fellate him.

'She does that well, doesn't she?' Kate said.

'I suppose so.'

'Perhaps that's why he prefers her?'

Martin Bell gulped. Perhaps it was her hand that rested on his thigh.

'Perhaps.'

'Perhaps she's better at sucking cock than I am.'

Her hand moved and he didn't stop it.'

'Mrs Adams . . .'

'Kate.'

'Kate. You are a beautiful woman and I believe you are attempting to coerce from me a promise I cannot make.'

'I am?'

'The soonest we could have your papers ready would be late Monday.'

Her hand discovered the erection in his trousers. She stroked it absent-mindedly.

'Sunday lunchtime,' she said.

'Mrs Adams, Kate, this is unethical.'

'I thought it was a stiff cock. Shall we see if I can do better than the lady on the screen?'

'But it's not possible . . .'

'Anything's possible.' She unfastened his belt. Her fingers hovered at his zip. 'Even Sunday lunchtime.'

He gulped.

'But, that means . . .'

'That means I suck your prick now, and I let you fuck me on Sunday morning.'

'Oh, my God.'

'I told you. Call me Kate.

'All right,' he said. 'Sunday.'

Kate unzipped his trousers and unfastened the restraining button at the top. She slid onto the floor between his knees and uncovered his erection. It was not as big as the detective's.

Her head dipped and she took it into her mouth and sucked. He quivered and shook, his hands by his side on the leather as if he was not taking part, as if he were the victim of an assault by a deadly mouth. She squeezed the base of his prick, she rubbed the length with deft certainty, and she pushed the glans into the back of her throat and he came.

His spasm filled her mouth with sperm which she swallowed as if it were the elixir of life. When he had finished, she got to her feet and crossed to his desk where there was a glass of water. She drank to clear her palate.

He remained on the chesterfield. On the screen, her husband and his mistress had moved to the bedroom.

'I'm staying at The George,' she said. 'I'll expect you on Sunday morning.'

Martin Bell stared at her. He was drained. perhaps it

had been the elixir of life. Men were such fragile creatures. He nodded.

The two sexual encounters had satisfied her ego and assuaged her desire. They also made her uncomfortable for her dinner date with Paul.

What would he think if he knew what had occurred with the detective and the solicitor? How would it affect the love he said he had had for her when she was a lost soul with long hair and a repressed personality?

He was a good man. There were a few of them about and she knew, in her heart, that Paul was one of them. But she did not know if she wanted a good man. Once, perhaps, but now?

Kate also wondered what Paul really thought of her now. Did he still love her or was he really frightened of her? Perhaps he disapproved. Her motives were open to question in inviting him to dinner. He had been a good friend when she thought all she had needed were platonic relationships but perhaps it would have been kinder to have kept their friendship distant.

In fact, she had sought to drag from him his declarations of love. Perhaps she had instigated the dinner date to keep his interest, to maintain him as an admirer. She knew she could attract most men and had that day demonstrated her powers of persuasion and manipulation. So why was Paul so important? Why would she be sad to lose him as an admirer?

Kate knew her powers but knew she could not use them on Paul as blatantly as she had on others. To be at ease with him, she wanted to go to bed with him. But was that because she now equated all relationships with sex? He offered something more and it disturbed her.

The dinner passed with civility and affection. He had made an effort and had combed his hair and wore a shirt and tie with a corduroy suit. His hair looked better uncombed and she did not tell him that the plaid tie did not go with the check shirt.

He marvelled at the amount she ate.

'Where did you get your appetite?' he said, and she laughed at a secret not to be told.

They laughed a lot and she relaxed and wondered if he would make a pass at her. Wondered whether she could entice him to her room and privacy where they might instigate intimacies in the dark, but she should have known better.

Paul was the perfect, diffident gentleman and his slow smile was all he was willing to share with her. He waited with her by the lifts and they said goodnight.

'Not even a kiss?' she said.

He took her hand instead and squeezed it.

'It wouldn't be appropriate,' he said.

'When will it be?'

'When you have left your husband. When you have made your decisions. When you have placed me.'

'Placed you?'

He smiled.

'We used to be safe together. We didn't threaten each other. But that was before you believed in yourself. Now you have so many options, Kate, and I don't know if I'm one of them. Eventually you'll decide, and I will know.'

Paul raised her hand to his lips and kissed her fingers,

then walked away into the night. Kate went to bed as confused as she had been a week before.

Chapter 27

Kate telephoned from the station. His voice was unmistakable and it still sent a shiver down her spine.

'Toby?' It's Kate.'

'Kate?'

'I thought the horses might need exercising.'

'Kate?' The confusion left his voice. 'Where the hell are you?'

'At the station.'

'What are you doing here?'

'I came to see you.'

'I'll come straight away and pick you up.'

'No. Please don't. I'll take a cab. I'd rather take a cab.'

'I can be there in five minutes.'

'No, really. Let me do it my way.'

'All right. If that's what you want. Are you coming straight here?'

'If that's okay.'

'That's fine.' He laughed. 'How are you?'

'I'm good.' She wondered why she had chosen such a word. 'But I'll tell you when I get there. I won't be intruding, will I?'

'Intruding?'

'Wife? Family? Girlfriend?'

He chuckled.

'There's nobody, Kate. I'm all alone.'

The taxi went past the hotel where she used to live but it held no happy memories for her. It turned along the drive that ran through the copse of trees and came out on the track that went through the fields to the converted farmhouse she remembered so well.

Two horses grazed in the top field. Three more were in the east field. The house was just the same. A Range Rover was still in the drive, although it was this year's model. She felt like she was returning to the past after a long journey. Even the sun was shining and the temperature had climbed into the sixties.

Toby was in the open doorway. He hadn't changed much. He was still tall and handsome, his hair grey, his features perhaps a little craggier, casual in a check shirt and cord trousers. He was fifty-two. She had always known his age because he had always been too old. Until now.

'Hello, Kate.'

'Hello, Toby.'

He held out his hands and she held them and they stared at each other.

'You're beautiful,' he said. 'But you always were.'

'Not always.' She glanced at the farmhouse and back at him. 'Nothing's changed.'

'I'm older.'

'It doesn't show.'

They smiled and he led her inside. She was aware they

hadn't embraced. She wondered what she would do if they did?

'Here. Let me take your coat.'

He took her trenchcoat and hung it on the wooden hooks in the hallway. Beneath it she wore a white cotton dress, simply cut, with a pleated skirt.

They went into the living room. Even the furniture was the same. A bottle of champagne sat in an ice bucket on the table. He spread his hands in a helplessly male gesture.

'I didn't know what else to do?'

Kate laughed.

She said, 'I always drink champagne at one o'clock in the afternoon.'

He wrapped a towel round the bottle, popped the cork into it and poured the wine into two crystal flutes. She accepted one of the glasses and they touched rims. The crystal tinkled. Like her nerves, she thought.

'To you, Kate.'

They drank and she walked around the room and used the glass as a prop. Another production, another performance. They talked and exchanged details of a decade and more. He sympathised to hear she was in the throes of a divorce. He had never been tempted into marriage again, he said. He had spent a year in Kenya before returning to England. He hadn't seen her mother since but he had often thought about Kate.

'I wanted to find you. Make sure you were all right,' he said. 'But I didn't know how. I didn't know if you would want to see me.' He shrugged. Besides . . .'

'Besides?'

The silence lay between them just as the years lay between them.

'I always loved you, Kate. I suppose I still do.'

'You married my mother.'

'That was a mistake.'

'Did you love her?'

'In a way. I was very fond of her. I suppose she was second choice. Because I couldn't have my first choice.'

'You married her because you couldn't marry me?'

He looked uncomfortable.

'It wasn't even that simple. I was much older than you. I didn't know how you felt. Men, particularly older men, can be very insecure, you know.'

'You could have told me how you felt.'

'No I couldn't. I was too involved with your mother.'

'You could have told me. Perhaps I would have understood.'

'I was afraid you would laugh.'

Her eyes widened. 'Laugh?'

'You were so beautiful. So sensual. I always felt clumsy around you. That's why I couldn't talk to you about things that mattered.'

Even then, she had had the power and had never realised it.

'Do you still have my letters?' she said.

'Yes.'

'You kept them?'

'They were the only love letters anybody ever sent me.'

'Didn't they tell you how I felt?'

'I thought it was a teenage crush.' He shrugged and

shook his head. 'I suppose, when it comes down to it, I was a coward. I thought it would be too dangerous to tell you, to talk about it.'

'In case I made a fuss?'

'Something like that.'

He sounded helpless.

'Why did you and mother get divorced?'

'It wasn't working. What we told you that day, that was the truth.'

'Did my mother know?'

'About us?'

'Yes.'

'No. Of course not.'

'She didn't find the letters?'

'She never found the letters, Kate. We divorced because of differences between us.' He sighed. 'Perhaps you were a factor, from my point of view. You were so beautiful and vibrant and your mother, well, your mother . . .'

'Yes?'

'You don't really want to know.'

'Yes, I do.'

He licked his lips and stood up straight.

'We did not have a satisfactory sex life. It was as if once we got married, she stopped trying. She became, I don't know, dowdy. Happy to be the little woman. There was no excitement. She looked upon sex as something rather distasteful that she had to put up with.

'Her personality was different at the hotel. When she was there, she made herself attractive. She dressed well and flirted better. But that was because she liked an audience, she needed one. Before we married I was part of the audience. Afterwards I was just part of the furniture.'

Kate said, 'The announcement you made. The separation. The timing always made me wonder. It was a week after we made love.' Her eyes stung as she used the words. He bit his lip. 'The first and only time we made love. Is that why you decided to separate?'

He shook his head.

'We had decided before that night. Before we ... made love. I had no excuses for my behaviour, except that I was mad about you. But the only reason I lost control that night was because I already knew the marriage was over. We had already made the decision to split. We were working things out before we told you.'

Kate felt like laughing. She had served a sentence for a crime she didn't commit. She had always thought her mother had known; had found the letters. She turned and stared out of the window at the horses in the east field. He came and stood behind her. His body closed in on hers and he put his arms around her and held her arms.

'I've missed you, Kate,' he said. 'Do you forgive me?'
'I never blamed you. I blamed me.'

His arms tightened around her and his body was strong against her. He was still using the same aftershave. The memory came back after all these years. She moved against him and felt his stiffness in the groove between her buttocks. It still fitted. The excitement still burst when they touched.

A hand moved up her body and cupped a breast. His

lips went to her neck and kissed her.

'I'm so glad you came back,' he said.

'So am I.'

She tipped her head backwards and her lips found his. They kissed and her tongue was bold in his mouth.

'Kate,' he said.

'Don't speak.'

He turned her in his arms and they kissed and pulled at each other and she remembered the first time. They had been so eager, so hungry for each other. After so many years their passion was the same.

They staggered from the window and he pushed her onto the couch, throwing up her skirt as he fell upon her. His hands went over her legs, across the stockings and onto her flesh, then beneath her and into her panties and over her buttocks.

Kate pulled at his shirt and ripped it open. Buttons flew. She bit his chest and pulled the shirt from his shoulders. He ripped the panties and they snagged on her white garter belt as he pulled them down. He shredded the silk in his frustration and they hung from one leg.

Her hands reached between for him but he pushed them aside in his hurry to unfasten himself. Instead, she pushed her fingers between her own legs. She was wet already and she opened herself and pushed fingers inside, as he had taught her many years ago.

He pushed the trousers and undershorts down over his hips and tore off his shirt. He was panting like a sprinter and she moaned and thrust her hips in enticement. For a moment he paused and watched her finger digging into herself, masturbating herself, making her squelch, and then he could wait no longer and positioned himself over her.

Kate gladly moved her hands and he guided the head of his weapon into her sex. Her eyes widened and he adjusted, pushed again and thrust inside her all the way.

They fucked wildly and she screamed, wrapping her legs around him, trying to take him ever deeper. They rolled upon the couch and fell from it onto the floor but remained united. His hands went beneath her, dug into her bottom, slid beneath her thighs and the tips of his fingers went inside the lips of her vagina as he pounded to a crescendo.

Kate had come and was coming again. It felt like she had always been coming. The emotions swept her, drowned her, threw her assunder and dragged her back for more. And in the midst of it all Toby orgasmed and shook and his embedded weapon stirred and invoked yet another coming.

They lay on the floor in exhaustion until finally Toby rolled away. He pulled down her skirt so that she was decently covered and fastened his trousers with his back to her. He poured more champagne and drank it. Kate stared up at him. He poured another glass and offered it. She sat up and drank.

He shook his head. As before, he was robbed of words.

Kate smiled and got to her feet. She refilled the glass and walked from the room. He watched and, after a few seconds, followed. She went upstairs and stood in the doorway of the bedroom that had been a massage room.

The wine was cold and delicious. Her body was on a

plateau of pleasure that she did not yet want to leave.

'Do you still have the rubber sheet?' she said.

'Yes.'

Kate put down the glass, unfastened the dress and stepped out of it. He stared at her tanned body in the white underwear.

'Get the sheet,' she said. 'I want a massage.'

Kate lay on the rubber sheet face down, with her eyes closed, and the ritual commenced. His hands caressed and rubbed in the oils and the lust gathered like a lurking storm. His fingers slid along the crevice of her bottom and teased her anus and the open petals of her sex.

And when she was slithery as a serpent, he lay upon her. His hardness slid in her crease and they lay silently, their flesh oozing against each other.

His oiled palms went beneath her to hold her breasts and he moved with a firm rhythm upon her back and upon her buttocks.

Kate moved and realigned her bottom. She enticed his prick between her legs and it slithered into the swampland there. Again he was content to move it without penetration, to continue feeding the storm inside.

She remembered the ritual but that was then and this was now.

'Fuck me, Toby,' she said.

His rhythm faltered.

'Kate,' he whispered, his hands moving to stroke her neck.

'Fuck me!'

Her voice was low but definite. The heat inside her

needed release. He probed tentatively with the head of his penis and the mouth of her sex found it, sucked it in and devoured its length.

He gasped as he sank upon her softness, his iron staff buried in her furnace and in danger of melting. She squirmed her bottom against him, bucked against him and made him fuck her.

The ritual was gone and he held her hips and fought back and she came and he came and she came again.

This time she left him lying in exhaustion. She showered and dressed and adjusted her make-up. In the kitchen, she took a can of Coke from the refrigerator and poured it into a glass. He came downstairs, still damp from the shower, wearing a towelling robe.

'Are you staying?' he said.

'I've called a taxi.'

'Stay.'

She shook her head. She sipped the drink. It was cold and effervescent. It felt alive, like her.

'Will you come back?'

'I don't think so.'

He stared at her. His incomprehension showed on his face.

'Why did you come?'

'To find a perspective. To find a truth.' She smiled. 'To place you, Toby.'

'To place me?'

'You wouldn't understand. I don't think you would ever have understood.'

But Kate did, at long last. She left the farmhouse in the taxi without regrets. She understood that her guilt had been unjustified and that she had been a victim. She understood that her love for Toby had been as much a mirage as her marriage.

It had been an infatuation that had grown in the silences when he had not spoken but had taken advantage of her. An infatuation compounded by a near-rape experience that had taken her virginity with an orgasm of such power that she had feared she would never experience the like again.

But she had. And it had not depended upon rape or imaginary love. Sex and love still confused her but she felt she was getting closer to understanding. Placing Toby had helped.

Maybe love was something different to sex, but an ally of it, nonetheless. Maybe Lorna was right, that the combination of the two was an added dimension of experience. That sex was there to be used by love. That the experience of both could grow together.

But not with Toby. He had his favourable points. Her mother would think the settlement he made on her after their divorce was in his favour. She did not know it had been prompted by his guilt.

Kate did not believe Toby had ever been capable of real love. He could give money but she doubted if he could have given of himself, despite the illusions he liked to cast, the illusions that he lived. Even now, he probably believed he had loved Kate. He would probably embrace a broken heart for as long as it suited him.

He was not a bad man but he was not a good man. He was faulted, as most people were. But he was now part of her past. The journey had been another part of

her process of rediscovery but it was time to move on.
It was time to place other people.

Chapter 28

Martin Bell did not look like a solicitor on Sunday morning. He wore an expensive grey tracksuit and white running shoes. The briefcase he carried was incongruous.

Kate greeted him with a smile, opened the door of her hotel room wide, and said, 'Come in, Mr Bell.'

He coughed and stepped past her nervously. She wore a white silk peignoir, high heels and pearls and a touch of perfume.

'It's all prepared. Adultery requires two parts. The act of adultery has to be admitted or proven. And the petitioner, which is you, of course, has to find it intolerable to continue to live with your spouse. The evidence proves the first conclusively and a judge would accept that living with your husband would be totally intolerable, particularly after all that he has said.'

Kate said, 'And Miss Hudson?'

'She is, of course, named in the petition and we shall be asking for costs to be awarded jointly against her and your husband.'

'That's nice.'

He opened the briefcase and removed a grey folder which he gave to her.

'Three copies will be delivered to the court first thing in the morning along with a copy of the marriage certificate. They will send a copy to your husband in due course. I doubt if he will dispute the financial arrangements but, to be safe, we will also ask the court to transfer the house at twenty-three Maple Drive into your sole name.'

Kate opened the folder and spread the contents on the dressing table. There was the divorce petition form and three copies of the financial agreement the solicitor had prepared.

'I also need your signature,' he said, and placed several documents nearby with a pen. He coughed, and she knew he was nervous of the bargain they had made. Perhaps he wondered if she would keep it. 'I hope everything is to your satisfaction?'

'It looks as if it is totally satisfying.'

She stood up, opened the pegnoir, and shrugged it from her shoulders. His gasp was gratifying. All she now wore was a white garter belt and tan stockings, high-heeled shoes and the pearls around her throat. She leaned with both hands on the dressing table and stared into the mirror.

Kate had to admit she looked good. Martin Bell looked as confused as he had in his office when she had unfastened his trousers. His eyes bulged and his hands reached out as if warming themselves on her flesh, but he did not touch.

'We had our own arrangement, Mr Bell. Did we not?'

'We did, Mrs Adams.'

'Perhaps you would like to help yourself while I read my future?'

'What?'

His eyes met hers in the mirror.

'Fuck me, Mr Bell.' She leaned forward a little more and pushed her bottom back against his tracksuit. 'I have a schedule to keep. I'm sure you won't mind if I sign while you fuck?'

Kate lowered her eyes and continued to read. The solicitor was put off only for a moment. His hands touched her, he palmed her breasts and she murmured with a hint of pleasure. Perhaps it would make him try harder and come quicker. He pushed down his tracksuit trousers and his penis, already erect, went between her legs.

His fingers slid down her belly and into her undergrowth. They probed her vagina and found it wet. These days, it was always wet. He grunted and groaned and his hands did not know where to go next or what to touch. She cantilevered her hips to give him a clue. He pushed his penis inside her.

Kate was surprised that she felt as aroused as she did. She had planned on being ice cool. The solicitor was close to gibbering. He licked the back of her neck with a slobbering mouth as he jerked in and out of her in an unsteady rhythm. His hands clawed at her breasts. She picked up the pen and began to sign the documents he had prepared.

His grunts were a distraction. His thrusts were getting stronger and making her writing shaky. She signed the last one and put down the pen. Her own breathing was difficult to keep under control and when she looked into the mirror the heaviness in her features gave her away.

'I've finished,' she said. 'How about you?'

His mouth opened and he emitted a strangled cry, gripped her hips and came. His eyes were closed and he did not see her slip her hand between her legs and finger her clitoris. She, too, shuddered but he did not notice.

After the climax came his embarrassment.

He collected the documents she had signed and put them back in the briefcase. She did not bother picking up the peignoir but watched him from the other side of the room, comfortable in her *deshabille* and her beauty, knowing that if he delayed he would be aroused again.

But she had things to do and the bargain had been for one sexual encounter, which he had had.

The young man held his briefcase in front of him. Perhaps he thought he needed protection, from himself as much as from her.

'When the courts get in touch we will need to meet again.'

'I look forward to it.'

'Affidavits, Directions for Trial,' he explained.

His eyes wandered her body.

'Of course.'

'Then we'll get a date for the *decree nisi*.'

'Excellent,' she said.

'As long as it remains undisputed.'

'It will be undisputed.'

'Well, then.'

'Well, then.'

Kate opened the door for him and he left, hesitantly, looking back from the corridor.

She said, 'I'll be in touch.'

'I look forward to it,' he said.

Kate smiled as she closed the door.

The sky was grey and overcast as if looking for a row. With luck, it might rain, she thought.

Kate took a taxi to the corner of Maple Drive. The van and the lorry that carried the skip were waiting. She walked down the polite tree-lined avenue along the tidy pavement. The houses were detached and substantial. There was no BMW in the drive of number twenty-three, only her car, and she turned and waved and the van and lorry driver put their vehicles in motion.

A neighbour across the road was unloading his golf bag from the back of his car. He stared in surprise as she went up the drive of her house. She waved.

'Hello, Bernard. Good game?'

His look changed slowly to one of amazement.

'Kate?'

She laughed and unlocked the front door.

The lorry driver's mate jumped down from the cab and guided him as he reversed into the drive and lowered the skip from the back of the wagon. The driver got down and the two of them came into the house.

'Where do we start?' he said.

'Upstairs.'

Kate took them to the loft and the land that Bob built.

The driver and his mate surveyed the landscape and the villages and stations.

'Very nice,' he said.

She picked up a train and looked into its carriage but couldn't see anyone fucking in the lavatory. She dropped it casually and it broke.

'It all goes,' she said.

'Shame,' said the driver's mate.

'Land reclamation,' she said. 'I need it for redevelopment.'

'You're the boss,' said the driver.

Yes, thought Kate, I am.

In the bedroom, she began by pulling his suits from the wardrobe and dropping them on the floor. But why stop at *his* clothes? The ones hanging in her wardrobe were a total mess – his choice because he preferred her to be The Little Woman. Perhaps his anytime girl would like them?

The few items she had affection for, including her outdoor pursuits gear and sports equipment, she put to one side. Everything else, she told the men, could go. Also the tools in the garage. She took the sign that said Bob's Place and hung it on the end of the skip. The briefcase at the bottom of the cupboard she put in her car.

On her way out, she collected a new set of house keys from the workman who was changing the locks. A good morning's work, she decided. Now for lunch at The Red Lion.

The encounter with Martin Bell had given her an appetite and the food in The Red Lion carvery was excellent. She parked on the street rather than in the car park so that Bob would not be alerted to her presence until she was ready to make an entrance. She would eat first.

How many times had she been here before? Countless. But this time was different and she viewed the pub through different eyes. Before, she had arrived with her nerves frayed, wondering whether she would be able to cope with the conversation of Mrs George Mellish and the other wives. She had worried about being adequate.

Now she appreciated what a handsome building the hotel was. It was on the High Street at the corner of the bridge across the river. The side bar and the restaurant above it looked onto the waterfront and was glass fronted. Standing on the bridge, she could see into the bar.

George Mellish was in his usual place and she supposed the other members of the clique that her husband liked to think of as being highly influential would also be there. Yes, there was Bob, leaning against the window and being forthright and boring as ever.

Kate entered through the front door instead of from the car park at the back and went straight to the carvery. She had plenty of time. The men always enjoyed two hours in the bar before either going home with their Little Women as chauffeurs or ascending to the restaurant to dine and have more to drink.

The waiter was most attentive. He had never been so before and she could tell he was puzzled. He knew her from somewhere but could not place her. It was somewhere she had escaped from, she wanted to tell him. Somewhere she would not be placed again.

With the roast beef and Yorkshire pudding she had a half-carafe of red wine. The meal was satisfying and she paid for it with the Gold Card that was debited to her husband's personal account. She declined a pudding. She had her own plans for afters.

Kate looked at her watch and judged the time was right. She checked her appearance in the ladies room. The hair, the tan, the pearls, the navy blue Chanel suit. She looked good.

The door opened and Mrs George Mellish and another wife entered, smiled distantly in her direction and continued chattering about a forthcoming Rotary dinner. They had not recognised her.

'Nancy, Beryl,' she said, with a smile.

They paused and stared at the uncalled for intrusion. Their minds were so wrapped in safe tweed skirts, three-pack tights and Safeways shopping they still didn't know who she was.

'Is Bob here?'

'Bob?' Nancy Mellish said.

'My husband Bob.'

'Good God!' she said, and put her hand to her mouth. Kate smiled and left.

There were three steps down into the bar that looked over the river. Bob was in his usual place at the far end and the others would be gathered around, the men on high stools at the bar, the wives sharing a table and perhaps a packet of salted peanuts.

Make an entrance, Lorna had told her. But she had not known how. She smiled. It had come naturally to her. As it did now.

Kate descended the steps into the bar. The talk from the far end monopolised the room and few other tables were occupied. They were all there. George Mellish, Harry Burns, Maurice Smythie-Brown, a solitary Little Woman waiting for the other Little Women to reappear, and, of course, Bob in Bob's Place.

George was talking but the thread of his conversation faltered as she strode towards them. He could not stop looking at her and the others turned to follow his gaze. She understood their confusion. Why would a beautiful young woman be walking towards them?

Bob was staring and had stopped lounging against the window. He actually had a leer on his face. It began to change. Like the waiter, he was thinking, where have I seen her before?

'Sorry I'm late,' she said. 'I had things to do.'

'Kate?' her husband said. 'Is that you?'

'Close your mouth, Bob. You're a danger to passing flies.'

'Kate?' George Mellish echoed. He got off his stool at the bar. He glanced at her husband and back at her at a loss. 'We thought you were away.'

'I came back. I had business to deal with.'

Her husband tried to laugh but it didn't quite work.

'Business?'

Nancy Mellish and her companion returned from the ladies and her audience was complete. Kate opened her shoulder bag and removed a copy of the divorce petition. She held it out and Bob took it.

'What's this?'

'Divorce papers.'

'Divorce?'

'You'll be properly notified by the courts but I thought

you'd appreciate the personal touch.'

'Divorce?' he repeated.

'You will see that Miss Valerie Hudson is cited as co-respondent.'

Nancy Mellish took a deep breath from somewhere behind her at being present as a real-life scandal unfolded.

'Valerie?'

'You haven't forgotten already, have you, Bob? She's the one in the black stockings who calls you a sex pig. The one you fucked in the lavatory on a railway train.'

Nancy Mellish murmured, 'Oh my God,' and collapsed in a chair. Her husband coughed and tried to move discreetly down the bar but Kate was blocking the way.

Kate handed to George Mellish a still photograph that had been taken from the video. It showed her husband and his mistress having sex on the sofa. Mellish glanced at it and tried to look away but the curiosity was too great. He stared at it again.

'Do you know her, George?' Kate said.

'Sorry, my dear. Can't say I do.'

She had several copies of the same photograph and handed them to the others present.

'Does anybody know her?'

They all stared at the photographs with stony faces, pretending to be motivated by her request. They all shook their heads and said no. She did not ask for the return of the photographs and they did not offer. She handed a copy to her husband and his face drained of colour when he saw it.

'Remember her now, Bob?' Kate said.

He looked round at the silent crowd of witnesses to his embarrassment.

'Look,' he said to Kate. 'We should go somewhere and talk.'

'I agree.' She presented him with the document that set out the financial agreement her solicitor had prepared. 'For instance, I think you should sign this.'

'What is it?'

'All my worldly goods. I want them back.'

'I don't understand.'

'It's a financial settlement. My financial settlement.'

'Look, Kate, you're going too fast. I mean,' he looked at her, 'what happened, for chrissake?'

'I got wise.' She turned to the bar. The barman was as enthralled by the confrontation as anyone. 'A large whisky,' she said.

He poured a large whisky and gave it to her.

'He'll pay,' she said.

She put the whisky on the nearest table and pulled out a chair.

'Sit,' she said. 'The whisky is for you. Read the paper and sign it.'

'Now look here, Kate.'

He was trying to assert himself. She gave him a photograph of himself wearing the stockings and garter belt of his mistress.

'Sit.'

He sat and, when she pointed at the agreement, he began to read. Kate sat on one of the high stools at the bar and crossed her legs high. The men stared, their wives gasped.

'Gin and tonic,' she said.

The barman presented her with the drink and George Mellish offered to pay.

'Thank you, George, You're very kind.'

'Bad business,' he said, trying to commiserate beneath the gaze of his wife. 'If I can be of any help?'

'Of course.'

Her husband had finished reading. He stared at her. He looked as if he had been cast adrift in a storm on a leaky raft. She joined him at the table.

'You've taken everything.'

'It was mine anyway.'

'I'll fight it.' He found his bluster. 'I'll fight you every inch of the way.'

Kate placed another photograph in front of him.

She whispered, 'You can get away with porno pics of you fucking a bit on the side, Bob. All lads together eh? But wearing ladies underwear? How would that go down? You sign this agreement now or I circulate them to everyone I can think of who would enjoy a laugh at your expense.'

'No!' he gasped.

'Besides. When you think about it, I'm being generous. I have videos, documents, photographs and you confessing to your girlfriend how you've been screwing me. And I don't mean sexually. My solicitor mentioned something about malpractice? Sign, Bob. You'll still have sixty-k, the BM and the anytime girl.'

'But?'

'Sign.'

He signed.

Kate said, 'George? Would you witness this signature?'

'Of course, old girl.'

'Bitch,' her husband said, under his breath.

It reminded her of another time and another place and she leaned over and whispered in his ear as George Mellish countersigned the agreements.

'Rich bitch,' she said.

Men were so easy.

When she had put the documents in her shoulder bag, he tried to recover his composure.

'Look, Kate. Let's talk at home. We can still work something out.'

'You don't have a home. You've been moved out. I've had the locks changed and I don't want you coming anywhere near.'

'Moved out? But all my things . . .?'

'Taken care of.' She looked at her watch. 'If you care to come with me to the car park, I'll show you.'

Kate walked from the bar followed by her husband, George Mellish and the rest of the in-clique, and the barman. They crowded at the back door of the pub. The lorry had reversed into the car park and had lowered the skip next to his BMW. The sign still hung over the end. Bob's Place.

'Tell him where to deliver it,' she said. 'He's paid for the rest of the day.'

On Gold Card.

Chapter 29

Cyprus was pleasant in early November; not too hot but enough sun to make them forget any winter blues they had left behind in England.

Paul looked good with a tan. He looked good in the denim shirt and jeans she had made him buy. He looked good naked. The hotel was in Paphos, not far from the place where legend said Aphrodite had emerged from the warm waters of the Mediterranean. The legend was in the guide books but Paul had filled in the details.

'You are very erudite,' she said.

'And you are very beautiful and I love you.'

'I love you, too.'

Kate had finally placed her librarian and she had rediscovered books at the same time. They read in between sex. It was a perfect holiday combination. He had also been a revelation as a lover.

'One thing I never asked,' he said. 'You changed so much in Malta. What happened?'

'I would be too embarrassed to tell you.'

'Married couples should have no secrets.'

'So we're getting married?'

'Most definitely.'

'If I tell you, you might not want to.'

'I'll want to.'

'Well, maybe I'll tell you in a letter. Several letters.' She kissed his nose. 'Love letters.'